THEY WERE ALL MEN THAT ANY WOMAN IN HER RIGHT MIND WOULD TRUST

Dr. Springer, Anne's doctor, gentle, kindly, understanding, who said he had done everything humanly possible to save the baby she had lost . . .

Dr. Rivers, her psychiatrist, who made her feel more safe and sane after every visit to his office to voice her suspicions and fears . . . **Doug,** her husband, so patient with her, yet so eager for them to make love again and have another child . . .

They were all men Anne could trust—if it weren't for the other mothers with horror stories to match her own . . . and the nurses who died when they strayed from the line of what their medical masters called their duty . . .

They were all men Anne could trust—if it weren't for what Anne began to find out about her baby. . . .

Premature

The Best in Fiction from SIGNET

☐ **EYE OF THE NEEDLE by Ken Follett.** (#E9913—$3.50)

☐ **TRIPLE by Ken Follett.** (#E9447—$3.50)

☐ **FORGOTTEN IMPULSES by Todd Walton.** (#E9802—$2.75)*

☐ **INSIDE MOVES by Todd Walton.** (#E9661—$2.50)*

☐ **FOOLS DIE by Mario Puzo.** (#E8881—$3.50)

☐ **THE GODFATHER by Mario Puzo.** (#E9438—$2.95)

☐ **KRAMER VS. KRAMER by Avery Corman.** (#AE1000—$2.75)

☐ **ONE FLEW OVER THE CUCKOO'S NEST by Ken Kesey.**
(#E8867—$2.25)*

☐ **KINFLICKS by Lisa Alther.** (#AE1241—$3.50)

☐ **FEAR OF FLYING by Erica Jong.** (#AE1329—$3.50)

☐ **HOW TO SAVE YOUR OWN LIFE by Erica Jong.**
(#E7959—$2.50)*

☐ **THE KILLING GIFT by Bari Wood.** (#E9885—$3.50)

☐ **TWINS by Bari Wood.** (#E9886—$3.50)

☐ **THE GIRL IN A SWING by Richard Adams.** (#E9662—$3.50)*

☐ **SOME KIND OF HERO by James Kirkwood.** (#E9850—$2.75)

*Price slightly higher in Canada.

Premature

Mary L. Hanner

A SIGNET BOOK

NEW AMERICAN LIBRARY

TIMES MIRROR

PUBLISHER'S NOTE

This novel is a work of fiction. Names, characters, places and incidents are either the product of the author's imagination or are used fictitiously, and any resemblance to actual persons, living or dead, events, or locales is entirely coincidental.

NAL BOOKS ARE AVAILABLE AT QUANTITY DISCOUNTS WHEN USED TO PROMOTE PRODUCTS OR SERVICES. FOR INFORMATION PLEASE WRITE TO PREMIUM MARKETING DIVISION, THE NEW AMERICAN LIBRARY, INC., 1633 BROADWAY, NEW YORK, NEW YORK 10019.

Copyright © 1981 by Mary Lundholm Hanner

SIGNET TRADEMARK REG. U.S. PAT. OFF. AND FOREIGN COUNTRIES REGISTERED TRADEMARK—MARCA REGISTRADA HECHO EN CHICAGO, U.S.A.

SIGNET, SIGNET CLASSICS, MENTOR, PLUME, MERIDIAN AND NAL BOOKS are published by The New American Library, Inc., 1633 Broadway, New York, New York 10019

First Printing, November, 1981

1 2 3 4 5 6 7 8 9

PRINTED IN THE UNITED STATES OF AMERICA

For Al Shapiro

ACKNOWLEDGMENTS

This book is fiction, but it came out of the experience of three miscarriages and the grief that results from losing a baby, a grief too often ignored by the medical community.

Many people helped with this story, and I want to thank David, Nathan and Karen, the P.M. crew at the hospital, for their unflagging enthusiasm; the Berkeley Writer's Group, Jud, Agnes Birnbaum, Charlie, and Bill and Pam, who read for me. I am especially grateful to Joan George, Dale Aycock, Lynette Fazio, and Will Crockett at San Jose State University, all of whom taught me how to love words.

1

August in the St. Helena Valley was hot and dry, a time of dust and hazy skies, fresh tomatoes and squash from the vegetable farms, and long days in halter tops and sandals. San Marco, one of the fastest-growing cities in California, stretched its suburban fingers deep in the valley, grasping at peach, plum, and apricot orchards that still dotted the foothills. August was a time for swimming pools, iced tea, and vacations. It was not a good time to sleep, since a blanket of smog oppressed the valley day and night until fall.

Maybe it was the morning air, smelling sour from sleep, that disturbed Anne, or maybe it was the quilt tangled around her feet, or even the pillow jutting too far under her left shoulder. She dreamed she was swimming against a torrent of white water and losing, no matter how hard she swam. Her body was heavy and cold. She slid under the icy surface of the water.

Anne jammed the pillow farther under her head and searched for the edge of the quilt, pulling it tight around her shoulders. But that didn't relieve her discomfort, and the realization of cold, wet sheets seeped into her half-waking.

At twenty-seven Anne Hart had not wet the bed, but in those early-morning moments she suffered all the humiliation of a child who had, the frantic need to hide her disgrace and hope it would dry before Mama noticed. Anne wrapped her arms around her head and caught a few strands of blond hair between her fingers. She twisted the hair that curled easily and then slipped from her fingers. It felt good. Something had to feel good. She shivered and then thrust her hand along her body to the hard knot in her stomach. Her fingers traveled the taut skin and gently probed the muscles beneath. It was like a muscle cramp, except in the stomach. Not in the stomach, she thought bitterly; like trying to swallow aspirin dry. It was a contraction.

Her water had broken. She lay very still, monitoring the rise and fall of the internal constrictions.

Anne tried to roll on her back, but she could barely get her right shoulder over on the pillow. The doctor had warned her about being overweight. Every month Dr. Springer shook his head and said she'd be uncomfortable.

Her hand touched the warm wetness around her. Now the sheets were soaked with blood, too much blood. She shivered and continued to tremble.

She'd bled once before, six weeks ago, and then it had stopped, miraculously. She closed her eyes tight. Doug groaned and rolled toward her. She didn't move.

"Annie? Are you awake?"

"Yes."

"What's the matter? Can't you sleep?"

"I'm bleeding. Oh, God, Doug, the baby . . ." She silently counted the months and only reached six. Not seven yet. Six is too early for the baby, she thought frantically. Can a baby live if it's born three months too early?

The sheets were a bloody battlefield, some silent nocturnal atrocity she wanted to hide beneath the quilt. She stumbled to the bathroom and found a box of sanitary napkins behind a stack of folded pillowcases.

"I'll call the doctor," Doug said.

"No, not yet. Please, Doug."

While he changed the bedding—sheets, quilt, and mattress pad—Anne struggled out of the nightgown that clung to her skin and finally slid off like a red ramekin. She caught a glimpse of her face in the mirror, her pale face with the wide blue eyes that now looked like knotholes in a whitewashed fence. She leaned against the chest of drawers and noticed her hands. They didn't look like hers. Her hands weren't so bluish white. But those fingers moved on demand, a fact that surprised her.

Doug wrapped her in a clean blanket and led her back to the bed. He rubbed her back in slow circular strokes with his large, warm hand. Doug was two years older than Anne, with a deep melancholy around his smoke-gray eyes, a mane of toast-colored hair, and the paradox of an easy smile never far from the wide, handsome mouth.

"Anne," he said softly, "you need to go to the hospital. This isn't getting any better."

"Another hour. Let's wait another hour. The bleeding isn't any worse."

"And the cramps?"

"Not bad."

"Please, let me take you to San Marco General."

"No, you remember the last time I lost the baby." She said it as if she were losing the same baby this time. There were no names, no faces, not even graves to differentiate the specific hopes lost in a miscarriage, just the words "the baby." She had miscarried twice before, long before term.

"They let me lie in a room for hours. Don't you remember?" Her throat felt very dry. "And I was so scared. It took such a long time."

She curled up when a contraction pulled her stomach into a rock. Anne closed her eyes and held her breath until the pain passed. "Mama used to say things changed so fast, but I always thought they were slow. Everything was so slow. She'd pick plums, and a day later there'd be twenty jars of jam on the kitchen counter. She'd say that was fast, but it wasn't really." Anne's head felt light and very far away. "It took half the summer for those plums to ripen. And years for the tree to grow."

Another contraction gathered in her back. The timbre of Anne's voice rose with her muscles. "Mama was so scared of cancer, because it killed you fast. But it took two years for her to die. Two years isn't fast, is it, Doug?''

"Annie," he said, "listen to me. I'm taking you to the hospital right now."

"I was dreaming. About swimming." Anne felt Doug's arms bring her body to a sitting position on the edge of the bed. The movement was an effortless denial of gravity, like getting off the tilt-a-whirl at the state fair. "It's funny to wake up feeling cold in August. What time is it?"

"Eleven."

Her ears buzzed. She was dizzy. "It's too early. It's coming too fast. The baby will die if it comes now."

He didn't answer, but carefully walked Anne out of the bedroom, steered her down the hall that seemed unusually long, and then outside to the car. She began to cry, a stream of tears more like sweating. She cried through the emergency-room examination at San Marco General.

"Please," she begged the young doctor, "can't you do something to stop it? Can't you help me?"

"We'll do everything we can," he reassured her.

"Where's Dr. Springer?"

"He'll be here shortly to have a look at you. Just relax, now. You're going to be fine, Mrs. Hart."

After an injection, a unit of blood was started dripping through the clear tubing attached to her arm.

"B positive," she said to the nurse in a startlingly white uniform. "I'm a B positive."

"That's right," the woman said with a thin smile.

But Anne wasn't satisfied. "I'm a lab tech," she insisted. The nurse let her read the label on the unit of blood, but tears blurred her vision, and she wasn't sure it was B positive.

Doug bathed her face with a wet towel. She begged for a drink of water, and when the hawk-faced nurse left the room, Doug brought a sip of cool water in a paper cup. It was the sweetest water she'd ever tasted.

"Thank you," she murmured, savoring the trickle of moisture down her throat.

She slept for minutes at a time, waking to the pressure

deep in her body, like a balloon blown up inside a drinking straw.

She strained to hear whispered conferences at the foot of her bed, but she couldn't understand what was being said. One after another, unidentified hands pressed their stethoscopes to her belly and probed at her insides while she wept, dislocated from her body that refused to hold on to the baby any longer.

"Does it hurt?" Doug asked softly.

"Not much."

Then it hurt. Two young men in clean-smelling surgical greens came with a gurney. Chatting to each other, they slid Anne from the bed to a stiff white pad. Her head rested in the crook of a well-muscled arm. At the door of the room Anne glanced back at Doug, who sat crumpled in a wood chair.

"She'll be back in no time, Mr. Hart," the nurse at the head of the gurney said quite cheerfully. "You can wait in the lounge down the hall. Or get something to eat. You must be hungry."

To Anne it seemed like forever. First she was left in a dim corridor and later wheeled to a small room painted monotonous blue and left alone again. Only when she cried out did a face appear at the bed rail to say, "Just take it easy. It'll all be over soon."

But it dragged on and on. She was sure they'd made a mistake. Forgotten about her, perhaps. Anne searched the walls for a clock. "What time is it?" she called. "Is anyone there?"

"One-thirty," the nameless face said beside her. "Just relax, honey."

She had time to think between pains that wrenched her body. Where was Doug? Why couldn't he come with her? Surely something had gone wrong. This was too long.

She groaned, and the face of a handsome black woman hovered over her. "Help me," she whispered to the serene black eyes. "Please help me."

Anne felt the woman's cool fingers against her hot face.

"Don't fight it," the nurse soothed her. "It'll be easier if you relax and just let go."

She only cared when the pain stopped, which seemed no more than seconds. It wasn't fast. She could no longer locate the pain exactly when it arched her back, pushing through her. A commotion of voices surrounded her. She couldn't open her eyes.

"Jesus, isn't she ready yet?" she heard.

I'm ready, Anne tried to call back.

"Is she out?"

I'm not out, she thought wildly.

"Snoozing like a kitten."

"Tell OR we'll do a section. Otherwise we get a dead kid."

Another pain swept her almost to unconsciousness. She thought she could smell blood. She screamed.

"Doctor. I've lost the fetal heartbeat!"

The gurney rolled sickeningly away from the wall.

"Shit!" someone bellowed beside her.

Overhead lights flashed by. A rush of cool air hit her face, strong hands lifted her like a feather, and her body seemed to tear open. Then a sharp buzz, a siren in her head.

In the fifth month of that pregnancy Anne had resigned from her job as a senior research assistant at Peralta Technology, Incorporated. For three years she had tested the osmotic capabilities of the synthetic media Am-E, or "Ammy," as it was called. Ammy was a transparent enzymatic amine polymer that PTI hoped would be a life-support medium for the catastrophically ill, supplying oxygen and nutrients and absorbing wastes through the skin and gastrointestinal tract.

Dr. Geoffrey Collier was head of Research and Development at Peralta. "We'll miss you," he said to Anne on her last day at PTI.

She handed him the final notes on the oxygen-transfer parameters of Ammy. "I'll miss you, too, and my work here," she said, somewhat relieved by the formality of their farewell. They had spent so many hours discussing the properties of crystalline substances and enzyme bondings on a protein molecule that Anne wasn't sure she could manage an intimate good-bye with Geoffrey.

He was a slight man with fragile-looking hands and sandy hair pulled back to a knot at his neck. Geoffrey usually dressed in blue jeans, blue cotton work shirt, hiking boots, and, of course, the ever-present white lab coat. He was one of those medical men who look like they were born in a lab coat.

The reasons why an M.D., fresh out of medical school, would accept the job as head of Research and Development at PTI remained a matter of speculation. Once he said he didn't inspire much confidence in patients. But Geoffrey maintained some patient contact, working two nights a week at the downtown free Unity Clinic.

"I hope everything goes well for you this time," he said quietly to Anne. "I know how much this baby means to you."

Twice before she had taken maternity leave, only to return to PTI several months later after two premature deliveries of dead infants. This time there was no baby shower or even punch and cookies on her last day of work. Her co-workers said "Good-bye" and "Good luck" in polite embarrassment. No one inquired about names for the baby.

"It's going to work out," Anne said to Geoffrey with a reassuring smile. "I just feel it."

"Right under the rib cage, I'll bet," he joked, glancing at the obvious bulge under her lab coat. "Will Dr. Springer deliver you?"

"Yes. Thanks for giving me his name. I saw him last month. He said everything's fine, except my weight. I threatened to just call in next month and announce my weight if he doesn't stop lecturing me."

Geoffrey hooted. "There's a special course for obstetricians in medical school called 'Persuasive Preaching to Portly Pregnancies.'"

"I believe it, but I wish Dr. Springer hadn't insisted I stop working this early. I hate to leave Ammy, you know, just when the testing is going so well. What will happen with the medium now?''

Geoffrey shoved his hands deep in his lab coat pockets. ''Well,'' he said slowly, ''we'll finish the testing and begin our animal studies by the end of the year. Then release it for experimental work on humans. Limited, at first, and subject to FDA approval, of course. Then the sky's the limit. Ammy will revolutionize the care of burn cases, multiple traumas, cancer victims . . .''

''My mother died of cancer,'' Anne said softly, ''and I think she died of malnutrition more than anything else after nearly two years of chemotherapy. Ammy might have given her a fighting chance.''

''We have very high hopes for Ammy,'' he said. ''But I don't want it released before it's ready. And there are people at Peralta who want it on the market today, at the latest. People like H. M. Schwartz.'' He gave her a knowing glance.

Anne smiled. She was well aware of the difference between rarefied theoretical research and the steely world of practical medicine. H. M. Schwartz, chairman of the board at PTI, pushed Research and Development for results, verifiable results just short of miracles. ''I'll be anxious to hear how the rest of the testing goes,'' she said. ''And take good care of Xanadu.''

''I was about to give him his dinner,'' Geoffrey said, and picked up a beaker of blue fluid.

On top of Geoffrey's desk sat a large jar filled with the clear, semifluid Ammy suspending a white mouse who tumbled as if he were weightless and assumed a languid, vertical position, nose down in the jar. Geoffrey opened the jar and slowly poured in the beaker's contents. The medium turned a delicate sky blue. The mouse stirred.

''Funny thing about Xanadu,'' Geoffrey said. ''After eight months in Ammy, he seems to have lost all sense of direction.''

''Well, at least you haven't,'' she said.

Geoffrey's smile was quick and affectionate. ''I've enjoyed working with you. Let us know about the baby, and when you're ready to come back to work, give me a call.''

"Thanks, Geoffrey."

"Good-bye, Anne."

She turned and walked out of his office, then down the hall to the reception area, decorated with stainless-steel sling chairs and a bank of green plants intended to reassure visitors and employees alike that the environment at PTI was as safe as their own kitchen windowsills. But all the employees knew those plants had been replaced four times in the last year, not because of poisons in the air, but because no one watered them. The obvious was a constant difficulty at research companies like PTI, Anne thought.

The pneumatic doors wheezed open. She could create a complex crystalline molecule that behaved like human blood, but automatic doors remained incomprehensible. The door closed silently behind her, and she was swallowed by the still summer air of the St. Helena Valley.

At her car she looked back at the unimposing gray building. That's the last good-bye for a while, she thought.

The first light was overhead, multifaceted, breaking through a slate-blue darkness of Sodium Pentothal. Anne was relieved to be out of the anesthetic. It was like waking from a nightmare, breathless and grateful.

There were two light fixtures, two curtain edges, two silver bars dangling two yellow bottles. . . .

She remembered double vision was an effect of anesthesia. The jagged edges of darkness approached.

"I can't see," she cried in a cottony garble.

The darkness overcame her.

She heard a voice crying and wondered why they didn't do something to stop it. Is that my baby? she wondered. Why is my baby crying?

She opened her eyes. Despite her blurred vision, she could make out several faces peering down at her.

"Everything's all right," one of them said.

Anne tried to concentrate on the moving lips above her, but the voice screamed, "Where's my baby?" She knew it was her own voice. The sound arched its way out of her lungs, throwing her head back. Her arms tore at restraints. And the scream went on and on. She didn't know how to stop it.

"Where's my baby? My baby!" she cried, thrashing at the weight of a thousand hands on her arms and legs.

"IMI," she heard a voice say.

"What?"

"IMI. Stat."

"My baby . . ." she called again to the disembodied voices above her.

"Your baby died, Mrs. Hart."

The words were dim in the haze of her mind.

"We did everything we could, Mrs. Hart. Do you hear me? The baby is dead."

Anne screamed. The sound streaked in a red line in front of her eyes. It grew brighter and brighter, until a face, a leering chimera face, formed from painfully pure crystals of red color.

"No!" she screamed again. A hole tore open the face, a merciful black pit into which she dived.

"What do you remember?" Dr. Springer quizzed kindly.

Anne was back in her hospital room. "Where's my baby?" she demanded. "What happened to my baby?" She felt her stomach, as deflated as a basketball and very sore. "I heard you decide to do a cesarean section. I heard you. I wasn't out!"

"You must have been dreaming, Anne," he said quietly. "We didn't do a C-section. Check for yourself."

Her fingers searched for a bandage, but there was none. "But I heard you! And this crying. They did terrible things to me. Things inside me. I *wasn't* sleeping. And they put the baby . . . in a jar. Just like Xanadu." She was sobbing. She barely felt the needle prick in her arm. Dr. Springer bent close to her, and her words began to slur slightly. "They held me down. Why didn't you stop them?"

"Anne, Anne," he soothed her, "just take it easy. You must have had some terrible dreams. We *did* restrain you in recovery. We had no choice. You were determined to get out of bed.'' He fished a penlight from his breast pocket and flashed it across her eyes, tipping her chin up and crossing her face again with the light.

Anne jerked her head away. She hated his hand on her face.

''We were afraid you might hurt yourself,'' he said.

Anne studied his sultry, half-lidded eyes. Dr. Ben Springer was a smooth, darkly enigmatic man with pale skin that rose to a fresh plum blush at the cheekbones. He had the shoulders of a gladiator and the walk of a panther. She noticed the wet, pink lower lip under his trimmed mustache.

''I wish they'd stop that crying,'' she complained.

''What crying?''

''That baby crying out there.''

He listened. ''Where? I don't hear anything.''

''*That* baby! Crying in the hall.''

''Anne, there's no baby crying in the hall.'' He edged toward the split in the white drape around her bed. ''I want you to rest now. You're upset, and you'll feel better after a little rest.''

''I'm not upset,'' she called after him. ''Dr. Springer, where's my baby?''

After that she was weighed down with sedatives. The time passed in light sleep. Once a nurse with large breasts bent across her. The warm, heavy body was comforting, like the times she had a stomachache as a child and her mother brought a hot-water bottle. Another time she recognized lemon cologne. Mama liked lemon, she thought sleepily.

Anne also recognized Jolie, the black night nurse, whom she'd first seen in that sky-blue room before surgery. Jolie's sculptured face, large black eyes, and cool hands reassured Anne again.

''I got three kids of my own,'' Jolie said to her one night. ''They're a lot of trouble, but I'd sure hate to lose one of them. I know how you feel.''

"The baby's not dead," Anne whispered through the vaporous sedatives.

"Your mind is protecting you," Jolie said softly. "Maybe it's too painful right now to face."

The smallest occurrences were interesting to Anne. She knew the sounds of familiar footsteps in the hall, the clink of meal trays, the elevator bell. Doug came several times that she could remember. Faces appeared over the edge of her vision as if she were lying in a deep well. A man spoke to her about the crying in the hall.

"Stopped," she whispered. The infant screeched hysterically from a corner of the room.

A spoon poked insistently at her mouth. "You must eat, Mrs. Hart. Eat. You don't want any more of those nasty drugs, do you?"

Anne swallowed the morsel of food, gagged, and swallowed again. Although the thought of anything solid in her mouth made her dizzy with nausea, she knew she would never get out of the hospital as long as she refused food. And, slowly, the weight lightened. She didn't ask Dr. Springer about the baby again, and never mentioned the infant's crying. When the nurses' aide brought her breakfast tray, Anne drank the coffee, mushed the poached egg on her plate, and flushed most of it down the toilet. She was quite clever with oatmeal, which was particularly offensive, reminding her of brains. One of the aides told her the woman in the room next door had given birth to an encephalic monster, a baby with no brain. They could tell by shining a light in the child's ear and seeing the light through its eyes. Anne shivered. The aide had also said the woman was being transferred to the psych unit soon because she wasn't getting better. So Anne poured milk on the oatmeal while she gazed out the window, and then she flushed only half the bowl of cereal, restirring it for appearance' sake.

Maybe they were right. Maybe she was crazy. She certainly couldn't explain the persistent crying of a baby, the cold sweat that beaded on her lip when anyone touched her, or her revulsion to food. She just wanted to go home, away from the hospital and that room. And certainly not to the psych unit.

"When can I go home?" she asked Dr. Springer.

"How are you feeling?"

"Fine." She smiled.

"Oh, why don't you hang around with us a couple more days. You had a reaction to the anesthetic, and we want to make sure that doesn't recur."

"A reaction? An allergic reaction? Is that what happened?"

"Not exactly an allergic reaction, Anne. It's very difficult emotionally to lose a baby."

"A psychological reaction?" She tried to hold her voice steady. He said "lose a baby" as if it had actually been lost, misplaced somehow. That wasn't true. The baby had come ripping out of her. The thin, frantic cry of an infant in the hall distracted her. She didn't turn her head toward the sound.

"It's something we should talk about, Anne." Dr. Springer rested his hands on the bed and leaned toward her slightly. "Do you remember Dr. Rivers? He's seen you several times."

Dr. Springer waited for her reaction. Anne couldn't remember a Dr. Rivers.

"He's a psychiatrist," he continued. "I think you should spend some time talking to him. You'll like him."

"A psychiatrist?" Her voice cracked nervously. She could outsmart the nurses' aides, but could she match wits with a shrink? she wondered.

Dr. Springer reached out to pat her arm, but Anne twisted away. "Don't . . ." She started to cry, and then stopped abruptly.

"He can help you, Anne."

"I don't want a shrink," she said. "I want to go home. Please, just tell me what happened to my baby."

Ben Springer studied her for several long moments. "It was nearly three months premature. Like seeds, you know. You put them in the soil, and some grow. And some don't."

"No," Anne said, shaking her head.

"Anne, listen to me. The baby died. We did everything possible. Dr. Jones, the best neonatal pediatrician at General

Hospital, was right there. Believe me, we did all we could."

She fought back the tears. "Was it a boy? Or a girl?"

"A boy, I think," he said softly. His chest and shoulders loomed over her. "I know this has been rough. But my advice is to have another child, Anne. You're young. Next time we'll see if we can't help you carry it to term. You know the old saying—if you can't stand heights, go climb the mountain." His face crinkled in a smile, an oddly fierce smile. "You can go home tomorrow afternoon, if Dr. Rivers thinks it's okay. He'll stop in later today. Otherwise, Anne, I'm afraid we'll have to move you to Six West." He exhaled softly. "The psych unit."

It was a clear threat. Anne held her breath and managed to nod solemnly.

"Good girl. You take it easy. I'll see you later."

She watched him walk around the curtain and heard his steps across the tile floor and then on the carpet in the hall. Anne covered her eyes with the backs of her hands and lay very still. Don't cry, she instructed herself. Don't ever cry.

2

Nina Phillips rarely cried. She was seventeen, squarely built, with lusterless gray eyes and brown bird's nest hair when she came into the emergency room of San Marco General complaining of stomach pains. Nina's mother, Mrs. Paula Phillips, sat in the waiting room while Dr. Springer examined the girl.

"Appendicitis," he told Mrs. Phillips, who nodded and signed the permission slip for surgery on her daughter.

Nina Phillips, twenty-two weeks pregnant, with an elevated white-blood-cell count and acute pain in the lower-right quadrant, went into the operating room, and two hours later, paste white and snoring, she was wheeled to her room on Fourth Central, not the maternity floor at General Hospital. Nina Phillips was now minus an appendix and her baby.

"She was pregnant, you know," Dr. Springer explained to Mrs. Phillips, who did not seem surprised. "The appendix had ruptured and infected the abdominal cavity. We had to take the baby."

Paula Phillips shrugged. "When do I have to pick her up?"

"Is she in school?"

"Quit last year. Been runnin' wild ever since."

Ben shook his head slowly. "She'll need a week to ten days here."

Paula Phillips cocked her head and looked up at him with her rheumy blue eyes. "You couldn't fix her, could you, doctor? So she wouldn't go and get herself pregnant again?"

"No, I'm afraid not." Ben smiled at the woman. "Nina's too young for that."

Mrs. Phillips nodded in resignation.

3

Anne was in a room alone on the maternity wing. It was an act of kindness, she thought. The other women, shuffling up and down the hall in bright pink robes and new slippers, had babies to look at, babies wrapped in white receiving blankets to hold several times a day. Anne saw the nurses carrying the small bundles to their appropriate mothers. Sometimes she heard those babies whimper. Her baby didn't whimper. It shrieked, just outside her reach.

Dr. Marc Rivers arrived in her room before lunch. The pale yellow walls seemed to swell with his presence, which was strange, Anne thought, because the man was quite unremarkable apart from his crackling dark eyes juxtaposed in a serene, softly lined face.

"Hello, Anne," he said in a voice that seemed to begin in the center of his body and radiate upward. "I'm Dr. Marc Rivers. I'm glad to see you looking much better."

"I'm fine. I'm ready to go home."

Marc Rivers sat down in the wooden chair beside her bed. Anne absently watched the soft paunch just above his belt line swell and then sink with each breath. She liked this man, but she wasn't sure why. The slight defect of an unathletic waistline pleased her, balanced her attraction.

"This place must get pretty boring," he said, glancing

around the hospital room. "How are you feeling? Are you really well enough to manage at home?"

"There's not much to manage. A couple Boston ferns, the vacuum cleaner . . ." She looked away from his piercing eyes. "I feel fine. Really."

"How about the crying? Do you still hear the baby crying?"

"No, I got over that."

"Or you got smarter and learned not to talk about it."

Anne glanced up quickly at him without agreeing or disagreeing with the statement.

"And the dreams? I understand you have bad dreams at night."

"Sometimes." A thick rope of anxiety tightened around Anne's chest. "I just want to go home. There are things I want to do."

"Like managing the Boston ferns." He smiled at her. "And what else?"

"I can go back to work. If I want to."

"Do you want to?"

"I don't know."

"So what will you do at home all day, Anne?"

"I paint. Or I used to. I'd like to do that again."

"Friends?" he asked. "Do you have friends here in San Marco?"

"Yes."

"And another baby?"

"Another baby?"

His smile was gentle. "One way to get over losing a baby is to have another one."

"I don't know," she stammered. "I need to think about it."

"Of course," he agreed, "of course you do." Dr. Rivers pulled a hand-tooled leather appointment book from his pocket. "How are Tuesdays and Thursdays for you? Could you see me at three both those days?"

"If I say yes, can I go home?" Marc Rivers was a man who made it difficult to say no.

"I see no reason to keep you here. As far as I am concerned, you can go home tomorrow, after Dr. Springer checks you out.''

Rivers rose elegantly from the chair and approached her bed. Anne cringed against the pillow and watched his hands. His knuckles were thick knobs of bone—from arthritis, she guessed.

''Where's your office?''

''Next door, in the Medical Building. Suite 103.'' He stood looking down at her. ''They tell me you don't like to be touched. Is that right, Anne?''

She nodded, desperately hoping he would not insist on testing that information.

''I understand,'' he said, nodding. ''I'm going to leave a prescription at the desk for you to take home and have filled. And I'll see you Tuesday at three.''

''I'll be there,'' she said, breathless.

Doug came after dinner that evening. He looked tired and uncared-for, with his shirttail hanging out where he had obviously tried to tuck it in his slacks. Doug Hart walked as if he were on a conveyor belt, a liquid gait, but that night he seemed slower.

''You look awful, Doug.''

He smiled self-consciously and made one more stab at the shirttail. ''I'm a little tired. And there isn't anything good to eat in the house. And I miss you.''

''Have you had anything to eat tonight?''

''Sure.'' A smile widened across his face. ''I had a peanut-butter sandwich with banana slices, except we were out of peanut butter.''

''A banana sandwich?''

He laughed softly. ''Maybe I'll have some dinner later. Not in the cafeteria. Everything down there looks like pressed sawdust with gravy on it. Even the Jell-O.''

''I get to come home tomorrow,'' she said.

Doug's face tightened. A small muscle jerked involuntarily under his left cheekbone. ''Are you feeling well enough, Anne?''

''I'm fine. Really. They want me to see a psychiatrist.''

His eyes opened wide, but Anne thought Doug looked relieved.

"I know," he said. "Dr. Springer talked to me. What do you think about it?"

"I met Dr. Rivers this morning. He seems nice—" The soft wail of an infant interrupted her. "Do you hear that?"

"What?" He glanced toward the door. "Someone's talking in the hall. Why?"

"Nothing," she said. The cry seemed to be coming from the other side of the room, near the window. "I thought I heard something."

"What about Dr. Rivers?" Doug asked.

"Do you think I should see a psychiatrist, Doug? Am I crazy? Is that what everyone thinks?"

"You're not crazy," he objected quickly. "You had a very bad time in surgery. Dr. Springer said it will take some time to get over that."

"They gave me all those drugs!" Her voice rose to a squeal.

"Look, Annie," Doug pleaded, "you're not crazy. Don't worry about things. Tomorrow, when you're home again, things will look better."

Anne tugged irritably at the sheet and fussed with a damp curl on her forehead. Her head felt muddy, and efforts to think exhausted her. "You're probably right," she finally admitted. "Go and get some dinner."

"Okay." He bent to kiss her. Anne half-turned away, then caught herself, but not before she saw the flicker of pain in his darkly rimmed eyes. He brushed her cheek lightly with his lips.

"Doug, I'm sorry. I didn't mean that."

He stood over her, his shoulders sagging in the brown shirt. "It's all right. I'll see you in the morning."

When he was gone, Anne considered the ceiling. Was she crazy? Doug certainly hadn't heard the baby cry. And she knew she didn't want anyone, not even Doug, to touch her. That was definitely crazy, she thought. She began to count the acoustical tiles on the ceiling. She'd done that many times, sometimes counting by twos or tens and multiplying rows, but she always arrived at a different number. Maybe that was crazy, too, or at least something else not to tell the shrink.

The P.M. nurse interrupted her counting. "Time for meds," the nurse chirped, shoving a white paper cup under Anne's chin.

"Two?" Anne asked, surprised by two pills in the cup instead of one, as on other nights. "Are they both sleeping pills?"

The nurse hesitated. "One is," she said. "The other's a vitamin B_{12}."

"For healthy red blood cells, I suppose," Anne quipped as she popped both capsules in her mouth and reached for the glass of water.

"And a good night's rest," the nurse crooned. "Good night, Mrs. Hart."

In a pig's eye, Anne hissed silently. Sleeping pills were used to keep patients out of the nurses' hair at night. They had nothing to do with the *patients'* rest. When the nurse's back was turned, Anne spit the pills in her hand. She might take them later.

"Tell Jolie to stop in when she comes on duty," Anne called after the bulging white figure in the door. "I might still be awake."

Anne concentrated on keeping her eyes open, counting ceiling tiles in diagonals this time for variety, and waited for Jolie. The two pills were tucked under her pillow. She didn't want to sleep. With sleep came the bad dreams, terrifying journeys through a world of brilliant red faces from which there was no escape, except waking.

The crying of the infant was worse at night. The cry could have been a cat. At home, she thought, a cat crying outside sounded like a baby.

Her eyes drifted shut. The baby's cry pierced the air in the hospital room until her ears rang. Finally Jolie's face jutted through the door.

"Hi," Anne said hoarsely.

"How you doin'?"

"Okay. I get to go home tomorrow, but I want to talk to you first. Do you have a minute?"

"You're supposed to be two hours into slumberland already," Jolie answered, gliding to Anne's bed in the noiseless crepe-soled shoes. "Didn't you get meds tonight?"

"Of course.They brought in the horse pills." Anne fished for her cigarettes on the bedside stand and lit one. "A sleeping pill to shut me up and a vitamin B_{12} to keep the oxygen going to my brain."

"You didn't take them!"

"I wanted to talk to you first."

"Anne Hart, you are making my night difficult," Jolie scolded in mock irritation.

"Jolie . . ." Anne whined, drawing out the name in long vowels.

"I'll get your meds. Or do you still have them?"

"Yes. Turn on the light."

Anne dug out the two capsules, but the blue-and-yellow one split in her hand and poured its contents on the sheet in a white spray.

"Oops, sorry," Anne apologized.

"It's okay." Jolie scooped the sheet from the bed in one brisk arm movement. "Give me that pill, and I'll get meds ready for you *again*. And a clean sheet."

She left Anne sitting uncovered on the bed finishing her cigarette. Nurses were so rushed. Anne wondered if they were really that busy or if they looked hurried as a matter of professional pride. Thirty minutes later Jolie returned.

"Had to restart an IV," she explained. "Here's your sleeping pill."

"Where's the other one?" Anne asked after inspecting the paper cup.

"The orders are for one Seconal. I can't find an order for vitamin B_{12}. Are you sure that's what the nurse said?"

"For heaven's sake," Anne cried, thrusting the sleeping pill back in the cup. "That's what I wanted to talk to you about." Her lower lip trembled. "Everybody thinks I'm crazy, and Dr. Springer says the baby died, and now I have to see a psychiatrist. *And* take all these pills. But I'm not crazy, Jolie. I remember . . . something. A jar. A big jar. Do they put babies in a big jar here?''

"Sometimes, Anne," Jolie said softly, "if the baby is dead."

"No," Anne protested, shaking her head defiantly. "No, they're trying to make me forget. I'm not taking any more of those pills."

"Anne, hey, it's okay. Everything's okay. I wouldn't give you anything to hurt you. Do you believe that?" Jolie spoke to her as if she were a frightened child. "The vitamin was probably a verbal order over the phone. We'll straighten it out in the morning. You'll live through the night without B_{12}."

"Do you think I'm crazy, Jolie?" Anne brushed away the tears. She hated to have anyone see her cry. Her eyes swelled immediately, and the tears left red splotches on her cheeks.

"No, I don't." The authority in Jolie's voice was reassuring. "Come on, let's get this sheet on, and then you take the pill." Jolie spread the sheet over Anne. "Take the pill, hon, and I have a surprise for you." Jolie's eyes twinkled mischievously.

Anne fell right into the game. "I get to go home *tonight?*"

"Not quite. Almost as good," the nurse teased.

Anne swallowed the pill, and Jolie, with a theatrical flourish of her slender hand, produced a cellophane package of crackers from her uniform pocket. "Genuine saltines." She grinned.

Anne moaned. "Some surprise."

"According to the best medical tests available, it is virtually impossible to eat two crackers at once and keep any pill—I repeat, *any pill*—hidden in the mouth. One cracker is evidently not enough, but two are absolutely unbeatable."

Anne laughed. "Why don't you get a flashlight or a probe and inspect between my teeth?"

"That's not as reliable as two crackers. You want to argue with the medical experts? Now, eat."

Anne dutifully munched both crackers. Jolie sat down in the armchair. "Lie back," she said. "You'll be sleepy in a minute."

"Tell me what happened to the baby. You were there—"

"Anne, I told you before. I was only with you *before* surgery, for an hour or so."

"Someday you will tell me . . ." Anne said softly. The words made colored stripes in the dark in front of her closed eyes.

"Someday you'll have a couple babies to take care of, and you'll forget about this one."

"I won't forget." Her tongue felt thick.

"It's best to forget, Anne. Go on living. Go back to work or to school, maybe. Nothing's going to bring that child back to you."

"Nothing . . ." Anne repeated in a semihypnotic drawl. "Except remembering . . ."

"Go to sleep now."

Then it was morning, time for coffee and one piece of toast eaten as a going-home celebration over the protest of her stomach. She flushed the rest of her breakfast. Nurses with stacks of sheets and white towels, clean gowns, strong-smelling soap, and pleated cups of pills filed in and out of her room. Anne was showered and dressed by the time Dr. Springer arrived.

"Dr. Springer . . ."

"All dressed and ready to get out of here," he said, leaning against the windowsill and flipping through the pages of her chart. "Everything seems in order. You're eating again. The bleeding has subsided. How'd things go with Dr. Rivers?"

"Fine." She sucked in a deep breath. "Dr. Springer . . ."

"And you're going to see him again?"

"On Tuesdays and Thursdays."

"Good." Ben Springer nodded several times in approval and reached in his pocket for a small envelope. "I want you to take these, one a day at bedtime, and come in to see me in two weeks."

Anne took the envelope, careful not to touch his hand in the transfer. "What are they?"

"Depletion vitamins. You're quite run down, you know."

She turned the envelope in her hands and studied the sealed flap.

"We get samples. I thought I'd save you a trip to the pharmacy," he said. Ben slapped the chart closed. "You're going to be fine, Anne. Take care, now."

"Dr. Springer . . ."

But the man had virtually evaporated from the room, and she hadn't asked him about the vitamin B_{12}. He hadn't mentioned it either. Anne tore open the envelope and inspected the pills. They were tiny yellow circles with the number 10 stamped on them. They certainly didn't look like the blue-and-yellow capsule the nurse said was vitamin B_{12}. Anne tucked the envelope in her purse and decided not to think about the pills right now. She could always check *The Physician's Desk Reference.*

By one o'clock she was home. Anne wandered into the spare bedroom, intended for a nursery. Doug had packed the crib with its butterfly mobile back in the closet. "Spare" was certainly the correct word for that room again, Anne thought. Once it had been a child's room wallpapered with blue-and-red clowns holding bouquets of balloons, and Doug and Anne had decided not to repaper when they moved in. Anne used the room for sewing and storage, and a plaid sofa bed stood against one wall, but they rarely had guests. Anne's father promised to fly out every year from Iowa, but he postponed the trip every year, too. Anne knew he was afraid to fly. And Doug's parents lived in Florida. They had never visited either.

Monday morning Doug went back to work at Lincoln Electronics, where he was an engineer, and Anne had the morning to herself. She was grateful he decided to go back to work instead of taking more days off to stay home with her. The weekend had been an ordeal of delicate avoidance, nicely keeping her distance from Doug in the kitchen and in their bed. Maybe she was crazy. She loved Doug and at the same time couldn't bear to touch him. Apparently he was aware of her efforts to maintain an invisible space between them. He had smiled and said he'd go back to work Monday.

The infant's crying softened during the day. The sounds seemed hidden deep in the kitchen walls as she sat drinking coffee. At nine o'clock Fay phoned.

"You're home!" she shouted when Anne answered.

"Of course I'm home."

"How are you?"

"I'm fine," Anne snapped. "How are you?" Fay hadn't seen her in the hospital, or even phoned, although she had sent flowers, bright yellow and orange pom pons.

"They wouldn't let me in to see you at General," her friend explained, as if she sensed the distance in Anne's voice and knew the reason for it.

"What?"

"They said you couldn't have any visitors or phone calls," Fay continued. "I tried to see you. Or at least talk to you. I was furious. I even thought about borrowing one of your lab coats and sneaking in, but Doug said you were really tired and needed to rest."

"Something happened," Anne said. "I don't even know what, exactly. But they gave me a lot of drugs, and I don't remember much."

"What happened?"

"I don't know, Fay. The doctor said the baby died and I had a psychological reaction. Now I have to see a psychiatrist."

"Are you serious?"

"No, I'm evidently crazy."

"Annie, that ridiculous. Are you depressed?"

"A little, maybe. How do you know if you're depressed or not?"

"Can I come over? I mean, are you feeling well enough?"

"Yes, come. The coffee's hot."

As well as a neighbor and friend, Fay O'Donnell was a potter, a very good potter, whose work was gaining some acceptance in the St. Helena Valley. She'd been invited to exhibit at the San Marco Art Museum in September and at the

Ocher Earth Gallery later in the fall. Anne knew she was busy getting the pots ready.

When Fay arrived at the door, she didn't knock. "Anne?" she called through the front door.

"Here," Anne answered from the kitchen table, where she sat huddled in a pale green robe. She poured another cup of coffee for Fay.

"I'm terribly sorry about the baby," Fay said simply. "Everything was going so well, wasn't it? What happened?"

"Well," Anne started slowly, "Friday morning I woke up with cramps and bleeding. I stayed in bed. I just couldn't believe it was happening all over again. Doug took me to the hospital. It seems like years ago. Maybe we weren't meant to have any children." She twisted the tie on her robe. She wouldn't cry.

Fay's eyes were wide with disbelief and a generous compassion.

"I was so scared, Fay."

"Scared of what?"

Anne felt the panic rise. She smelled the antiseptic recovery room and felt nauseated. "There were these awful dreams . . . faces . . ."

Fay looked stunned.

Anne swallowed hard several times. "I'm okay. It's just hard to talk about it. Something happened in surgery, but I'm not convinced it was a psychological reaction. I can't understand why I was taken to the operating room, instead of Delivery. When I lost the baby before, I was in Delivery."

"Maybe they made a mistake and were afraid you'd sue," Fay suggested. "I mean, they *do* make mistakes."

Anne agreed, but she didn't feel up to reviewing her collection of horror stories about surgical procedures gone awry. "I don't know what happened. . . . Sometimes I hear a baby cry, off in the distance."

The muscles in Fay's shoulders tensed, muscles developed by years of lifting and kneading wet clay and working at the potter's wheel. Fay's gray University of California T-shirt seemed to inflate. "I don't think it's good for you to sit around the house and think about this," she announced. "Get dressed and come with me to the supermarket. I have to buy Coke for me and whole-wheat bread for my organic son."

"Good. I'm out of cigarettes. Though I guess I should quit."

They drove to the market in Fay's Dodge Colt. Anne liked the car, with its cushioned leather dash and deep, contoured seats. They drove in silence.

"Go through the express lane," Fay instructed her at the market. "And I'll meet you there in a few minutes."

Anne picked up a carton of cigarettes. She tried to remember if she needed anything else. Shampoo, she decided. The cosmetic aisle was right behind the cigarettes, but when Anne turned, she was staring at rows and rows of baby-food jars. She'd never really looked at baby food before. She examined a jar of eggs, bacon, and oatmeal, pureed to a lumpy tan pudding. How old would a baby be when it ate that? she wondered. She picked up a jar of chicken soup. Her face burned. A sweet ether aroma of disposable diapers rose from the bottom shelf. The long rows of jars began to spin, and then Fay was there, prying the jar out of her hand.

Fay replaced the soup and steered Anne to the checkout. "Anne, are you all right?" she asked, glancing nervously at her.

They paid for their groceries and returned to the car. Despite the mid-eighty-degree temperatures, Anne was shaking visibly.

"Am I crazy?" she asked, examining her tingling fingers. "What's wrong with me?"

"You're upset, that's all." Fay started the car.

"Sometimes I feel awfully crazy."

Fay's response was careful. "Maybe the psychiatrist will be good for you."

"Maybe."

Tuesday afternoon Marc Rivers' face was calm and smiling when he met her in the small waiting room outside his office. Anne was relieved she did not have to wait in the main waiting room, full of chairs, magazines without covers, and people talking in hushed voices.

"Anne?"

She was tired of people smiling at her. Doug smiled at breakfast, and Doug was not, by nature, cheerful before noon. Fay absolutely beamed at her. The nurses had all smiled, as well as Dr. Springer, the receptionist in the main waiting room, and now Dr. Rivers.

"Mrs. Hart?" he asked again.

"Oh, I'm sorry. I guess I was daydreaming," she said quickly, and scrambled out of the chair.

"What was the daydream?" Dr. Rivers asked, holding out a gnarled hand to her, not exactly in a handshake, but more to guide her into the room.

Anne shrank away from him. His smile faded. The baby shrieked.

"Nothing," she said. "It was nothing."

"Tell me about nothing." He closed the door and sank down in a leather chair that wheezed softly.

Marc Rivers' office was a play of dark and light, contrasting white walls, a dark rug with a wide border of mauve and gold, and an enormous walnut desk. Three Chinese brush paintings hung on the walls, and a set of paned windows lit one end of the room with warm sunlight. Anne sat in a maroon wing chair, and Marc's armchair was chocolate brown, deeply cushioned, resembling a burned marshmallow, Anne thought.

Marc Rivers adjusted his feet on the ottoman and chose an exquisite meerschaum pipe from a rack on the table beside him.

"I wondered why you were smiling," she said. "People always smile at me. I wonder why."

"Maybe they like you." He lit the pipe.

"Maybe."

"You don't sound convinced."

"You hardly know me. But every time I see you, you're grinning . . . like a chimpanzee."

"I like you," he said with the pipe between his teeth.

Anne studied the pattern of footprints in the dark brown rug. The shrink would definitely not be as easy to outwit as the nurses' aides.

"How was the weekend? Any problems?"

"It was fine."

"How are you feeling?"

"Fine." The question was a ritual for Anne.

"Are you taking your medication?"

"Of course." Saturday, when the druggist filled her prescription for chlorpromazine, he gave her a twisted smile. She discovered that chlorpromazine was the generic name for Thorazine, a powerful antipsychotic. She threw the vial in the garbage at home.

"It hasn't slowed you down much," he observed thoughtfully, motioning toward the door, where she'd avoided his hand earlier. "You moved pretty fast just a minute ago."

"I hate being drugged."

"Keep taking the medication, Anne." He sucked deeply on the pipe. "Did you think I was going to hurt you at the door?"

"No."

"What frightened you?"

"I . . ." Anne hesitated. "I don't like being touched."

"Yes, I can understand that. You've been touched a great deal in the last few weeks." He relit the pipe, puffing and watching her out of his dark, bright eyes. "Was that a problem before you lost the baby?"

"No, it wasn't."

"What bothers you about being touched?"

"I just don't like it."

"I'm sure. But *what* don't you like about it?"

"None of it."

"Do you ever answer questions with more than five words?" he asked. A smile played around his mouth again.

"Rarely," she said, and then a smile broke on her own face, warming the cold tension in the room. "Is this what I'm supposed to do here? Answer questions?"

"You aren't *supposed* to do anything here. It's a time and

place for us to talk. What did you think you would do here?''

"I wasn't sure. I thought we would talk. About the baby. About what happened to me in the hospital.''

"What about the baby, and what happened to you at General?''

"I'm not *sure* what happened. I hoped you could tell me something. Why did they give me all those drugs?''

"You were very upset, Anne.''

"Of course I was upset. What did they expect?'' She traced the row of upholstery tacks on the arm of the chair. "I have this feeling that something happened in surgery.''

"What?''

"I don't know. I simply don't know.''

The bleat of the infant distracted her. The sounds seemed to come from the air vent above Dr. Rivers' desk. She listened.

"Anne? Anne.''

She pulled her attention back to him. He was staring at her, holding his pipe in his hand.

"What just happened?'' he asked, peering up at the air vent, too.

"Nothing.'' She shook her head. "I have some trouble concentrating sometimes.'' The continual questions annoyed her. Particularly when he asked them in that intense, fatherly voice. Besides, what else did he expect from someone swallowing Thorazine, she thought, waiting for the hour to end and the door to open.

"Do you hear the baby cry, Anne?''

"No, of course not. What makes you say that?''

He shrugged and laid the pipe back in its rack. "Just a hunch. You may have discovered it isn't wise to mention that to most people.''

"Well, you're wrong. I don't hear anything.''

"Possibly.''

"If I come back here Thursday, will you tell me what happened to my baby?'' She hurled the question across the room at him.

"The baby was dead, Anne.''

"Do you know that for sure? Or is it just another hunch?''

4

Most of the sessions with Marc Rivers ended in relief. She thought the hour was punishment for some unnamed crime so hideous that she deserved interrogation by this seemingly mild psychiatrist. Rivers told her that was a projection. But it didn't help. Tigers were never tamed by giving them a name.

The fact that much of the time was spent in silence did not alter Anne's feelings, and she studied the three paintings in Marc's office like new inmates in a prison cell. She used to paint, but not for several years now. She had nothing to paint, no interesting faces, no stunning scenes in her mind.

So she read from the psychology section in the San Marco library—Menninger, Freud, and Maslow. She discovered hearing voices was not a good sign.

"Take the medication," Rivers encouraged her. "It might help."

Dr. Rivers wrote prescriptions for Thorazine, and Anne tore them up. She choked on solid food, everything from lettuce to slivers of cheese, and she spent the night huddled on her side of the bed so Doug wouldn't brush against her, triggering the waves of nausea and dry vomiting. And the child wailed at her all day from a blurred and distant memory, so far away she thought it must be only fragments of a nightmare.

Marc's mouth and eyes turned down in sadness by the end of her sessions with him.

"I think I can help you, Anne," he would say quietly, "but you have to let me."

"Help me find out what happened to my baby."

"Your baby is dead."

Dr. Springer would have told her the same thing, but she didn't ask him. He'd threatened her once with the psych ward, and once was enough. As he bent over his desk in his office, Anne noticed the soft patina of a gold ring on his left hand and his dark, curly hair graying at the temples.

"I want you to take these pills," he said, glancing up at Anne, who sat across the desk from him. He held up two envelopes on which he'd written directions. "One is an antispasmodic to relieve the throat spasms, and the other is for nausea."

Anne nodded. "What about the vitamins?"

"Vitamins?"

"Yes. You gave me those 'depletion' vitamins when I left the hospital. I finished taking them."

His face relaxed in a smile. "Oh, just a multivitamin will be fine now. My concern is your weight. You've lost twenty-two pounds, you know," he said. "I think these new pills will help. I won't write a prescription yet. Let's see if they work when you come back in two weeks." Ben leaned back in his chair. "How's it going with Dr. Rivers?"

"Fine."

"Are you ready to consider having another baby?"

"I . . . I don't know. I'm not sure," she stammered.

"If we can get you pregnant again, I think many of your difficulties will disappear."

"Do you have children, Dr. Springer?" she asked. His solution to her difficulties sounded terribly simple to Anne.

Ben Springer motioned toward a picture of a child on his desk. She was about twelve years old, holding the lead of a horse.

"That's Chrissy, my daughter. And her horse, America."

"Does she ride a lot?"

"She jumps. She and America have won a number of area competitions. That picture was taken this summer at the county fair."

"Isn't jumping dangerous?"

Springer shrugged. "What isn't dangerous?"

"And has she solved all your difficulties?" Anne asked.

He smiled. When Ben Springer smiled, it was as if a light snapped on inside his head, illuminating his whole face. "Some of them."

"I'm thinking of going back to work," Anne told him.

"You are? At Peralta?"

"Maybe. Or maybe I can get a job at General in the lab."

Slight alarm ringed Ben's eyes. "Have you talked to Dr. Rivers about this? I think you should. I don't believe you're ready to go back to work yet."

But she would be ready, and soon. Anne swallowed the red tablets in the morning and the tiny yellow ones at night. She thought the yellow pills looked a great deal like the vitamins, except these had the number 20 stamped on them. She would look them up in *The Physician's Desk Reference* on her very next trip to the library.

Anne could eat as long as the food was liquid, and she began to look forward to lunch of eggs, milk, and honey blended to a frothy pale yellow.

And she called Personnel at General Hospital and asked them to send her an application form, which she filled out and mailed back promptly.

She could work part-time, and General had a half-time job available, even if it was at night. She'd have the day free, her evenings with Doug, and two or three nights of work every week. Two or three nights at General Hospital to try to find out what had happened to her there. Or what had happened to the baby.

Anne saw Dr. Rivers twice a week. She no longer felt her sessions were a punishment, but a pivot and an anchor for her week. If she was crazy, she needed a psychiatrist, and if she wasn't, maybe he would help her find out what happened to her baby.

Thursday, the middle of September, Marc Rivers eased back in his chair and said pleasantly, "We can help you with this aversion to touch. We can systematically desensitize you to the pain you feel when you are touched." He lit his pipe. "Perhaps you are afraid of another pregnancy?"

Anne stared at his dark fingers fondling the slender white pipe. "I'm not afraid."

"Good." He smiled and puffed vigorously on the pipe. A ribbon of smoke coiled over his head. "Now, I want you to sit back in the chair with your arms comfortably at your sides. Desensitization is slowly reexposing you to what you are afraid of, but under relaxed circumstances. Just relax . . . breathe slowly in and out. . . . That's good, Anne."

His voice merged with the in-and-out tide of her breath. She imagined the seashore with waves rippling over it, cresting in white curls of foam.

"Now, close your eyes . . . think of one person you like . . . someone you trust. Your husband, perhaps. I want you to picture this person standing about five feet away from you. Is that comfortable, Anne?"

"Yes."

"Now, picture this person. . . . Who is the person?"

"Fay, a friend of mine."

"Picture Fay three feet away now. She has moved a little closer." He paused. "Now Fay is moving toward you, but very slowly, one step at a time. . . . Now she is two feet away. How does that feel?"

"Okay."

"Imagine Fay's hand rising slowly from her side . . . just a little. Her hand is rising and reaching to you . . . but slowly. . . . How are you doing? Do you feel any anxiety at this point?"

Distant breakers crashed dimly in her ears. She sucked more air into her greedy lungs. "No."

"Good. Now Fay is holding out her hand to you. Her hand is ten inches away from you . . . palm up."

Sweat beaded on her top lip.

"Now, picture your own hand beginning to move toward Fay's hand. . . ."

Anne opened her eyes in terror and pushed herself far back in the chair. It creaked its objection.

"You did fine," he said gently. "You did just fine, Anne. It will get easier and easier. How do you feel?"

"I'm okay," she said. She thought her bone marrow must be quivering.

"Good." He rose from his chair. "We can continue to do this exercise until you are comfortable imagining yourself shaking hands with your friend. Then we can go on to other disturbing situations."

Anne's heart thundered. Marc pulled the door open for her, and she met a rush of cold air in the hall, chilling the polyester shirt clinging to her back. She put on her sweater and wrapped it around herself.

Anne's night dreams were livid with the brilliant crimson faces, red hands that clawed at her, inside her. Sweating and terrified, she woke to Doug's urgent pleas.

During the day the baby wailed and whined, puncturing her attention. Shirts hung from her shoulders in folds, and her usually crisp blond hair clung in oily ringlets on her forehead.

"This desensitization isn't working," she cried to Dr. Rivers after one of the anguishing exercises. "All I want to know is what happened to my baby. Why won't you tell me?"

"Your baby died," he answered softly. "That makes you angry and sad."

"No, you're wrong," she stated, mocking his calm voice.

"You aren't angry or sad?"

"The baby didn't die!"

"Why do you torture yourself?" he asked sadly. "What will convince you that your child was too premature to survive? What will convince you, Anne?"

Nothing, she wanted to scream, nothing will convince me. Both Dr. Rivers and Doug, she thought, treated her kindly, but much like an ailing parakeet, expecting her to sit up one day and fly right.

Doug brought home fresh asparagus and ripe kiwi fruit to tempt her appetite, and a periwinkle-blue negligee for her birthday. And his appetites.

"Is it better, Anne?" he asked one evening.

"I feel okay." Instant wariness tightened her throat.

"I think you need to get out of the house more, you know, go shopping or jog or something. I can't imagine what you do here all day."

Anne inventoried the disheveled room. What he meant was that she certainly wasn't doing *much* at home. Clean laundry piled on the sofa. A week of newspapers carpeted the family-room floor, and books balanced in precarious stacks on the coffee table and desk.

"I filled out an application for General Hospital, Doug. There's a half-time midnight job open."

His eyes darkened. "You want to work at *night?*"

'I don't know.' She watched him finish his Scotch and soda in one long gulp. "Maybe I'm bored. There isn't much to do around here. I read and—"

"I noticed." He knocked the stack of books out in a row. "Dream analysis. Isn't that what I pay Dr. Rivers for?"

"I know Dr. Rivers is expensive. I thought if I had a job I could help pay for him."

"It isn't the money."

"What, then?"

Doug raised his hands, prepared to catch the ceiling in case it fell. The gesture was helpless and frantic. "I don't know. But I'm sick of coming home and finding the house a mess, no dinner, and you're depressed. We never go out. And we haven't had sex—for a *long* time." His shoulders slumped. "When will it end, Annie? It's been six weeks since you lost the baby. When do we get to go back to living again?"

He was right. She'd neglected herself, as well as Doug and the house. That night she sat up and made a list of things she needed to do.

The transformation took three days. Anne and Fay cleaned

the house in one marathon session, reordering books on their appropriate shelves or returning them to the library, dusting and waxing floors from one end of the house to the other, and restocking the refrigerator. They sat in the living room in the leather wing chairs when they finished.

"You couldn't pay me to do this kind of work for a living," Fay gasped. "I'd rather go out and sell my beautiful body on Sawyer Street."

Anne giggled. "Listen, Fay, I really appreciate your help. I don't think I could have managed this alone."

In a session with Marc Rivers, she practiced a mental haircut, and two hours later a plump beautician, wadded in a green nylon smock, styled Anne's overgrown hair and chatted about children, weather, taxes, and the price of gasoline. Anne left the shop bobbed and curly-headed. She caught a glimpse of herself in a full-length mirror near the door and barely recognized the image.

"Looks like Oliver Twist," Doug commented on the haircut that evening. "But I like it."

She'd worn most of her old clothes even after she lost weight, a total of twenty-eight pounds now. Every few days she adjusted the safety pin at the waist of her jeans. So she and Fay went shopping for clothes.

"How's this?" she asked Fay, holding up a white blouse with a thin velvet bow in Rainbow Rags downtown.

"Too tailored. You don't want to look like a school girl, do you?"

Maybe, Anne thought.

"Here's one," Fay said, pulling from the rack a white gauze shirt gathered at the neck and wrists. "It'll make you look like a sexy artist."

The shirt hung loose from her shoulders. When she looked down, she couldn't see her feet. "I'm a tent." Anne laughed. "Again."

"Try a belt with it."

She wrapped the white macrame belt around her waist. "It still surprises me sometimes, how far *in* I go. I didn't used to go in at all. I went out."

"Well, you look gorgeous now," Fay said softly, raising her eyebrows.

Anne bought a leather blazer, camel wool slacks, the white shirt, soft blue denims with meticulous white stitching, and a silver necklace.

"It's just what I wanted," Anne crowed happily over coffee at the Jelly Belly sandwich shop.

"Do you think Doug will like it?" Fay asked, her dark eyes gleaming.

"I hope so. I don't think he'll like the bill for all this, however." Anne studied her coffeecup. "Fay, I have to go back to work. I think we need the money—Dr. Rivers is expensive—and I want to work again."

Fay nodded.

Anne looked up quickly. "Did you hear that?"

"What?"

"That crying."

"No, I don't hear anything."

That was the last time she would ever ask anyone about the cries.

That evening Anne modeled the jeans and shirt for Doug. He sat reading the San Marco *Times*.

"How do you like it?" she asked, feeling slightly foolish turning slowly for effect.

He laid the newspaper in his lap. "Well, it matches the hairdo, at least."

"What?"

"You look like a street urchin!"

Anne affected an aristocratic snobbery, half-turning away from him, arching her back, and planting both hands on her hips. "A street urchin, my dear, couldn't possibly afford these jeans."

She studied her reflection in the bathroom mirror. The shirt opened wide on her neck, revealing deep pockets above her collarbones. She tousled her hair. Not a bad street urchin, she thought.

Doug watched her from the bathroom door. "The Conways are having an open house Sunday afternoon. They bought a place in the foothills. Can I tell them we'll be there?''

Anne swallowed hard. "No, not yet, Doug. Please, not yet.''

His head dropped slightly, and he turned away.

"I'm sorry," she said softly, but he was halfway back to the living room. She punched at a curl. Diversions were almost intolerable. Anne felt caught in an undertow so powerful and unwieldy that only the most necessary of normal human functions, those needed to keep her on a fine balance, were acceptable. The Conway open house was definitely not one of them.

And when Geoffrey Collier, her old boss at Peralta, called a few days later to offer her the research job back, it would have been easy to say yes. It would have meant a day job and a paycheck. And she hadn't heard from San Marco General Hospital about the lab job there.

"No," she decided, "I'm not ready to come back to Peralta. But I appreciate the offer, Geoffrey."

"Well, I tried." He sighed. "But I have another offer you might like. I work two nights a week at Unity Clinic downtown, and we sure could use somebody to read throat cultures and Gram stains. I hoped you might be interested in coming down Wednesday and Thursday evenings.''

Anne hesitated. "To be perfectly honest, Geoffrey, I've applied to General Hospital. I'm hoping to hear from them any day now.''

"General? Why do you want to work at General?''

She laughed softly. "Why do *you* want to work at Peralta?''

"Okay, okay. But until you hear from them, why don't you come down and help us out at the clinic? You might like it.''

"Sure," Anne agreed, "I can come in for a few nights.''

"Come early on Wednesday, say six-thirty? The clinic opens at seven. I'll get someone to show you the ropes.''

Wednesday evening Anne found the Unity free clinic, located in the basement of the Unitarian Church. She had to park three blocks away.

The area was littered with old men in worn parkas; struggling bushes were planted along the street, glints of beer cans beneath them. Stick-thin teenagers wearing dirty flannel shirts and blue jeans hung outside the clinic until it opened at seven. They could get coffee and soup on Wednesday nights at the clinic, as well as any needed medical attention. One fellow's hand was bandaged with a T-shirt. The blood seeped through layers of cloth. His girlfriend hovered beside him. They turned as Anne opened the door to the clinic.

A young woman with transparent skin and heavily penciled eyebrows sat at a library table guarding the door. "The clinic doesn't open till seven. You'll have to wait outside, please."

"Oh, I'm not a patient," Anne explained quickly. "I'm working here now, I guess." She glanced around the cavernous waiting room. "My name's Anne Hart. I talked to Geoffrey Collier, and he said to come at six-thirty."

"Jaaaafreeeee!" she called toward the door at the back of the waiting room.

"Yeah?" a voice responded.

"Someone here to see you."

Geoffrey stuck his head through the door. "Hi, Anne. Come on in."

Anne threaded her way through the cluttered waiting room. Folding chairs and painted benches clustered between battered Danish-modern coffee tables strewn with torn magazines and chipped ashtrays. She zigzagged behind Geoffrey past a maze of white-draped examining rooms to a small room equipped with dull yellow Formica counters, one microscope, and an antique metal incubator for throat cultures in one corner. There were bottles of red and blue stain on a TV tray beside the stainless-steel sink. A young man stood at the counter with a stack of plastic culture plates.

"This must be the lab," Anne said with an amused smile.

"Gary," Collier said, "I have some help for you."

The man turned to them. His face was heavily scarred from acne that still boiled under his skin. He surveyed them with large green eyes.

"This is Anne. She's a lab tech. Will you show her around?"

"Sure," Gary agreed, but without enthusiasm.

Anne wondered if she was invading Gary's territory at the clinic. His welcome was less than overwhelming.

"I'll talk to you later, Anne. Have to go polish my stethoscope," Geoffrey excused himself.

"It's pretty busy when we open," Gary murmured, and turned back to the culture plates.

He showed her the throat cultures he was reading, ingenious small plastic squares of media that inhibited all bacterial growth except the offending streptococcus. The plates were checked against a light for the typical Group A beta hemolytic strep which caused sore throats and often required penicillin.

"Are you a licensed tech?" Gary asked shyly.

Anne had been particularly careful not to threaten him or his dignity, and he began to thaw. "Yes," she told him.

"That's what I want to do," he continued. "Do you like the work?"

"It's really an interesting field. Are you in college, Gary?"

"I was. I dropped out for this semester."

He showed her a rack of smears. There were sixty or seventy slides for gonorrhea waiting to be read.

"Who reads these?" Anne asked.

"Well, the doctors do when they have time, but there's only two doctors here during the week, and then only for a few hours. People call back to see how their smear was. And then, if it's positive, they have to come in again for treatment."

"Who stains the slides?" she asked, dubiously inspecting the dark, almost opaque slides.

"I do. In the sink."

The lab was equipped to do liver enzymes too, because hepatitis was popular with addicts on the street. The tests were quite simplified, and Anne had some reservations about their accuracy.

"What about white blood counts and differentials?" she questioned Gary again.

"No one does them here. Well, not until now." He blushed in confusion.

A torrent of noise rumbled through the clinic, interrupting their conversation. Voices rose and fell, chairs and impatient feet shuffled and skittered on the waiting-room floor.

"Sounds like an invasion," Anne said.

"It is," Gary agreed without a smile.

All evening she searched smears for the evasive bacteria, and she taught Gary to stain the slides properly, since most of those in the rack were virtually unreadable. They cultured throat swabs brought from the examining rooms to the lab.

"How's it going?" Collier asked, coming through the lab to stand by Anne. "Didn't I tell you you'd have fun down here with us?"

"Yes, you told me," Anne answered in a flat voice without looking up from the microscope. "Has the flood let up out there?" she asked, referring to the patients at the clinic.

"We're shipping a pretty little lady off to General. I'm just waiting for the ambulance. Appendicitis. I'm almost positive."

Anne looked up from the microscope. "Get me a tube of blood, will you? We can do a differential count, at least."

Geoffrey stuffed his hands in his lab-coat pockets. "Oh, I don't think that's necessary. She has all the symptoms. And the ambulance—"

"I'd like to show Gary how to stain a differential slide," she said. "It would be a good chance."

Geoffrey returned a few minutes later with a tube of unclotted blood, and Anne struggled through the stain with a kit outdated six months previously.

She studied the white blood cells under the microscope, and asked Gary to get Geoffrey.

"Doesn't look like an appendicitis," she said. "This is a normal count, no bands. . . . Are you sure about that woman?"

"She was three or four months pregnant. The cell count doesn't always elevate in pregnant women. You should know that, Anne," he chided her.

She looked at the slide again under the scope. She'd never

heard of pregnant women's white-blood-cell counts remaining low in severe infections. Theoretically it was possible. "That stain kit was old," she said quietly. "I suppose it could have disintegrated some of the cells."

"Well, they'll figure it out at General," Geoffrey said, and left the lab.

"I hope so," Anne whispered as he disappeared through the door.

By eleven o'clock people were fed, bandaged, medicated, and counseled. While Anne wiped down the counters, Gary got her a cup of hot coffee.

"Are you coming back?" he asked, setting the coffee almost reverently on the counter for her.

"Sure, I'll come tomorrow night."

"I hope you'll teach me how to do some more. How hard is it to learn to read differentials?"

Anne remembered the long months spent at a microscope in Hematology while she trained. "Well, it takes a while," she said.

Gary walked her back to her car, and she was grateful for his presence. A sheer mist of fog disguised bushes, litter barrels, and bodies that emerged and vanished on the street. Safely in her car, she felt better and said good night to Gary.

Doug was waiting up for her. "How was it?"

"Interesting. The lab is a real antique."

"It isn't a very safe place to be at night," he said. "How often are you going to do this?"

"Wednesdays and Thursdays, for a while."

He shook his head. "I hoped you could find something to do during the day, not half the night."

"It's only for a few weeks, Doug. It'll be okay." At least she hoped it would be okay. So many things weren't.

She woke from a bad dream near dawn, escaping once more the world of threatening red faces that pursued her. She wondered if the small yellow pills Dr. Springer had given her were a sedative. She didn't seem to sleep, but fell into a deep state of immobility whenever she took the tablets. She decided to ask the doctor when she saw him again.

Anne watched Doug sleep. His long, pale hand rested lightly on the blanket. She thought about how it felt to sleep tight against him, the way she used to sleep, before the baby and the dreams. She thought she could sleep with Doug if she wanted to, tucked in the curve of his body. Anne inched toward him, and he wreathed her with his warm, heavy arm.

"Is it time to get up yet, babe?" he asked, yawning in her hair.

"No, not yet." Anne slipped out of his arm and fled to the bathroom.

5

Despite the cool temperature in the operating room, sweat drizzled down Dr. Ben Springer's forehead. At two-thirty A.M. Mrs. Claire Anderson was about to deliver her second child, six weeks premature. They'd held off for ten hours, but the baby crowned, and Mrs. Anderson was whisked off to OR Delivery.

Jolie McKinley had seen a hundred births like this, but the drama never failed to seize her. She watched Ben ease the child's head into his hand.

Claire Anderson giggled strangely and then began to cry. Jolie turned to the woman, but the anesthesiologist, Dr. Wintrobe, had already tucked himself tight against the patient's head and covered her face with the black mask. Mrs.

Anderson sank into a limp sleep, but not before the sharp peal of a cry issued from between her legs. Ben Springer pulled a struggling, puny infant into the world, along with the umbilical cord.

Jolie was ready with the incubator when Ben handed her the child, a boy, who had ceased his cry and started a choked mewling. Jolie quickly sucked mucus from the infant's mouth and throat.

"Doctor!" Jolie yelped. The baby was blue, rapidly approaching cyanosis, and shuddering rhythmically.

Springer glanced up. "Meconium aspiration," he growled. "Might as well forget that one."

Jolie suctioned the baby several times, but it made no response.

"Get it in the jar before there's tissue damage," Ben yelled at her.

Mrs. Anderson stirred on the table.

"She's fighting it," the anesthesiologist warned.

"Give her more. Keep her under a few more minutes."

Ben Springer thrust the infant headfirst into a large jar of pink gel that stood waiting on the tray. He clipped the umbilical cord at eight inches, clamped it, and let it coil into the jar.

Jolie stood paralyzed against the wall. A shiver brought her attention back to Claire Anderson, deathly pale on the operating table.

"She's going," Dr. Wintrobe bellowed. "For God's sake. What's happening?"

The blip on the cardiac monitor fluttered, peaked erratically, and finally settled to a slow, steadier rate. The anesthesiologist was almost as pale as Mrs. Anderson. His hand shook as he adjusted the mask on her face.

"Somebody switched the lines," he said, nodding up at the colored tanks above their heads. "She was getting pure nitrous oxide."

In the back of Claire Anderson's throat a low, thick growl quickly rose to a shriek, a mindless monotone wail. Springer grasped her hand that clawed at the mask.

"She's rigid," he barked. "McKinley. IMI."

Jolie remained frozen against the wall.

"McKinley!"

When she didn't move, Ben grabbed a small vial from the tray, a syringe and needle, and injected the medication himself. Claire Anderson's voice sank to the growl again.

"Get out of here!" he ordered Jolie.

She didn't think her muscles would obey, but they did, propelling her through the heavy door and as far as the wall in the hallway. She tore off the mask and wrapped her thin arms tightly around herself.

Moments later Ben towered over her. "What the hell is going on." It wasn't a question.

Jolie's breath caught in the back of her throat. "Why did you give her IMI?"

Springer's head and massive shoulders leaned closer to Jolie. "Because she is epileptic. Do you have any other questions about my medical decision, Nurse McKinley, or can I get back to our patient?"

"*Why is that baby pink?*" she screamed at him. Her back pressed tighter against the wall.

Springer's eyes narrowed. "You're off Delivery service, as of right now! I'll speak to the supervisor," he hissed.

Jolie clenched her surgical mask in her hand and stamped out of OR back to Maternity. Tears streamed from the corners of her eyes.

She was removed from Delivery service. She would remain on Maternity, but postpartum care. Jolie knew the action was disciplinary, and when she demanded to know the exact reason, her supervisor told her that Dr. Ben Springer had complained about her emotional instability and poor judgment in a crucial medical situation.

On the maternity wing, Claire Anderson's pleas racked the nerves of staff and patients alike. After she was found wandering the halls several times, her arms were tied to the bed rails with soft cloth restraints, and she rattled the metal bars day and night. She begged for her baby, claimed it was alive, and grew increasingly disruptive, elevating her own temperature to 103 degrees with her unceasing activity. When Dr. Springer ordered massive sedatives, everyone was relieved, but even drugged, the woman called for her child.

"Please, please, nurse," she cried to Jolie in a husky voice. "Please, let me hold him just once. Please, just once."

Jolie wondered if Mrs. Anderson knew her baby had been a boy. Had someone told her? Or was it a lucky guess?

Claire Anderson was transferred to Six West, the psychiatric unit, quite suddenly. Rumors spread that her husband had filed for divorce, and the news, added to the loss of her second child, had put her into a completely psychotic state.

Several days later Jolie saw Anne, stopping by her house after work because she wanted to know if Anne was all right.

Jolie told her about Mrs. Anderson and IMI, imidazole methyl iozide, a powerful psychogenic anticonvulsant. Hallucinations were one unfortunate side effect, but it was a very effective nerve block used in surgery for epileptics when administered carefully.

Shaking and ashen, Anne sat at the kitchen table. Her stark blue eyes filled with terror. "They said that to me, too," she said in a whisper. "They said IMI."

"They gave *you* IMI?"

Anne nodded. "I remember. Somebody said that. And I'm not epileptic."

Anne asked Dr. Springer about the medication at her usual biweekly appointment later that same day.

"What's IMI?"

His expression widened to a smile edged with curiosity, or possibly anxiety.

"IMI?" he repeated.

"It's a drug."

"Why do you ask?"

"I don't know," she said slowly. "I remember someone said that to me in the recovery room."

Ben shrugged.

"It's odd you don't know. One of your patients got IMI

when she lost her baby. Mrs. Anderson? Claire Anderson? She's on the psych ward now."

"How do you know about Mrs. Anderson?"

"She's a friend of mine. For several years now." Anne knew she couldn't tell him Jolie disclosed information about a patient at San Marco General.

"That's very interesting," he said. "Mrs. Anderson just moved here from Utah. But of course, you knew that already."

"Of course," she lied boldly.

"Then you're aware that she is also epileptic."

"No, I didn't know that. But doesn't it seem strange to you that both Mrs. Anderson and I were given IMI? *I'm* not epileptic. And both of us believed our babies were alive."

Springer's voice was brittle. "You were extremely agitated in Recovery. You appeared to be having convulsive seizures, and IMI was given as a precaution."

"It makes people hallucinate!" she said.

"It doesn't make people believe their babies are alive. And it certainly doesn't make them stop eating! You've lost another six pounds in two weeks. Are you taking the antispasmodics and the antinausea pills?"

The infant shrieked suddenly. Anne stiffened in the chair. "I'm not taking any more pills."

"You *must* continue taking those," he said sharply. "I'll write you a prescription. Or I can give you samples, unless you are convinced of some crazy notion that I'm trying to poison you."

"No," she said softly. "Of course I don't think that."

"Then I'll give you the samples."

"I'd rather have a prescription," she said, but he ignored her and plucked several small brown envelopes from his desk drawer.

How could a request for a prescription be interpreted as psychotic? she fumed on her way to Unity Clinic that evening. But Anne couldn't afford any more doubts about her sanity, especially if she wanted that job at General Hospital.

This time the girl at the front desk of the clinic recognized Anne and smiled. Gary was already at work with the cultures, and Geoffrey brought in one of the new colorimetric pregnancy-test kits.

The work load was light. Gary helped with patient exams, and Anne read Gram stains. It gave her time to think. Was Jolie imagining the dangers of this IMI? Would Dr. Springer risk his medical practice giving unorthodox drugs for no apparent reason? Drugs that made people crazy? A woman's scream interrupted her thoughts.

Gary dashed into the lab and said Geoffrey wanted her help in Number 4. Anne's heart skipped, but she followed Gary.

Geoffrey was trying to examine a young woman who was bleeding profusely. Her thin white legs were parted and secured in metal stirrups on the examining table, but she twisted and pulled away, arching her back violently.

"Help hold her still," Geoffrey said. Blood covered his gloved hand and the front of his lab coat.

Anne quickly wrapped a blanket over the woman and leaned heavily across the shaking body. The woman moaned. Her eyes were wild. Rabbit eyes.

"That's placental tissue," Geoffrey announced, producing a scrap of it to show Anne. "Definitely an abortion. Get an ambulance," he called to Elaine outside the curtain. Then he stepped close to the woman's head. "Who did this to you? They almost killed you, you know."

The woman screeched and turned away. Geoffrey jerked open the white drapes and left the examining room.

"You'll be okay," Anne assured the woman when the ambulance drivers arrived only moments later.

After the doors closed to patients, the clinic staff met in the waiting area for a conference, a chance to discuss any difficulties and assess the evening's work.

"What about that abortion?" a young woman asked, referring to the woman recently removed to the hospital. "Will she be okay?"

"Somebody butchered her," Geoffrey said. "She'll live, but she'll never have another baby."

Anne felt very tired and queasy. "I didn't know that kind of thing still went on in the valley," she said softly.

Geoffrey leaned back in his chair. "There are over two hundred thousand abortions a year in California, and we do forty or fifty thousand right here in San Marco. Those numbers are estimates. We don't know for sure. It's complicated in this valley because of the number of runaway kids, girls who can't find jobs or a place to live in San Francisco. They end up pregnant and here because the system is easier to work in this county and cheep housing is still available."

One of the volunteers snorted. "If you can call three hundred a month cheap!"

"But aren't abortions covered by medical insurance?" Anne asked.

"Not since the tax cutbacks." Geoffrey's voice was low. "And too many women can't afford the hospital costs. We try to keep them out of the back-room-abortion business in the valley and get them to M.D.'s like Ben Springer."

Anne glanced up quickly. But her thoughts remained on the forty or fifty thousand babies no one wanted. A river of babies. A city of them. Ten times more babies than the little town of Avery, Iowa, where she grew up. Thousands of babies. And all she wanted was one.

"I guess it's the injustice," she explained to Doug, who had waited up for her again. "That woman didn't want a baby. We do. It makes me sick."

"Maybe you shouldn't work at the clinic if it upsets you," Doug suggested.

"I'm *not* upset. It just isn't fair. That's all."

"Nothing's fair," he added quietly.

Maybe he was right. Anne ran a glass of water at the kitchen sink and fished out one of the yellow pills from its envelope. She considered not taking it, but she certainly didn't want the nausea or that terrible choking sensation to return. Of course Dr. Springer wasn't trying to poison her. Geoffrey trusted him. But next time, she wanted a prescription. She replaced the envelope on the windowsill.

*   *   *

October brought the first rains to the St. Helena Valley, squelching four months of dust and summer heat.

Anne eased her way into the parking lot of Nyman's Department Store. She had to find a birthday gift for her sister, Linda. Something pretty, she decided, shutting off the ignition.

Racks of striped and muted plaid blouses attracted her attention, but none of them looked like something Linda would ever wear. Anne drifted through rows of velvety bathrobes and sleepwear, and suddenly she found herself staring at layettes and tiny baby shoes, miniature saddle shoes, in clear plastic boxes. She shivered and turned back to women's sportswear, only to find herself face to face with furry winter buntings for infants.

A row of cribs—white ones with delicately turned spindle sides, dark walnut ones, and rusty maple beds decorated with laconic bunnies—blocked her way.

Her chest tightened, and she gripped a display rack to steady herself.

"May I help you?" a clerk asked.

Anne gasped. The clerk's face was crimson. Anne's head felt strange, like she was wearing a thick helmet. The walls began to circle, and her stomach went with them.

"I'm not crazy," she cried and staggered down the aisle.

That same leering red face she'd seen in the night dreams, that crystalline chimera face, gleamed at her from a pile of baby blankets, and lunged out from winter coats. Every way she turned, it met her, laughing and sneering at her.

She searched frantically for the door to the parking lot, bumping into shoppers who turned to her with their bright red faces. Their words were red bolts of lightning that hurt her eyes.

"I have to get out of here," she cried to stacks of pastel sheets. "Help me."

Small clots of people gathered around her, and Anne barged past them. She had to find the door. A man caught her arm once, and she started to run. The door was in front of her, and she dashed through it to the street, four lanes of traffic and blue sheets of drenching rain.

All she remembered was the wet squeal of brakes and the ungiving concrete. She tried to stand, but slid to the street on her shaking legs. There were sirens, and finally a young policeman with a smile that reminded Anne of her brother, Victor. He covered her with a dry blanket.

"You okay, miss?"

Anne looked down at her arms covered with blood and rain. Her knees hurt, and so did her head.

"There's an ambulance coming," the policeman said.

"No. I'm not going to any hospital!" She scrambled out of the blanket and tried to stand, but a crush of the policeman's solid body brought her easily back to the street. "Don't touch me!" she screamed.

A cry, the cry of a helplessly enraged child, tore open her mouth and spewed into the air around her. She hated the sound. It swirled around the face of the policeman bending over her. Cry after cry rose from deep inside her, and she let them go in an off-key chorus with the rain and the wail of sirens.

They treated her for abrasions and contusions in the emergency room at Good Shepherd Hospital, where she calmed down and answered their questions. After an X ray of her left arm and a light gauze bandage on her knee and forehead, she called Doug to come and get her.

"I just didn't see the car," she explained to him. "It wasn't anybody's fault."

Or maybe it was those pills Dr. Springer gave her, she explained to Marc Rivers. But he looked skeptical and doubted antispasmodics or antinausea pills would cause her to get lost in a department store or dash in front of a car.

Or maybe it was the IMI. Or maybe she was crazy. The terrifying red dreams not only invaded her sleep but also threatened her waking moments as well.

"I'm not getting better, am I?" she said softly.

Marc Rivers made no response. He sat with his feet propped

on the ottoman, and he nursed a pipe in the corner of his mouth.

Anne watched drops of rain dribble down the windowpane. "They write little stories in the dirt on the window," she murmured, mainly to herself, "little secrets, if you could read them."

"If you could read them, what would they say?"

Anne glanced at him. He seemed far away. Light from the floor lamp beside him sectioned his face into distinct planes. "They would say I am I, and you are you."

"That's very oblique."

"Raindrops are that way, you know."

Marc's smile was wistful. "Anne, I am a very patient man. I will wait here with you for as long as it takes you to tell those little stories."

"I know you will," she said.

In the parking lot of the Medical Building Anne considered checking the infant whimpers coming from somewhere behind a row of cars. The crying sounded different this time. She edged between the cars and looked down a row of polished hoods. A child sat on the concrete, sniffing and patting a car bumper.

"Hi," she said.

He looked up. Tears ran in grimy stripes down his face. He turned his attention back to the car bumper.

"Where's your mom?" she asked.

He didn't answer. The boy looked about two years old. His yellow shirt almost met his green boxer jeans with a blue denim patch on one knee. His feet were bare and dirty. He must be cold without shoes or a jacket, Anne thought, as she inched toward him and crouched three feet away.

"Are you lost?" she asked.

He stopped crying and glanced at her again. "No," he said clearly.

"Is this your mama's car?" Anne asked, encouraged by one response.

"No," he sniffed, and began the eerie wail again.

"Where's your mama?"

"Noqooo."

"I won't hurt you. I'll help you find your mama. Come on, let's get you off the ground. I'll bet it's cold down there." Anne shivered inside her own windbreaker. October was proving unusually cold this year.

"Nooooooo," he persisted, and patted the car bumper.

Maybe he's two, Anne thought. Two-year-olds don't talk much. "How old are you?"

"No."

"No," she agreed softly. "I doubt I'll get much more than that out of you."

She reached for the boy, and then she saw his right arm, peppered with small red burns oozing a greenish-yellow fluid. Anne stared at the arm. "What happened to you?" she gasped. She swept him off the concrete. He offered no resistance, but continued to whimper.

"It's okay," she said, patting him on the back and pressing him against her for warmth. "What is that on your arm?"

He screamed when she tried to examine the burns. A man trudging across the parking lot stopped when he heard the scream.

"Sir!" she called to him. "Are you going to the Medical Building?"

The man nodded almost imperceptibly.

"I found this child sitting in the parking lot. I don't know who he belongs to. Will you tell the receptionist . . . or ask what I should do with him? I hate to leave, in case—"

"Ask her yourself," the man growled, and continued to tromp to the side door of the building.

Anne didn't want to carry the child from the car, in case his mother returned. At that moment a woman in flapping blue jeans and a loose maroon sweater hurried out the side door of the Medical Building. She stopped and then ran over to Anne and the child. The boy, still weeping, reached for her. Anne let him go, regretting the sudden absence of his weight in her arms.

"Jay, sweetheart," the woman cooed, "did you get out of the car, baby?"

"Noooo," the child moaned.

"He was sitting on the ground crying . . ." Anne offered, feeling like an intruder. "What happened to his arm?"

"Oh, that. He got up against a vaporizer a few days ago." The woman opened the car door and plopped Jay in the front seat. He continued to cry. "I just had to run in for a minute to pay a bill at the clinic," the woman said. "Jay's had such a bad cold, I didn't want to expose him to anything else in that waiting room. And they're so quick at this age. I certainly didn't think he could open the car door." Jay's mother whisked around the car to the driver's seat.

"Shouldn't he have a jacket on?" Anne asked loudly. "And I think his arm is infected. He should see a doctor."

The woman's smile was thin and ugly. She rolled the window down. "You didn't *take* my baby out of the car, did you, lady?" she sneered. "Why don't you mind your own business?"

The car jolted out of the parking space and whipped out of the lot before Anne could memorize the license plate. Anger and shock paralyzed her for a moment. The car merged with the traffic, and Anne saw only the first three numbers of the license.

A few days later she told Dr. Rivers about the child in the parking lot. "I am furious that people who obviously don't want a child have one and then burn his arm with a cigarette. And some of us . . ."

Marc removed the pipe from his mouth and peered across the room at her. "Did touching him bother you?"

"I didn't even think about it."

"See how the desensitization is working?" He smiled with satisfaction and resumed the gentle chewing on the stem of his pipe.

Anne grinned. "You know, sometimes you are positively Pollyanna."

At the door that day Marc held out his hand to her. Anne placed her own hand in his and then quickly pulled away.

"No," he said, pressing her hand gently, "I won't hurt

you. Does that hurt? Think about your hand. That doesn't hurt, does it, Anne?''

She searched her hand, muscle by muscle and bone by bone, for some sensation of pain, but there was none. In fact, his dark hand on hers was pleasantly warm. She noticed a thatch of small black hairs on the back of each of his fingers.

"You're right! It doesn't hurt."

And it didn't hurt when Doug began a circular entreaty on her right breast early in the morning.

"Is it okay?" he asked.

"It's okay." There was no pain, and she felt only one shiver of nausea. Afterward they lay together in a tangle of sheets.

"Dr. Springer thinks I should have another baby."

Doug's eyes opened in surprise. "I think that's a marvelous idea."

Finally, Mary Wold, the lab manager at San Marco General Hospital, called Anne about the part-time job, and she was inhaled by the medical bureaucracy, inserted back in a white lab coat, assigned a pay-scale level and acquainted with lab procedure during her first week. Blood banking was the most difficult, since no blood had been cross matched at Peralta. But it all came back to her quickly, and the techs at General were pleased by her intelligent adeptness. They were also relieved that someone had been found to fill the part-time midnight position, someone other than themselves.

Anne was scheduled for an employee physical. She filled out the form under Nurse Bennett's watchful gaze. Covered by a flimsy paper drape, she waited for the doctor in one of the examining rooms in the Employee Health Office and mentally reviewed several desensitization exercises for a physical. Anne had time to study the decor, what there was of it. The rug was olive green and the walls were painted a shade lighter. The drab color gave the place a military flavor.

Dr. Jeanne Petri bustled in fifteen minutes later. "Hello," she said, breathless. "How are you this morning?" Dr. Petri was a petite, energetic-looking woman in a cream-colored blouse and tweed skirt under her white coat.

"Fine," Anne answered after assessing the woman. Anne had mentally prepared for a male doctor, and she wasn't sure how she'd react to a woman. Don't panic, she coached herself.

"This is one of my favorite jobs at General," the doctor said with a saucy grin, "examining healthy employees! Did you walk in here?"

"Yes." Anne knew she was in for the old joke about employee physicals.

"Good, then you passed the physical."

The friendly banter relaxed her. "Does that mean you don't want to know about my slipped disk and bleeding ulcer?"

"And not your recent heart transplant, either," Petri quipped. She listened to Anne's heart and lungs, flashed the ubiquitous penlight across her eyes, and said, "I see from your form you lost a baby last August. How have you been feeling since then?"

"Bored."

"Time to get back to work." Petri poked and pressed gingerly on Anne's belly. "And you have a positive HISS—the hepatitis test."

"Ever since my training."

"You know you should never have another one, don't you? A second one could be very dangerous. Even fatal."

"Yes, they warned me about that."

Jeanne Petri grinned. "Well, you seem quite healthy to me. Welcome to General Hospital."

6

Anne returned to Unity Clinic after a week's absence, but this would be the last time. She couldn't work at the hospital and give much time to the clinic.

Geoffrey was waiting for her when she arrived. "Hi," he said, "I'm glad you came back."

"I've been training during the day at General Hospital, and I was just too tired last week to come in. I'm afraid this is my last night at the clinic," she said. "It's more that I can handle at the moment."

Geoffrey looked surprised. "You took that job at General?" Then he nodded, in resignation, rather than agreement. "Well, I'm glad you came back tonight, anyway."

After the initial rush, the clinic was slow. Most people came to drink coffee and eat a sandwich or to get out of the cold. One of the local churches had collected coats and jackets. They were piled in a cardboard box in the waiting room, and by nine o'clock the clothes were gone and only a few egg-salad sandwiches remained.

Geoffrey brought a cup of tea back to the lab. It was nine-thirty, and Anne was reading the last of the smears from the week. Geoffrey propped himself against the counter and sipped his steaming tea. "Don't *ever* drink the coffee they make here," he said.

She looked up from the microscope and then into her Styrofoam cup. A definite metallic scum had formed on the top of the coffee. "I won't, I promise." She pushed back from the counter.

"How do you like it at General?" he asked her.

"So far, it's really interesting. I won't be doing anything exotic on the midnight shift, but just the basics should keep me entertained."

"You're working graveyard? Why?"

They heard footsteps in the hall. Anne looked across the room to the door, expecting Gary, who was cleaning exam rooms. Instead, she saw a dazed, very young woman, seventeen years old at the most.

"Hi," Geoffrey said, "can I help you?"

"Please, I want to talk to someone," the girl said softly.

"Sure." Geoffrey shrugged at Anne and steered the woman down the hall.

Anne finished the slides and wiped down counters with alcohol.

Geoffrey came back to the door of the lab. "Anne? Will you come with me?" he asked. "Maybe you can talk some sense into this woman."

Anne followed him to the exam room. The girl, hardly a woman, sat stiffly in a wooden chair beside the long white table. Her face seemed to pinch her eyes, swollen and red from crying. Two bright pink splotches glowed on her cheeks.

"This is Kathy," Geoffrey said to Anne. "That isn't her real name, but that's okay. Kathy's pregnant, over three months, and she doesn't want to keep the baby."

Anne's breath shortened.

"It isn't that I don't want the baby," the girl explained in a nearly inaudible voice. "I *can't* keep it."

"Why not?" Anne asked her.

"See, I'm living with this guy. And he doesn't want no kids around. You know how it is."

"Is it his baby?"

"No, he just moved in a month ago. I don't have a job right now, and he takes care of me."

"Does he know you're pregnant?" Anne pressed her.

"Yeah. He knows." She broke each statement with a long pause. "He said I should get an abortion or something."

"It's too late for that," Geoffrey said. "An abortion after the third month is dangerous."

"I was going to do it last month, but I just couldn't. See, I was raised Catholic, and even if I don't believe all that stuff now, I just couldn't go through with an abortion."

Anne and Geoffrey waited for her to continue.

"So I told Mike, that's the guy I'm with now, I told him I was going to. Do it, you know. And now I don't have enough money to get it done right. At the hospital and everything. They wanted the money before they'd do it. And tonight I was supposed to go to this other place—"

"What other place?" Geoffrey demanded.

The girl twisted the strings on her macrame purse, but she didn't answer.

"You still have the option of carrying the baby and giving it up for adoption," Anne offered, touched by the girl's dilemma.

"No," she almost shouted, her blue eyes wide and frantic, "I'd rather kill it than do that. *I* was adopted. I'll never do that to a baby."

"So what are your choices?" Geoffrey's voice was rough. "The baby isn't going to evaporate."

She searched their faces. Then she turned back to Geoffrey. "Somebody told me you could help me here." Her lower lip trembled.

"Who told you that?" Geoffrey asked without looking at the girl. He doodled on a clipboard.

Tears squeezed from her eyes. "Somebody. I promised I wouldn't tell. Please, I need your help." The young woman's mouth opened and closed, catching the stream of tears that ran down her face. She twisted and jerked the purse strings.

"Do you want a drink of water?" Anne asked.

"No," she gulped. "Please, can't you help me?"

Geoffrey tore a scrap of paper from the clipboard and wrote on it. "I'm going to give you the name and address of an obstetrician here in San Marco. You make an appointment with Dr. Springer. Tell him I sent you. Then, if you're not satisfied with his suggestions, you come back to the clinic. Is that okay?''

The girl's face relaxed a little, and she nodded.

He handed her the name and address and a bottle of vitamins he produced from his lab-coat pocket. "And take one of these a day, too," he instructed her.

When the girl had left, clutching the slip of paper and bottle of vitamins, Geoffrey picked up his clipboard again and studied a small drawing. "We try to keep these women out of back-room abortions and talk them into less risky decisions. But chances are she won't give up the baby for adoption *or* contact Springer." He added a few flourishes to the drawing. "Do you still want a child, Anne?"

The question hovered in the air, birdlike and sudden. "Of course I do," she finally said.

Geoffrey pursed his lips thoughtfully. "How bad? I might be able to arrange something."

Anne stared at him, afraid to breathe. Was that possible? Or legal? "Are you serious, Geoffrey?"

"Pretty serious." He held up the clipboard for her to see. "There are ways. That's a sketch of my son, Toby. We've had him for almost three months now."

Anne studied the cherub face of the child Geoffrey had drawn. "A black-market baby?" she whispered.

"Call it whatever you like. I think about it as providing choices."

"Geoffrey?" a woman's voice called outside the drape, "are you busy? We got a stoned kid in Number 2."

"Coming," he answered loudly, and then, in a softer voice to Anne, "Think about it. Call me if you'd like to talk about it sometime."

The kid in Number 2 was seventeen years old and overdosed on crystal. Two of his friends dragged him into the clinic, but he was already dead. Gary told Anne about it.

"My God," she groaned.

"You kind of get used to it after a while," he said mildly.

"Some of these guys swallow anything that will fit in their mouth."

At eleven o'clock she said good-bye to Gary and asked him to keep in touch, but her head whirled with Geoffrey's offer. A baby. But she had a baby. It cried continuously at her. For something. First she had to find out about her own child, she decided.

Ben Springer picked up the phone. "This is Dr. Springer," he said pleasantly. He laid his book down on the low side table beside his large leather chair.

It was Cheryl Kev. She was bleeding, finally. Ten days earlier he'd begun her treatment with progesterone and then withdrawn the hormone suddenly. Cheryl Kev was sixteen years old and nearly sixteen weeks pregnant.

"Come into General Hospital," he said. "And don't worry. Everything's going to be fine."

He hung up the phone gently and smiled. He'd keep her in the emergency room for a few hours and then to Surgery. She'd be home by the next day, with only a sixty-dollar hospital bill to pay, the emergency-room fee. There would be no charge for the surgery and no doctor's bill.

Ben Springer stared up at the beamed ceiling in his study. He counted silently to March. Yes, the end of March.

Anne paced Marc Rivers' office. "I can't get it out of my mind. This thought that the baby didn't die. I dream . . ." She stopped and shook her head, trying to clear her thoughts.

"Anne, this refusal to face the fact that your baby is dead is one way to relieve the pain. You are protecting your feelings, refusing to experience the grief and anger."

"Said like a true shrink," she mocked him.

He continued without acknowledging her sarcasm. "What would happen if you admitted that your baby died?"

"I'd cry. Or scream for a very long time."

"You can cry here. Or scream."

"Yes, but I'd need more than an hour if I ever got started." Countering Marc Rivers depleted her. Anne returned to the armchair and sat down. "When I worked at Peralta, I tested this medium we called Ammy. It's a synthetic gel that can transfer oxygen and carbon dioxide, as well as urea and glucose and other essential things like that, through the skin, or at least through any semipermeable membrane. And Ammy is really beautiful—clear and crystalline. In the sun you can see rainbows reflected in it."

"You seem to have changed the subject, Anne."

"No, I haven't. What I wanted to say is that I dream about that gel. And a face—not a red face, not the face that scares me. This one is only part red." She caught her breath. "I can see rows and rows of glass jars of Ammy making rainbows on a wall or a window. And this face. Isn't that strange?" A nervous burst of laughter erupted from her. She didn't look up at Marc. She *had* changed the subject. "Please, try to understand. I can't think about the baby being dead. Do you know what they do with dead babies?" She raised her eyes, brimming with tears, to look at him.

He chewed the end of his pipe and shook his head slightly.

"They put them in jars of formalin. I saw them once in a lab where I worked—shelves of yellow, shriveled-up babies in big glass jars."

Silence engorged the room, interrupted by street whines of rubber on concrete, a branch demanding entrance at the window, and the steady beat of her heart in her ears.

"Are you afraid they put your baby in a jar of formalin?" he asked.

"No, that didn't happen to my baby. Something else happened. And no one will tell me what, exactly. Not you, not Dr. Springer—he just looks concerned and says I should have another baby and keep taking the pills."

"And what do you think happened?"

"Maybe they made a mistake with the baby. It happens. Maybe they're afraid I'll sue them if I find out what really did happen. I don't know. But I'm going to find out."

Marc replaced the pipe in his mouth. "How do you intend to do that?"

"I've been thinking about hypnosis."

Rivers snorted. "Hypnosis! Whatever gave you that idea?"

Anne glanced at the degrees hung over Marc's desk. One of them was from the Northern California Institute of Hypnosis in San Francisco, California.

"I doubt you're ready for hypnosis," Marc said. "It can be a valuable tool in therapy, but I can't imagine how it would benefit you."

"I have to remember something."

"Remember what?"

"If I knew, I wouldn't need your help to remember it, for heaven's sake. Why are you talking in circles?"

"I'm just trying to follow you," he said with an amused grin. "Anne, have you considered painting this face you see in your dream?"

"No." She hadn't painted anything for six months.

But she wasn't getting better, either. She picked at her food; nausea plagued her mornings at General Hospital, where she was still training for the midnight job; and when the baby cried, she tried to lip-read conversations of the other lab techs, Fay, the newsboy, Doug, and even Dr. Springer, whom she still saw every two weeks.

"These pills don't help at all," she complained to the doctor.

"They don't?" He looked surprised. "You haven't lost any more weight in two weeks!"

"I'm still awfully nauseated."

A smile crept over his face. "You aren't pregnant?"

Anne straightened in the chair. She tried to remember her last menstrual period. "I have a period due in a week or so."

"Then we'll know soon."

And that wasn't all she would know, she decided. If she was pregnant, she had to find out what had happened to the August baby, the crybaby.

Both Dr. Springer and Dr. Rivers said it died. Even Jolie. But *why* did the baby die?

Maybe they waited too long for the delivery. She'd lain in that blue room for hours. Many hours. Maybe the baby died before birth.

Or maybe . . . She chewed on a fingernail and gagged.

Maybe they did something to the baby. She'd read about savage deliveries, the severing of limbs, accidental decapitations with forceps . . . Her head reeled.

No, not that. Had they dropped the baby? Was that possible? Did it slide out of Dr. Springer's hands like a slippery trout fresh from the water? No. She clamped both fists over her ears.

Or had there been something wrong, badly wrong, with the baby? Something they didn't want her to know? Was it born with no brain, like the other infant? The encephalic monster? She shook off the thought.

But who would tell her the truth? She rested her head in her hands. Pathology. Of course. They would know in Pathology.

October 30 was Anne's last day of training at General. During her lunch break she went to Pathology and stood in front of Mrs. Hanson's desk. The path office kept the records and computerized data from autopsies and examinations of surgical and histological specimens.

"Mrs. Hanson?"

"Yes?" The woman's gaze was sharp.

"I'm looking for some information. I'm from the lab."

"What sort of information? Are you a student?"

"Sort of."

The door to an inner office opened, interrupting her. Dr. Ted Bell, a pathologist at General, glanced from Anne to Mrs. Hanson. "Can I help you? Oh, you're one of our lab techs, aren't you?"

"Yes, I'm a night tech."

"Well, Mrs. Hanson, we have a special policy for night techs. Keep them happy at any price." Bell grinned at Anne. His blue eyes twinkled. "What can we do for you?"

"I need some information. I want to know the diagnosis on a baby. Baby Anderson. The mother was Claire Anderson."

"Do you know the hospital number?"

"Of the baby?" Anne stared at him. "No. The baby died."

Bell nodded and motioned Anne to the postmortem room off the main office. The smell of formalin hit her like a wet gauze curtain.

"We can check the path log. Do you know the date of death?"

"August, I think." Anne followed him to the ledger on a counter. She jammed her hands in her lab-coat pockets to keep them from shaking.

Ted Bell flipped the ledger back to August. "Do you know the exact date?"

"No, I'm afraid not." Anne read the names just behind his index finger that ran down the rows of names and hospital numbers. Campman, Seliz, Reed, Butler, Rose, Hernandez . . .

"Anderson, Anderson," he chanted softly. "Maybe this is it. Anderson, Julia."

"No, her name is Claire Anderson." Anne's voice shook. "Maybe it was September." She had discovered something she hadn't expected. Her own name was not on the pathology log in August. It wasn't there!

Dr. Bell scanned September. Finally he stood up. "Claire Anderson? Are you certain of the name?"

"Yes, that's her name."

"I don't see it here. If you could find out the exact date, I'm sure we could find the diagnosis for you."

Anne nodded. "Yes, of course. I'll do that. Thanks." She hurried out of the prickly aroma of formalin and the rows of specimens she'd seen behind the counter in the post room. *Her name wasn't on the log.*

She phoned Jolie that evening to check on the date of birth of Claire Anderson's baby. Jolie told her it was September 12. She remembered. It was the day before Jolie's own birthday.

"Claire Anderson's name isn't on that path log, Jolie." Anne said each word slowly. "I checked. Claire Anderson's name isn't there. Neither is mine."

There was a huge silence on the other end of the phone. She heard Jolie's breath escape in a sharp whistle finally.

"My baby *isn't* dead. And Claire Anderson's baby isn't dead. And who knows how many others."

Doug studied her over his dinner of beef stew and cornbread muffins. She mashed a bit of potato and ate a tiny bite. She didn't want to gag.

"You okay?" he asked.

"I'm fine."

"You didn't . . . you didn't get your period today or anything?"

"No."

His smile was hopeful. "Good. That's terrific." He did not take the large spoonful of stew. "Annie, if you aren't pregnant, it's okay. We can keep trying, you know."

She nodded and mushed a carrot. "I checked in Pathology, Doug. My name isn't on the log for August."

His spoon clattered to the bowl. "Should it be?"

"The baby would go to Pathology. There's no entry in August for Hart. I checked." Her dinner threatened to rise from her stomach.

"Annie." He caught her hand across the table. "Please don't torture yourself like this."

"Our baby never went to Pathology. It *isn't* dead."

He let her hand slide out of his. Doug picked up his spoon again and kept his eyes on the stew. "You can talk to Dr. Rivers about it tomorrow."

Anne dashed to the bathroom just in time to lose the little supper she'd managed to swallow.

Jolie was filling in for one of the nurses in the neonatal-intensive-care unit at San Marco General. Over the past three years she had taken eighteen hours of postgraduate work in primary neonatal care at the state university and had applied for a position at General, but there hadn't been an opening yet. So when the chance came to fill in for an ill nurse, she jumped at it. Maternity service was monotonous now that she was off Delivery. Jolie was eager for a change.

"All you have to do is watch," Mrs. Sands, the head nurse,

told her. "Watch that baby breathe. If it doesn't, the alarm rings, but the first thirty seconds are critical."

At six hundred and fifty grams, Baby Boy Kahler was thin, bluish-pink, and curled tightly in his incubator.

"He doesn't look good," Jolie said, watching the cardiac monitor over the incubator.

"We've got three bad ones tonight. I'll watch the other two."

For two hours the infant's monitor beeped erratically. Jolie bathed a second infant and suctioned mucus from a third while she kept an eye on Baby Kahler's chest rising painfully and dropping back. The infant's matchstick ribs struggled feebly beneath the mottled skin. Shortly after one A.M. Jolie turned to check his breathing and realized there wasn't any.

"Mrs. Sands!" she called.

By the time Sands reached the incubator, the alarm on the baby's monitor shrilled. Mrs. Sands reached up and flipped it off.

"The baby's a no-code," she said, and deftly swept it from the end of the incubator, blanket and all. A no-code infant meant cardiac arrest was greeted with relief rather that the rush of lifesaving measures ready at a thirty-second notice for a viable baby. No-code was a death sentence, but more humane than letting an infant die of exhaustion in the backroom of the nursery, a method not unknown in the early days of premature neonatal care.

Jolie kept her eyes on the infant she was changing, sliding a blue pad under the child to absorb urine. She wished she'd checked Baby Kahler a few seconds earlier, just to touch the baby. A baby should be cuddled and stroked, at least once, she thought. Baby Kahler's short life of two days had been nothing but tubes, needles, and only a sharp electronic alarm at the last.

Two other infants died that night, both suddenly, both no-codes. No doctors shot into the ICU to try something miraculous. There was an alarm, then silence.

From the small storeroom, Mrs. Sands carried in two more large jars filled with a thick pink gel. Baby Kahler already rested in a jar on the counter. Jolie helped slide the other two still-warm infants into the jars.

"This preserves the O_2 level," Sands explained, capping the last jar. "It's some help determining cause of death."

Jolie read the label on the jar. "What's this RDS lab?"

"The respiratory-distress-syndrome lab. It lost its funding." Sands set the three jars on the dumbwaiter. "The jars go to Pathology now."

Jolie and Anne met for the two-A.M. break in the cafeteria. It was Anne's second night on graveyard. The two women eyed a rack of sugared doughnuts but chose fruit and coffee instead.

Jolie shook her head. "I never took a course on how to watch those babies die. Three of them tonight. Oh, Anne . . ." She caught herself. "I'm sorry. You don't need to hear about that."

"It's okay, Jolie. Really." Anne quickly relieved her distress. Jolie obviously needed to talk about babies dying.

"They were all premature. You have to watch premies every second. They take one breath. And then they don't take another one. If you miss it, they die."

Jolie told her about the jars of thick gel into which the infants were placed. Anne's mind jogged, like going around a corner in a strange city.

"Can you get me some of that gel?"

"Sure, I guess so. But why?"

Anne mushed the last of her banana to semiliquid. "Just curious."

She listened to Jolie's account of an RDS research unit that had lost its grant to find a solution to the respiratory-distress syndrome, or hyaline-membrane disease, in newborns, affecting the membranes lining the alveoli of the lungs and resulting in decreased oxygen supply and eventual death.

"Listen, Anne," Jolie said softly. "About what I told you a couple weeks ago? That woman, Claire Anderson? Well, I was wrong. I had a long talk with John Wanaker, the hospital administrator, and he told me Claire Anderson was epileptic, a borderline case, and that's why they gave her IMI."

"Can you explain why her baby never showed up in Pathology? Or mine?"

Jolie's head dropped. "Maybe you missed the name. I don't know. I'm sure there's some explanation."

"But *I'm* not epileptic, and they gave *me* IMI."

Desperation washed over Jolie's face. "It may have been a precaution. Listen, Anne, let's forget about it. I can't afford to risk my job. It feeds my kids."

"That's exactly why I can't forget about it, Jolie. I don't have my child to feed."

Between erratic CBC's that night, Anne checked the hospital directory for the RDS unit. It wasn't listed. She phoned the operator to see if a phone number was available for the unit.

"The what?" the operator asked.

"The RDS research unit," Anne repeated slowly. "The respiratory-distress-syndrome research lab."

"Never heard of it. No, there's no number listed for an RDS research unit."

"Thanks anyway."

By November 5 Anne had definitely missed a period, and she began counting days. If she were pregnant, the pregnancy test would be positive in ten days.

And if she wasn't pregnant, she worried whether Doug would be so willing to try again. Every time he looked at her, the possibility of a child burned in his eyes. She was afraid he might be deeply disappointed.

That was the reason for her visit to Unity Clinic the following Wednesday evening. She had to talk to Geoffrey.

Gary was managing the lab quite well without her. Anne noticed his reddened face, fiery from the acne and abrasive cleansing. Her own face felt suddenly warm and tender when she remembered the sore lumps she'd tried to wash off her nose and forehead as a teenager. She wanted to tell Gary he had beautiful green eyes and not to worry.

"Jeez," he said, "I'm glad to see you."

"I'll bet you're doing just fine."

"Geoffrey expects me to do white counts and pregnancy tests!" Gary complained. "Since you quit, he's *so* grumpy."

"Who's grumpy?" Geoffrey said behind her.

Gary blushed deep purple.

"Me. I'm an old crab tonight," Anne said quickly.

"Please don't mention crabs. I have enough troubles tonight without *that!*"

"Geoffrey, I need to talk to you. I . . ." she started.

Gary excused himself, looking like a banished child. "I'll help Nadine set up suture trays. 'Bye, Anne."

When he was gone, Anne studied Geoffrey for a moment. Dark rings edged his eyes. "You look tired. Are they working you too hard at Peralta?"

"If they are, it's your fault for not taking your old job back." He smiled halfheartedly. "I've got a new assistant who isn't worth shit."

"Geoffrey, I may be pregnant again. That's why I came tonight. I won't know for another week or so." She said it quickly.

"I guess that's great news." He looked more like it was bad news.

Anne's heart thumped noisily. "But if I'm not . . . How long . . . how long before we could get a baby? From you."

He lifted his heavy-lidded eyes. "Three weeks. Maybe four."

"I'm not sure I could talk Doug into an illegal baby . . ."

He smiled mildly. "A baby is never illegal."

"You know what I mean. I'd always worry that someone might claim it later."

"That's impossible. There's no way to trace our babies. We send in the birth certificate with your name and fingerprints. It's simple. There is no evidence that a child is not naturally born to its adopted parents."

Anne was shaking. "I'll let you know."

He nodded and crossed silently to the door. "I trust you won't mention this to anyone else, Anne."

"No," she assured him. "I wouldn't do that. And, Geoffrey, you take care of yourself."

He didn't acknowledge her concern. She noticed his shoulders held rigidly under the lab coat.

Some nights on Maternity were very slow. Those were nights when the patients slept peacefully, and the call panel at the desk remained dark. And tonight was Jolie's last night on Maternity service. Tomorrow night she would don the soft pastel greens to start training in Neonatal ICU.

Mrs. Sands had liked her work the night she filled in in Neo ICU. So when Cynthia Reik resigned, Mrs. Sands had recommended Jolie for the job. The first thing Jolie did was make an appointment with the orthodontist for her oldest boy, Sammy. She hadn't been able to finance those braces until now.

But there were things to do on a slow last night. The other RN disappeared into the lounge, and Jolie was alone at the desk. She typed in the name of "Anderson, Claire," added the code instructing the computer to do a name search, pressed the transmission bar, and waited.

Jolie stared at the screen. Claire Anderson was still in the house, Room 614.

"Angie," she called to the RN. "I have to go upstairs a minute. Will you keep an eye on things?"

The nurse came to the door of the lounge. "Sure. Go ahead."

Jolie used the elevator and let herself in the psych-unit door with the passkey kept by the night supervisor on Fourth Central.

She recognized Ruth Moyer, the night nurse on Six West. The dim corridors gave Jolie a moderate case of the creeps. It smelled strange on Six West. She knew the smell of disease on most of the wards at General, but this was different.

"Ruth," she said quietly. "How's it going?"

"Fine. Very quiet up here. The moon must not be full tonight."

"Listen, I want to ask you about Claire Anderson. I took

care of her on Maternity. I wondered how she's doing.''

Nurse Moyer's face clouded at the mention of Claire Anderson. ''She's being transferred to Park State Hospital tomorrow. She's catatonic.''

''What? Catatonic?''

Moyer nodded gravely. ''Go see for yourself.''

Jolie stood frozen in front of the desk.

''If you ask me,'' Moyer said softly, ''they gave her too much shock. Of course, no one *does* ask me, but that's my opinion. She wasn't that bad when she came up here. It's been downhill ever since. One of our more classic failures.''

''She's in Room 614?'' Jolie asked.

Moyer nodded down the hall behind her, and Jolie glided down the hushed hallway, reading room numbers until she saw 614.

Inside the room, a single night light cast its soft glow on the scarecrow face in bed. Jolie remembered Claire had been a rather pretty woman, dark snapping eyes and short, lively black hair. Now her eyes were wide open and glazed, watching some horror scene with total absorption. Those eyes didn't flicker as Jolie approached the bed.

''Mrs. Anderson, how are you tonight?''

The woman made no response. Jolie held one of the cold, stiff hands in her own.

''Claire?''

Was anyone in there? Jolie wondered with a shiver. Were there any remains of a person crouched behind those great, staring eyes? She laid Mrs. Anderson's hand back on the blanket and tiptoed from the room, feeling slightly foolish, like asking directions from a deaf man. Claire Anderson certainly didn't care about noise. Possibly she never would.

After that Jolie had trouble falling asleep, even after long nights at work. She was sharp with the children, who looked up at her with their darkly hurt eyes. Whenever Jolie closed her own eyes, she looked into the sightless stare of Claire Anderson. That woman's mind was burned from the inside of her head. But why? Because she thought her baby was alive? Jolie asked the same questions night after night, day after long day, and there weren't any answers. There wasn't much sleep, either.

Anne waited for Jolie at the elevator, and finally she was there, looking exhausted. That was becoming the norm: Jolie with cavernous eyes and Anne numb with the necessity of sleep. But first there was breakfast.

"Meet you at King's?" Jolie said with a slow smile.

"In ten minutes."

King's was a grease-stricken but homey cafe that reminded Anne of the restaurants in Avery, Iowa. Their menu was handwritten, prices blacked out and rewritten in pencil, and the friendly banter of cook and customer filled the air amid random tables covered with lavender cloths.

"Peter John," Jolie said to the cook, an older man of Chinese extraction, "what you need in this place is decor."

He looked up in playful surprise. "Decor? I don't think that's on the menu today."

Anne and Jolie settled in a far corner table and ordered breakfast.

"I have something for you," Jolie said quietly. She took a plastic urine container from her purse. "A jar of the medium broke this morning in Neo ICU, and I cleaned it up—right into this jar for you. Slippery stuff, isn't it? Makes your hands feel funny. By the time I finished, my hands were buzzy."

Anne carefully opened the container and looked in. A translucent gel stared back at her like some prehistoric creature with pink dome eyes. She dipped in the jar and produced a glob of the medium on her fingertips. Through the crystals she saw the typical rainbows.

"It's Ammy. I'm sure of it." She held her breath. This was the first solid evidence that someone at General Hospital was using the medium. Her impulse was to snatch the sample and drive to Peralta to confront Geoffrey.

She replaced the cover. "Why is it pink? Why would they tint it?" She was thinking out loud. "Unless . . . to hide a pink baby. Jolie, this is real evidence, not just suspicion anymore. Now I have to find that unit. And *who* is using Ammy at General.''

The waitress brought two plates of scrambled eggs, toast layered with melted butter, and cups of coffee. She glanced at the urine container and shrugged slightly.

"Jolie, listen to me." Anne pushed the plate aside. "My head is working a mile a minute, and all of it doesn't make sense. But just listen."

Jolie nodded between bites of egg.

"The reason your hands felt funny is that Ammy is oxygenated, and that oxygen is enzymatically transferred through the skin or any mucous membrane. So are glucose, antibiotics, and a number of other things. I mean, if I sat here and held Ammy long enough in my hands, I might not have to eat breakfast. Or take a breath."

Jolie stopped chewing a nibble of toast.

"But it isn't a preservative. Not in the least. So I still don't understand why they use it for dead . . . expired babies." She lowered her voice. "Or abortions." She bolted upright in the chair. "Unless those babies aren't dead. I mean, not *really* dead."

"An infant wouldn't have to breathe in Ammy," Anne continued. "Oxygen would be transmitted through its skin. We kept Xanadu alive for months in the gel, and he never took a breath."

"Xanadu?"

"A white mouse. But that's not important. Where do these jars go? Do you know for sure?"

"They're all marked 'RDS.' Mrs. Sands said they go to Pathology. I don't know for sure. There's a dumbwaiter."

"We have to find out more about this RDS unit. And soon. Come on, think, Jolie. Where would it be in the hospital?"

She stared down into the cup of coffee. "I can't think. I'm too tired."

"Somebody must know where it is. You can't hide a whole research unit in the hospital, not even at General."

Jolie's gaze riveted on Anne. "I saw Claire Anderson just a few nights ago, just before she was moved to Park State

Hospital. She may never leave there. She's catatonic after shock treatments and drugs. I wasn't going to tell you. I thought you'd be better off not knowing.''

Anne groaned.

"Maybe you should go to the police," Jolie suggested weakly. "That's what they're for. I think this is bigger than either of us."

"Who'd believe me? They'd think I was crazy, even with a jar of Ammy in my hand."

"I think I'd try, if I were you."

Anne noticed Jolie's hand shake as she reached for the bill. She knew Jolie was tired after a night of work, but her exhaustion seemed excessive.

"You're tired," Anne said gently. "I know how tired you are. Is it the work in Neo ICU?"

Jolie shook her head. "I'm not sure. I'd better get home. I'll talk to you tomorrow night." She slid her chair away from the table.

"Jolie, did I tell you I may be pregnant? I won't know until the fifteenth."

"No, you didn't tell me. Are you ready for another pregnancy, Anne, I mean . . ."

"I don't know. I have to wait and see, Jolie."

Barely inside the front door at home, Anne called Marc Rivers. He could see her at four o'clock. That sounded like next year.

Anne stripped off her lab coat and replaced it with a gray wool cardigan. She checked the coffeepot, but Doug hadn't made coffee.

She wandered to the bedroom. Maybe, she thought, she would fall asleep in a horizontal position. Fully dressed, she crawled in the burrow where Doug had slept. Just as she closed her eyes, she heard a scraping noise at the front door. Anne bolted upright.

Only the mailman, she thought. But that ended any thought of sleep. When the baby began a sulky whimper ending in short, cranky sobs, Anne slipped on a raincoat and dashed to Fay's. A fine winter mist had begun, drizzling from the trees.

"Hi, kiddo," Fay said. "Come on in."

Fay's house smelled of wet clay, ferns, and cinnamon toast all mixed together.

"I didn't want to be alone this morning," Anne explained, meandering to the kitchen. "Do you have any coffee?" The kitchen counters were piled high with dirty dishes, half-filled cans of tomato soup, several moldy grapefruit, and other debris Anne did not care to look at. "Is there a coffeepot in this house?" she asked in dismay at the mess.

"Creativity is inversely correlated with neatness," Fay announced with a smile. She poured Anne a cup of coffee from the pot on the back burner of the stove.

Anne took the coffee, gratefully, in both hands. "I don't want to interrupt you. Go on doing whatever you were doing. I'll watch for a while."

Fay had obviously been working. Red clay streaked her workshirt and jeans. "Okay," she said, "come on down to the studio. I'll throw a few more pots."

Anne settled on the corduroy-covered mattress Fay kept for reading or napping in the studio. She watched her friend hunch over the potter's wheel and force the lump of wet clay upward, then out and finally into a narrow neck.

"That's beautiful, the way you do that," she said with a yawn.

"Actually, I'm thinking of going back to coil pots," Fay said with her back to Anne. "After you've thrown five hundred pots, it gets real boring."

Anne set the cup next to the mattress and lay back. It was safe next to Fay, the reassuring sounds of the wheel, and Fay's running talk about coil pots. No one would come and take her off to Park State Hospital. No one would put electrodes on her head and wipe out her brain. No one.

"At least with coils, you never know . . ."

It was the last thing Anne remembered until she awoke that afternoon. "Uh," she groaned, "I must have fallen asleep. What time is it?"

"Two-thirty." Fay handed her another cup of coffee.

"Fresh," she said. "You are not a terrific sleeper, did you know that?"

"I'm not?"

"No. You moan and mumble and toss around."

"I was just overtired. Listen, I have to go home. Thanks for letting me get some sleep."

"Anytime."

An hour later in Dr. Rivers' waiting room, Anne sipped more coffee from a Styrofoam cup, and her stomach grumbled unpleasantly. She promised her protesting insides she would remember to eat something, right after she saw Dr. Rivers.

She had to eat. It was important, especially now. Five more days, she counted. In five days the pregnancy test would be positive. Or negative. It was the uncertainty—guessing, hoping and not hoping—that weighed on her. She liked things certain.

She liked the certainty of that waiting room. In a glance she scanned the entire room. All the corners were visible and secure. But when Dr. Rivers opened the door to his office, Anne jumped and the coffee poured down her gray corduroy slacks. She stared down at the spreading wetness on her thighs and the dark splotches on the rug. The baby screeched, and Anne dropped the cup and covered her ears.

There had been other times when she'd accidentally wet her clothes, and other cries a long time ago. She'd lain awake most of the night as a child for fear of wetting the bed. But it rarely worked. She remembered her mother's disgust. Anne had been forced to wash her own bedding, standing naked in the basement of the house in Avery, Iowa. And when not even humiliation cured her of the habit, her mother resorted to other means, more drastic means. Anne still had the scars.

"Is it possible you are afraid to have a child, Anne?" Marc Rivers asked. "Are you afraid you might hurt it?"

"I'd never do that!"

"Your mother hurt you."

"You're saying I lost those babies on purpose? Is that what you think?"

"I don't think it was a conscious decision, Anne."

"No," she sobbed, but the memories flooded back, the attempts to increase the bladder capacity with enormous amounts of water, a series of strange doctors and even stranger methods to break her bad habit, and finally the electric-shock sheet that caught fire one night. That was when Anne's father intervened.

When she left the office, a late-autumn rain masked her tears.

Rain pelted the windows and roof when Anne woke Monday morning. After three days off work, her body had finally learned to sleep at night and stay awake all day. It wasn't easy. Her body was stubborn.

Doug slept soundly beside her. It was five-thirty A.M. She listened to the steady rap on the shingles and glass.

When she was a child, in Iowa, it rained only in the summer. They could watch a storm coming for hours, building a great gray wall across the prairie sky, long before the rain started. She had always been afraid of those storms.

"They'll kill you," she'd said to Victor, barefoot and with water streaming from the hems of his jeans after running out in one of the rainstorms.

"Don't be silly," he'd said, and dragged her outside. Soaked and cool, they'd dashed back to the house, their shirts as near to them as their skin.

Victor. The young, wet, laughing face of her brother stuck to her memory like those wet clothes. He would be thirty years old now, if he had lived. He'd be in Canada. Not dead.

The day the telegram arrived telling them he was dead, after only three days of military service in Vietnam, Anne screamed the accusations at her mother. "You did it! You killed him!"

Her mother turned away. Anne remembered how the woman's shoulders sagged and heaved under the old brown sweater she'd been wearing. After that they rarely spoke to each other. Anne left for college in California and never returned to Avery, even when her mother was so sick. And not when she died three years ago.

The rain's drumming no longer frightened Anne. This was California. Not Iowa. She closed her eyes.

During the next few days Jolie and Anne asked discreet questions about a respiratory-distress-syndrome lab, but it wasn't easy to find information. Fellow employees looked blank or offered only cursory knowledge.

The yearly financial budget of the hospital was a matter of public record, printed each year in a nearly unreadable form. Jolie and Anne pored over the book night after night, and they finally found one small entry for an RDS lab, followed by the names of Dr. Benjamin Springer, Dr. Andrew Jones, and Dr. Harold Malachi Schwartz.

Harold Malachi Schwartz, or "old H. M.," was chairman of the board at Peralta Technology, Inc., when Anne worked there. She knew she'd never forget a name like that. And Ammy was developed at Peralta. The coincidence was unlikely, and Anne was certain the gel in the jars from the neonatal ICU was Ammy.

And her own obstetrician was connected with this RDS research. Anne looked at Jolie without really seeing her. It was a special kind of thinking, like seeing movies behind her eyelids, but difficult to translate into words. "They're using it for experiments. On babies. Now I have to get a look at that RDS unit."

7

The night of November 15, Anne removed the pregnancy-test kit from the laboratory refrigerator. The kit had to come to room temperature before she could use it.

She finished the differentials on two CBC's and then turned back to the pregnancy test. She placed a drop of urine in one circle on the slide and a drop of control in the other, added reagent, and waited. She counted the seconds. The test was positive. She stared at the slide and waited for the pleasant bubble of excitement to burst inside her. But it didn't. She was simply staring at a positive pregnancy test on a black slide. She shivered.

"I'm pregnant," she said aloud.

What she experienced were long, crawling fingers of fear that reached out and entangled her. She replaced the test kit in the refrigerator. Her hands remained cold the rest of the night, and in the morning she went home and crept into bed beside Doug without a word.

"Mmmm," he sighed, "you're cold."

And that's not all, she thought, curling up under the quilt.

Two days later Dr. Ben Springer was radiant when Anne saw him at his office. She'd already decided to find another

obstetrician, but first she wanted to ask him about those pills.
And the RDS research.

"Congratulations," he said. "I've confirmed your test,
and you most certainly are pregnant, Anne."

"Yes," she said, "but I—"

"You don't look very happy about it," he said, easing
down in his chair behind the desk.

"Oh, I'm happy about it," she said, forcing some enthusiasm into her voice.

"This is a very critical period," Ben went on. "We are
finding that the first three months are the determining factor
in fetal viability. So we'll want to watch you closely now.
You are taking the medication I gave you?"

Anne looked up slowly. "I . . . Yes."

"You mustn't forget. Particularly not now. That is, if you
want this child." His gaze seemed to pierce her forehead.
"We'll start you on a hormone, too. Think of it as an
insurance policy. With your weight loss, your body may not
be able to produce adequate levels of progesterone to maintain
the pregnancy, so we'll help it out a little. You do understand?"

"Yes, I understand."

Ben took three brown envelopes from his desk drawer.
"You can take all three together, in the morning. That should
be fine."

"I want to know the names of the pills," she said softly.
"I don't know the names."

He glanced at her and smiled. "Of course. Would you
prefer generic or trade names?"

"Generic."

Ben was still smiling when he brought the envelopes around
the desk to her. He'd scrawled a name in the corner of each
packet. "Still don't trust me?"

"I just want to know the names," she said. "Dr. Springer—"

"Have you told Marc Rivers yet?" he interrupted her.
"How's it going with Marc, by the way?"

"Fine. It's going fine." Damn it, she thought, ask him.
"Dr. Springer, what do you know about this RDS research
unit at General?"

He blinked several times. "It lost its grant."

"It's still listed in the hospital annual report. With your name."

Ben Springer's smile had lost some of its warmth. "As head of Obstetrics, I was part of that research." He started for the door. He obviously did not want to talk about the RDS unit. "Get an appointment for two weeks on your way out."

"I'm going to find someone else," she said quickly. Her hand shook as she tucked the pills in her purse.

Springer turned sharply. "If you do that, I can almost guarantee you won't carry the child for more than six months. That would be stupid, particularly in your mental and physical condition." He slammed the door behind her as she left the office.

She hadn't asked him about Ammy. And she hadn't asked him to explain why her infant's name never showed up on the pathology log. Even though he claimed the best record in the valley for bringing difficult pregnancies to term, Dr. Ben Springer was acting like a man who had something to hide.

Anne heard the front door slam. That was Doug.

"Annie?" he called. "Where are you?"

She smoothed her sweater over her hips and straightened her hair. "Here, Doug. I'm in the bedroom."

He joined her in front of the dresser mirror. "Well, are you?"

"I am." And they both laughed, flinging their arms around each other like playmates. "Yeah, I really am!"

He ran his fingers through her hair and cradled her head. "I thought you might call me at work. I jumped every time the phone rang," he said softly. "It'll be okay this time. It'll be okay."

She laid her head on his chest, and they rocked each other.

"Oh, I almost forgot," he announced. "Wait right here. Don't move." He dashed out of the bedroom, out the front door, and returned a moment later looking boyish and shy, with both hands behind his back.

"What are you hiding?" She laughed.

He handed her a bouquet of tiny yellow rosebuds and fragile white baby's breath.

"Oh, Doug, that's lovely. Thank you." Anne touched each rose. "I know this wait won't be easy, but—"

"But you're going to take care of yourself, and take your pills. And eat right. And quit working," he finished the list.

She looked up quickly. "Not for a while. I want to work a few months."

"You need your rest." His brows knitted with concern.

"It's only a few nights a week. Just for a few months. Okay?"

"Okay," he agreed without enthusiasm.

Fay, of course, greeted the news with wild anticipation, offers of milk, gluten bread, and even wheat grass. She told Anne wheat grass had a remarkable effect on the premature birth rate in some country. She couldn't remember which one exactly.

And Anne continued to take all three pills from Dr. Springer. She hated swallowing them, even if they were small. And she *was* going to find another obstetrician, but she didn't want to risk losing the baby, either. A little hormone couldn't hurt.

The red dreams renewed their violation of her days and nights. From the corner of her eye she saw the red prism face rushing at her, and two deeply veined red hands dangling the crimson heads of two babies. The infants' mouths gaped in a soundless cry. Anne turned and fled from the kitchen. She slammed the door of the bedroom and locked it.

"Why is this happening?" she cried out loud. "What's wrong with me?"

Jolie studied the darkness under her eyes. She smoothed on more moisturizer, knowing it wouldn't help, even if she had paid an extra two dollars for that brand of black cosmetics. Sleep was the only thing to remove those purple circles, and sleep was the one thing she couldn't manage lately.

She'd come home to breakfast dishes stacked high in the kitchen sink, beds to be made, and a load of washing every day. With three children there was always more housework than she cared to think about. Then Kevin, the baby, got sick, and the nursery school wouldn't take him with a fever. So for a week Jolie caught naps during the day and tried to sleep a few hours before she went back to work at the hospital.

But she was exhausted. She thought she couldn't sleep because she worried about all those babies. The pressure in the neonatal ICU to keep the babies alive was immense. There was never a break in the stress, always some infant struggling to breathe, going into shock or convulsing. But more than that, there was the moment when nothing else could be done. A baby either lived or died by some inborn will, some internal stamina or lack of it.

She studied her face again in the mirror. As expected, the moisturizer hadn't helped. Jolie sighed, picked up the car keys, and left the house, nodding to Mrs. Goodson, who stayed with the children at night.

Jolie liked to drive. She never turned on the radio. She needed those times of silence to think. She had to think. She believed if she thought about things long enough and hard enough, she could figure them out.

But not this time. If she could only sleep for a whole eight hours, she might be able to figure out something, anything, if only how to get through the next day.

Maybe she was too involved in Anne's problems, she considered. It was hard to talk to Anne lately. She was depressed since she found out she was pregnant. Jolie tried to keep their conversation pleasantly light at break time or during breakfast at King's Café. Anne was frightened, and Jolie knew Anne had good reason to be frightened, even more than Anne guessed.

That was why Jolie phoned Marc Rivers. Or part of the reason. She just had to talk to someone. A psychiatrist was an expensive need, but Jolie put that out of her mind. Besides, the medical insurance covered part of it. But a white shrink!

She waited for the light at Pine Street. There hadn't been time to look for a black psychiatrist. They weren't listed by color in the phone book. She had bothered to check.

And there was something else she had to check, a nagging cocklebur thought, one she had a chance to investigate that evening.

Anne said her baby never went to Pathology. Could that be true, or had Anne overlooked her own name, a kind of denial of the truth?

Jessica Haus, the night nursing supervisor, gave Jolie a ring of keys and asked her to drop off a cytology specimen in Pathology. The sputum had to be covered with a fixative to preserve its cellular morphology, and they'd run out on Fourth Central.

Jolie opened the door to Pathology and flipped on the light. She shuddered and tried to shake off her own very unprofessional reaction. Her nose shrank from the smell of formalin, sharp and slightly sweet. Pathology reeked of death itself.

She wound her way through the office to a second door, where Nurse Haus had told her the cytological fixative was kept, along with rows of gray metal shelves stacked with specimens in various-sized jars and bottles. Nurse Haus hadn't mentioned that.

Jolie glanced quickly around the room. The overhead fluorescent lights threw deep green shadows around the room, glinting on a stainless-steel postmortem table mounted on a black pedestal and the shining electrical saw on a counter. A tray of instruments lay next to the saw. Jolie looked away. At the opposite end of the room were three doors, pathologists' offices, and a row of smaller shelves lined the back wall.

Jolie edged down the first aisle of shelves and stared up at a large jar filled with a rubbery gray mass, like a preserved manta ray. The label indicated it was omentum tissue from someone named Sanchez, #1881, 9-6. That meant surgery was done on September 6, a full month after Anne's baby.

Her heart hammering in her ears, Jolie rounded the corner and traced dates on rows of specimens that stood like plastic gag-shop attractions: part of a foot with small black hairs still

curled on the yellow toes; part of a liver; two infants, one of
which was macerated to a fibrous pulp; at least six crumbly,
cheese-gray uteruses, all the once live pieces lined up in their
museum without patrons. Finally Jolie saw 8-3 on a label.
August 3.

She scanned the shelf above. Uterine scrapings, thick coiled
bowel, a small twisted hand . . .

She turned a jar and saw a sectioned infant. Her hands
trembled as she read the label. It wasn't Anne's. That baby
was labeled "Encephalic monster." Jolie remembered the
child had been born the day before Anne's.

A soft click sent her leaping back to the front counter. Jolie
listened. The clock clicked again. It was only the clock. She
let out a long sigh.

She checked all the specimens labeled 8-4 and found no
specimen marked "Hart." Anne's baby wasn't there. Then
she followed the dates to September, searching for another
specimen, Claire Anderson's baby. And she couldn't find
that one either.

As she poured fixative over the sputum, she noticed the
pathology logbook open on the counter. She checked August
and had just begun to scan September, but a brief movement
behind the shelves caught her eye. When she looked up, there
was nothing. She stared through the soft, thick silence to the
back wall.

"Who's there?" she called. "Is anyone there?"

The clock clicked again, and she jumped. Her breathing
didn't ease until she reached the bright hallway outside Pathology again.

"How long do they keep path specimens?" she asked
Nurse Haus when she returned the keys.

"A year."

"That's what I thought," Jolie whispered. She would talk
to Dr. Rivers about this. Maybe he could help her understand
what was happening at General Hospital.

Jolie knew Dr. Rivers from Maternity service, but she
doubted he would remember her. He had a good reputation at
General, but it was his eyes that Jolie liked. When he looked

at you with those dark, gentle eyes, he really seemed to see you. Jolie remembered his eyes when she talked to him once about a maternity patient who attempted suicide one night.

"Hello, Jolie," he said with a smile the following afternoon. "Come in, won't you?"

Jolie, suddenly feeling foolish about being in a psychiatrist's office, hesitated and then walked past Rivers into his office. She noticed the afternoon sun spattering the dark rug with light. "Do you remember me, Dr. Rivers?"

"Of course I do. You're one of the nurses on Maternity."

She relaxed immediately and told him about her inability to sleep. Sometimes she stumbled on a word or lost her train of thought.

"We have plenty of time this afternoon, Jolie," Marc said softly. "Tell me a little about yourself."

"About me?" Jolie studied her long slender hands stretched out on the arms of the rocking chair. "There's not much to tell. I'm thirty-three, and I've got three kids. Sammy, he's fourteen, Jill is nine, and Kevin is three. I grew up in Oakdale, California, and my mama and daddy moved to Tucson when I was sixteen. I stayed here and finished school. Daddy had high blood pressure and asthma. He died nearly five years ago." She hesitated. "I guess that's about all."

"And you're married? What about your husband?"

"I *was* married to Richard, but he's gone now. Richard got real tired of bills and kids crying and a lawn that had to be mowed."

"So you're alone with three children to raise."

Jolie intertwined her hands and rocked a few times. "They're good kids, Dr. Rivers. Real good kids. I'm not worried about them a bit." She leaned forward in the chair. "It's this job. I mean, it's a good job. This year my kids can have what they want for Christmas." She frowned and studied her hands furiously. "It's the babies, I think. I can't sleep because of those babies in the ICU." Tears rushed to her eyes as though she'd turned on a tap. "Some of them die. I can't stand it when they die."

"No, of course not," he said. "You care for them, and

despite that care, some of them die: I can understand your distress.''

"That's only part of it. Sometimes I don't believe they're dead. Not *really* dead.''

Marc's eyebrows shot up. "Have you talked to your supervisor about this?''

"The last time I asked Dr. Springer about it, he had me taken off Maternity delivery.''

Marc looked as though he didn't believe her.

"It's true. I couldn't understand why they'd given a woman IMI after a delivery. And Dr. Springer said it was none of my business.''

"Ben Springer said that?''

"Yes, he did,'' she said decidedly. "I did ask Mrs. Sands about how they know a baby is dead. She said viability has a lot to do with it. Babies with an Apgar below four are no-codes. If they stop breathing, they're just plopped in a jar, like a big mayonnaise jar full of preservative or something.'' Jolie closed her eyes. "Some of those babies don't look dead. The Wilks baby . . . I thought that baby moved in a jar.'' She opened her eyes and leaned forward again. "That baby was supposed to be dead, and I could almost swear it moved its arm.''

The silence in the room was enormous. She thought she could touch it if she tried.

"But maybe I was mistaken. I get so tired I think I don't know what moves and what doesn't.'' She took several deep breaths. "Maybe I'm wrong, Dr. Rivers, but I've seen a lot at General, both in Maternity and in Neo ICU. And I think something very bad's going on there.''

Marc laid down his pipe. Jolie told him about the elusive respiratory distress research unit at General, a unit run by Dr. Jones and Dr. Springer and funded by a doctor from Peralta. She also told him Anne believed the preservative in the jars was Ammy, the life-support medium developed at Peralta.

Marc looked skeptical, but Jolie told him that Anne was not the only woman who'd lost a baby at General and claimed it was alive. There was Claire Anderson. "You weren't on her case, were you?"

"No, the name's not familiar."

Jolie began to shake and cry at the same time. "They're taking those babies. I can't stand to think what they're doing to them. And I don't know what to do about it."

Marc handed her a box of tissues, and she blew her nose hard. "I know I sound pretty freaked-out," Jolie finally said. She wadded the Kleenex in a ball. "But deep down, Dr. Rivers, I think Anne's right. You know that feeling? Just something I can't shake."

Marc nodded. "Anne's your friend. That may make you *want* to believe her."

"I went down to Pathology two nights ago." She met his wide, dark eyes. She heard her voice change to the nurse's voice, the cool reasoning part of herself, and she told him about her grim search. "Anne's baby isn't there. I looked. Neither is Claire Anderson's."

"Are you certain, Jolie?"

"Yes, I'm sure. They aren't there."

Dr. Rivers gave her a prescription for a mild sedative, but she didn't want to take one until morning, after work. Then she could look forward to a long, long sleep. Kevin would go back to nursery school. His fever was finally gone.

Tuesday night Baby Cavalero wasn't doing well at eleven o'clock when Jolie came on duty. Mrs. Sands watched the cardiac monitor and turned the oxygen flow to thirty-seven percent. Baby Cavalero had an Apgar of five, with respiratory distress and cardiac insufficiency, but he had managed to hang on for ten days now. His mother came twice a day to the incubator window to see him, but tonight his O_2 was very low. His heartbeat was slow and irregular.

"He won't last the night," Mrs. Sands said as she prepared a syringe of mother's milk for the baby. She passed a small tube through the infant's mouth directly into its stomach and injected the milk. "He's too weak to breathe."

The night passed slowly while they watched Baby Cavalero fade. At breaktime Jolie called the lab and asked Anne to meet her in the parking lot at eight for breakfast at King's. Anne sounded more cheerful, which pleased Jolie. They would have breakfast, and then Jolie could sleep until four, when the kids came home from school.

When Baby Cavalero's warning buzzer sounded, signaling cardiac arrest, Mrs. Sands was the first one at the incubator. "Call Dr. Bronson. He's at 397."

Jolie picked up the phone and told a sleepy Dr. Bronson to get to Neo ICU stat.

Three minutes later the doctor, tousled and only half-awake, listened for the baby's heartbeat, shook his head, and signed the death certificate on the counter.

Jolie tended Baby Carr, dabbing antibiotic on several badly infected areas of skin, but she watched Bronson and Mrs. Sands, too. Before the doctor was out the door, Sands had a jar open and the baby half in it. Jolie looked away, and then back when she heard a cry, a weak, curdled cry from the other side of the room, from Baby Cavalero, being slid into the jar of thick gel.

Horrified, she watched as the infant's head submerged. "Stop!" she cried to Mrs. Sands, who clapped the lid on the jar and turned to Jolie, blocking her view.

"That baby's alive!" Jolie exploded. She rushed at Mrs. Sands in time to see the infant struggle in the jar and then stop abruptly. "Mrs. Sands!" Jolie cried.

The nurse grabbed her by the shoulders and shook her. Jolie tried to twist away. "Jolie. Get hold of yourself. That's a shock reaction. The baby's dead."

"No! That RDS unit. They're using—"

"Jolie!"

She started to scream, and the next thing she knew she was in the nurses' lounge in the ICU with Dr. Bronson.

"Calm down," he kept saying as he dug in the supply tray for a syringe.

Jolie saw the needle and backed away. "I . . . I'm all right," she gulped. "Don't give me anything."

Mrs. Sands bustled through the door with a cup in her hand. Bronson stood poised with the syringe ready.

"It's okay," Sands said, smiling. "She'll be okay. She's just a bit upset."

Bronson capped the needle. "Call me if you need me," he growled, and left to resume his night's sleep.

"I brought you some tea, Jolie. You just sit down and relax for a minute. I called Ginny Olson from the nursery—she'll come over and watch the ICU for a minute while you get yourself together."

Jolie collapsed on the sofa. "I . . . I . . ." she stammered.

"It's okay," Sands reassured her. "Just drink the tea. Don't talk for a minute."

The hot liquid burned her tongue but seemed to clear her head slightly.

"What you saw was the Petrovitch response," Sands continued. "I'm surprised you haven't noticed it before. It's an immature brain response, no different from an egg hitting a hot skillet. A protein response."

Jolie's breathing eased while she listened to Mrs. Sands.

"I remember the first time I saw it. Lord, I thought I was seeing things. Dr. Jones explained it to me. Nothing to be ashamed of. Listen, I have to get back to the babies. You drink your tea and rest, and come back when you're ready."

Jolie closed her eyes. The Petrovitch response. . . . Sands was probably right. She sat up and took two more quick swallows of the tea and leaned back. That would explain things, she considered. But what about that cry? Protein doesn't cry. And wouldn't Dr. Rivers have known about such a response when she told him she had seen a baby move in that jar?

Jolie started to get up from the sofa. Her heart thundered violently in her chest, and she fell back on the couch. She thought she would vomit, and leaned forward, grabbing at the coffee table. The cup of tea crashed to the floor. Her heart exploded, but not before she looked up to see Mrs. Sands watching from the lounge door. A thick, liquid gasp gurgled in Jolie's throat, and she was dead before her head hit the floor.

Nurse Sands waited at the door, and when Jolie fell, she

knelt and checked for a pulse. Then she slid a small vial into Jolie's pocket, careful to keep her own fingerprints off the plastic. A thin smile, like a stripe, crossed Nurse Sands's face. She picked up the lounge extension phone to call Dr. Bronson.

8

Anne waited at the door of the parking lot for Jolie. She checked her watch. Jolie was late. Anne waited five more minutes and then took the elevator to the third floor. Mrs. Sands was just leaving.

"Where's Jolie?" Anne was still wearing her lab coat with the hospital I. D. badge dangling from her collar.

"You didn't hear?" Sands asked in a hushed voice. "No one told you?"

"Told me what? Where's Jolie?"

"She committed suicide tonight. Took a drug. She died right here in the lounge."

Anne backed away from Nurse Sands. "That can't be. She—"

"She was terribly upset. We had to call Dr. Bronson."

Anne backed against the wall, turned, and dashed for the elevator. Not Jolie! was all she could think. Not Jolie!

But it was. Jolie was buried Saturday morning at Rolling

Hills Cemetery. Anne and Doug attended services at the funeral home and graveside. Marc Rivers came, too.

The three round-eyed children stood bravely around a tall older woman dressed in a navy suit. Even the baby, who was just three, was there. The black minister in a flowing gown sprinkled earth on Jolie's casket.

Anne was terrified they would lower the casket into the ground right then. She kept her eyes on the winch and tried to keep it from turning just by the power of her mind. Then the service finished, and the casket remained on its Astroturf blanket, sheltering the bereaved from the sight of the opened earth.

Anne smiled weakly at the oldest boy. "You must be Sammy."

He turned to her, his braces flashing in the brittle November sunlight. "Yeah. How'd you know that?"

"I was a friend of your mother's. She talked about you all the time. All of you. At the hospital."

His face turned down, exquisitely sad. "My grandma came," he said quickly. "We're going to move to Tucson soon."

"That sounds nice," Anne said. "What will you do in Tucson?"

"Go to school. Maybe learn to ride a horse. My grandma says there are lots of horses in Tucson."

"I'm sure there are, Sammy." Anne walked with him to the car where his grandmother waited. "I want you to know how sorry I am," she said, bending to speak to the elderly woman sitting in the car. Jolie had had her eyes, piercing and dark. "I worked with Jolie. If there's anything I can do . . ."

The woman lifted her sad face to Anne. "I don' believe no girl of mine would do such a thing," she said, her voice edged with anger. "I jus' will never believe it."

"I don't either," Anne told her. "Not for a minute."

The woman brightened for an instant and then sank back in her misery. "I jus' don't believe it."

Anne pulled on slacks and a heavy white sweater. Her socks fought back. She tugged angrily. Her feet were sweating, although numb with cold. The baby whimpered down the hall, but Anne ignored it.

She unlocked the deadbolt and opened the front door slowly. A wave of cold, bright December air tumbled into the entryway. The rain had stopped during the night. Anne watched the corner of the house, where her car bumper was visible in the drive. Nothing stirred. The sounds were familiar, and she picked her way down the wet sidewalk to the car. Inside she locked the doors, inserted the ignition key, and waited. They could rig cars with dynamite, she remembered from television. But she also felt suddenly foolish sitting there in her own car in front of her own house. Anne started the car. Her heart leaped with the engine.

She knew Jolie didn't kill herself. Her death was too convenient, even when Marc Rivers told her Jolie was extremely upset and exhausted by her work at General, and potassium cyanide was a favored method with hospital staff, due to its accessibility and almost instantaneous effect. But Anne was convinced someone made Jolie's death look like suicide.

At home she huddled behind the deadbolt locks and drawn drapes. The baby wept a thin insistent cry, and over its irritable whimperings Anne tracked every strange sound in the house, at the front door, at each window. Someone had murdered Jolie. And she might be next.

This was the time to run. Anywhere. Anne packed a bag and then unpacked it while the room spun, leaving long red tails in front of her eyes. She couldn't leave. She knew that. And, in fact, there was no place to go.

Doug was attentive but wary of her suspicions. She ran out of pills and decided to find another doctor that very week. Dr. Benjamin Springer would never touch her again. Or her baby. At least not this one.

At the hospital Saturday night Anne poked down the dark halls on the first floor. But doors were locked, and she could make out very little by peering through the meshed glass windows. She considered the morgue, but it seemed unlikely that research would be carried out there.

Who knew the hospital? San Marco General sprawled its four hundred and forty-seven beds in four buildings built over the last fifty years. To outsiders the place was a maze of corridors, elevators, and color-coded doors, red arrows, warning signs printed in three languages, strange sounds, haunting odors, and the aura of mystery.

Max, the night maintenance man on the first floor, swept by Anne as she wandered the corridor back to the lab. Max, of course. The cleaning people knew every square inch of General. He nodded and smiled.

"Hi," she said. "How's it going?"

"Fine, just fine." He braked the broom that was leaving a damp, medicinal-smelling path down the hall.

Some nights Max stopped his sweeping long enough to explain to Anne the latest in antibacterial detergents, static control in the operating rooms, or the relationship between bacterial growth and amounts of water used for cleaning. Anne was glad he had never seen her kitchen floor.

"Max," she said, catching up to him, "let me ask you something."

"Shoot," he said, resuming the broom's swath, but slower, so they could talk.

"You must know this hospital like the back of your hand." She noticed the silver ring of keys hanging on his belt.

Max beamed. "Like I know my own wife," he said.

Anne felt her cheeks get hot. She hadn't exactly meant that. "Do you know where they do research at General? I thought it was down here on the first floor . . ."

"You interested in research?"

"Of course. I used to work at Peralta Technology. We researched and marketed pharmaceuticals, bacteriology media, things like that."

He nodded.

"Weren't they doing some very fancy research at General on TB? Seems like I read something about that. Or was it RDS—respiratory distress syndrome?"

"TB. Two years ago," he said slowly. "Before they remodeled Five South. I used to clean that section. Nice people up there."

They had almost reached the door to the lab. Anne didn't want to arouse any suspicions, but Max obviously knew every activity in the hospital.

"I was just trying to think," he said. "McConnell has the second floor at night, and he's always complaining about that wing back of surgery. Used to be recovery. I dunno for sure. Haven't worked up there for years, but there's some kind of research going on in part of that wing."

"Next to OR?" That seemed incredible to Anne. Operating areas were generally isolated from all possible sources of contamination.

"It was all walled off," Max explained, "when they remodeled up there. McConnell says it can take him twenty minutes just to get into that back area to clean."

"Do you know what kind of research they're doing there?" Anne ventured.

"Nope. And I don't ask. Asking too many questions at General can be downright unhealthy, if you know what I mean."

Marc Rivers waited in Medical Records at General. The obese young secretary glanced quickly at him and then back to the computer terminette.

"I'm sorry it's taking so long," she apologized. "It's just that most doctors use the computer to go over a chart."

"Well," he said, smiling nicely, "I guess I'm old-fashioned. I like something I can hold in my hands and read."

Marc had requested Anne Hart's medical file. All weekend something about it bothered him, so Monday morning after rounds on Six West he went to Medical Records. He wanted to see the autopsy report on Anne's baby, just to quell any further questions. If there was an autopsy report, then certainly Anne's premature infant was received in Pathology.

He couldn't remember the other name Jolie McKinley had mentioned. Anders, or Anderson, or something. To request a chart, he would have needed a full name and medical number, so he contented himself with requesting only Anne's.

Marc realized he was staring absently at the secretary. She looked back at him uneasily.

"You know, I've thought about coming to talk to you sometime," she said, pushing at the dark curls drawn up on top of her head. "Especially when things get rough, you know."

He smiled again and hoped she wouldn't. He was up to his top lip in patients.

One of the Medical Records librarians bustled in with the chart, just in time to save him from a free instant analysis of the secretary.

The librarian waved the chart at Marc. "Here it is. Out of place. Wouldn't you know it."

"I just want to check on something." He paged through the chart. The pathology report was the second page, a perfectly usual report on a twenty-six-week female fetus, death due to prematurity, signed by Theodore K. Bell, M.D. Marc closed the file and handed it back.

"Thank you very much," he said to the librarian. He turned to the door. He knew that with a look at the secretary he could easily acquire one more patient, but at the door he gave in. "You feel free to come see me anytime things get rough," he said to her.

She blushed and murmured a "Thanks."

Medical Records was in the old section of General Hospital, and Marc walked the long corridor back to the elevators. Even though the tile floor had been polished to glass, this section depressed him.

Both Jolie and Anne were mistaken about Anne's baby. The fetus *had* been received in Pathology. And now Jolie was dead. Had he been inattentive, insensitive to her despair? He shook off the thought at the carpeted ramp to Second West, one of the newer sections of the hospital. His depression lifted slightly. He noticed his step lighten.

He made a mental note to add the name of Theodore K. Bell to his list of right-handed doctors. It was a kind of hobby with Marc, noting right- and left-handedness in M.D.'s. Someday he thought he might write an article on the subject. The data were already proving interesting in that more specialists were right-handed and general practitioners left-handed than could be expected in a normal population. Theodore K. Bell was right-handed, although his signature slanted to the left.

Having satisfied his question, Marc hardly gave the matter of Anne's infant another thought.

"Did your mother hold you as an infant?" he asked Anne later that afternoon. His voice breached the December afternoon. "Isn't it possible you are reexperiencing an old feeling that your mother murdered your brother by insisting he go to Vietnam?"

She hung her head. Her hair fell softly over her forehead. "I didn't murder my son. I would have named him Victor."

"And how about your daughter?"

"My daughter?" She looked up at him with a puzzled expression.

"Your daughter. The baby you lost in August."

"Dr. Springer told me it was a boy."

Mark Rivers rarely went to the doctors' lounge at General Hospital because most of the M.D.'s objected, however mildly, to his pipe smoking. But the following morning he'd been told in Pathology that Dr. Ted Bell was in the lounge, so Marc made his way down the dingy green-blue halls of the basement, past Central Supply, to the lounge.

He spotted Ted Bell at a table with several other doctors, involved in a heated discussion over their plastic cups of coffee or tea and heavily frosted sweet rolls. Ted Bell could have easily forgone the sweet roll. His belly, exposed in a soft roll under his open sport coat, completely covered his belt. But Ted Bell was an easy man to forgive any excesses. His blue eyes crackled with a good-natured disposition.

"Marc," he greeted him.

"Ted," Marc responded, "am I interrupting anything?" He looked at the ring of doctors, who stared back, obviously still involved in the argument.

"No, sir." Ted grinned. "We were just finished with the debate. And I won."

"But—" one of the doctor's objected.

Ted Bell threw him a dark look and glanced back to Marc. "Sit down, sit down. You so rarely grace us with your presence. How's Six West these days? And I see you're still sucking on your carcinogens."

"Each to his own," Marc replied mildly, clenching his pipe between his teeth and throwing a pointed look at Ted's beltline.

"Quite so," Bell admitted. "So what's up?" He picked up a pencil and doodled on a small pad of paper containing the hieroglyphics of the previous debate. The other three doctors wandered off politely.

Marc considered lighting his pipe and decided against it. "I stopped by Pathology to see you. They said . . ." He studied Bell's hand. "Do that again, will you?"

"What?"

"That little drawing."

Bell scowled at Marc. "Do you plan to send me a bill for this?" But he resumed outlining a series of boxes and squiggles on the paper. The pen was in his left hand.

"You're *left*-handed."

"Of course. Always have been."

"Will you write your name for me?" Marc asked, leaning across the table to watch.

"Love to," he said, and scripted "Theodore K. Bell" in a beautiful backhand cursive, crossing the T from right to left.

"Meet me in Medical Records." Marc pulled the pipe from his mouth and stood. "I think you'd better look at something."

Luckily Anne's records had not been refiled since the previous day. "We've been a little rushed," the librarian said, plucking it from the top of the file cabinet.

Dr. Bell studied his signature at the end of a report of an autopsy on "Hart, Girl."

"So?" he asked.

"Is that your signature?"

"Of course it is. 'Theodore K. Bell,' " he read, as if it were some kind of quiz game.

"You cross your T's from right to left. I watched you do it. This one is crossed from left to right. The signature on that report was done by a right-handed person."

Bell examined his name at the end of the report again. "You're right," he said. "Probably one of my assistants. Dr. Morely was here in August. He might have signed it to save time."

"Mrs. Hart claims her infant was a boy," Marc explained quietly. "Can you check with Dr. Morely?"

"He left in November. Took a position in South Carolina. I suppose I could write to him. Or phone. But I doubt he'd remember." Bell's eyes narrowed thoughtfully. "What's going on, Marc?"

"Anne Hart is a patient of mine. I can't tell you much more than that." They started down the corridor away from Medical Records. "Could you check with Dr. Morely? This might be important."

But when Dr. Bell called from his office in Pathology, Dr. Philip Morely was unavailable at Ehrhardt Memorial Hospital in Columbia, South Carolina. Bell left a message to have Dr. Morely return the call.

With a copy of the autopsy report in his hand, Bell typed an entry into the computer, giving the specimen number of "Hart, Girl." Marc watched, fascinated. He had no occasion to use the computer at General Hospital, since the records of psychiatric patients were confidential and kept only in written form. A screen finally flashed up.

Bell groaned, erased the screen, and typed in the information again. "These computers are great when they work . . ." he grumbled.

The screen appeared again.

"There must be some mistake," Ted Bell said softly, glaring at the screen. "The report lists that fetus as number 1682, but in the computer, 1682 is an ulcerated leg."

"Quite a difference," Marc chided. "Hardly an easy mix-up."

Bell shot him a scowl. "This doesn't happen, you know. It must be a computer error. Listen, I'll check on it and get back to you."

"Fine. Thanks, Ted." Marc left the pathologist still frowning and mumbling about these "damned machines."

Three days later Dr. Bell phoned Marc. "Sorry to take so long getting back to you," he apologized. "It took some checking to find out what happened."

"Did you get it straightened out."

"A series of mix-ups. A real snafu. Morely couldn't remember exactly. He said he signed reports when he assisted in the postmortems, and he *is* right-handed. He didn't remember the name of Hart."

"Was the infant male or female, Ted?" Marc leaned back in his chair and closed his eyes.

"Well, that's another problem." Bell cleared his throat. "The post reports the baby as female. But the PSD says it was male. Sometimes it's difficult to tell at birth. I'd go with the post findings."

"The PSD?"

"Permission for scientific disposal. The father signed it. They haven't requested the fetus for burial, have they, Marc?"

"No, nothing like that."

"As it turned out, Dr. Jones—Andy Jones, our neonatologist—has the specimen in his office. I should have thought of that. He sometimes pulls a specimen to study. So the data weren't entered in the computer yet. As I said, a real mix-up."

"Indeed!"

"But don't worry, Marc," Ted Bell assured him. "It's all taken care of now."

9

Anne's days were like a string of paper clips, connected, but not fastened to much. At the hospital she prowled the second floor, trying doors, peering into rooms, and finding nothing that looked like a research unit.

She called University Medical Center and made an appointment with Dr. Robert Bryant in Obstetrics and Gynecology. The medical center, including clinics and a modern 225-bed hospital, was well known for its oncology research and the treatment of spinal injuries. It also boasted a fleet of Ob-Gyn physicians and a recently remodeled maternity wing on the hospital. But Anne's main concern was that University Medical Center was *not* San Marco General.

And Anne decided to paint again, idly, with little purpose in mind. She dug out the case of acrylic paints in the studio of the house.

Several years before, she and Doug had converted the garage into a studio by adding skylights, floor-to-ceiling paned windows on the north wall, a sliding door looking out on the walled front yard, with a second set of glass doors that gave her a view of the back patio. At the time they had decided she could watch the baby while she painted.

The brushes were quite stiff, but salvageable. She stretched three canvases, dashing back and forth from the studio to the art shop, and then she sequestered herself in the room with *Water Music* deluging every corner to drown out the infant. This was an act of frustration rather than creativity, she decided.

Anne started with the largest canvas, applying layer after layer of Payne's gray and cadmium red light. A deep magenta cavern developed. On the second canvas she reproduced the dark depths and added silver metallic explosions with an air gun. But the third canvas she worked with a palette knife, texturing the background in raw sienna and earth green. A face formed slowly, capturing its features from lemon yellow light and umber, cadmium reds and blue and the raw sienna. This was not the red face of the dreams, but a rosy, enigmatic face, every line of which seemed familiar somehow, as if she had painted that same countenance before.

"All I have to do is be there," she told Doug over supper of a hasty quiche and winter tomatoes. "The knife seems to paint on its own. It's incredible."

"Mmm," Doubt murmured, barely acknowledging her excitement. "It certainly doesn't do much for your appetite. If you don't eat that quiche, I'm going to padlock the studio."

"I doubt if it would matter. I think I could walk through a wall at this moment." She nibbled the tomato. The nausea wasn't any better, but it wasn't any worse since she ran out of pills. And she would see Dr. Robert Bryant in three weeks.

But when Doug insisted they have Sunday brunch at the English Oyster, a small restaurant in Piedmont, Anne wondered if she would be able to eat anything without gagging.

"I'm not very hungry," she said, gripping the heavy china plate and staring at the ocean through huge bay windows across the restaurant.

Doug was already heaping his plate with thin slices of ham, crisply fried chicken wings, and cold oysters in a piquant butter-yellow sauce.

Anne shivered. That wasn't ham. That was slabs of thigh, pink and stringy, freshly carved. And not chicken wings.

Those were arm bones. Baby arm bones, snipped clean at the shoulder and elbow, and deep-fried.

Her plate remained empty, but her head reeled with the silver platters of delicate abominations. Cranberry gelatin looked like marrow, dark and clotted. She peered into a skillet of corned-beef hash. Scrambled lung.

Doug spooned sections of green leg bone, smothered in blood and a thick layer of fat, onto his plate. "That zucchini dish looks great." He held out a generous helping for her.

Anne backed away and stumbled against a portly woman in a green tweed suit. The woman's plate smashed to the floor, and food oozed out from the edge of the plate. Anne gagged.

Small belly oysters rolled around in their acrid sauce. Placental watermelon spit its dark seeds on her shoes. And she covered her face with her hands. Doug, at her side, steered her past the disgruntled woman and the waiter who busily cleaned up the mess on the floor.

"Annie, are you all right?"

They were back at their table. Anne's breath was heavy and slightly sweet, returned to her from inside the cup of her hands.

A man with quiet brown eyes and a too large nose bent over the table. "I'm a doctor," he said softly. "Is there anything I can do?"

"She's pregnant," Doug told him. "I think she had an attack of morning sickness."

The doctor smiled. "Try a few saltines. And tea. No coffee."

"Yes, thanks."

They sat in silence. Doug watched her closely. "Your color's coming back," he finally said.

"I feel better." She let her hands drop to the white table linen. "Doug, I know now why I haven't been able to eat." She unfolded the napkin. "When I was a kid, there was a story about how you got babies. It was food, something you *ate*, that grew into a baby."

"I heard the same story." His gray-blue eyes danced. "I think it was watermelon seeds."

"Yes, watermelon seeds, or something." She took a deep breath. "Or anything solid." Anything solid in her mouth had become a prospective infant, growing inside her. Rather than risk that possibility, she'd nearly given up food.

"But you want a baby, don't you, Annie?"

"*I* want a baby. That's the whole point." She clasped both hands around the icy water glass. "I'm afraid they'll get this baby, too. But they won't. I'll make sure of that." For the first time in months Anne was aware of her own pleasantly demanding hunger.

She stopped in at Unity Clinic to tell Geoffrey she *was* pregnant. He had progressed from looking tired to decidedly haggard. His eyes were blinking saucers.

"Congratulations." His voice was flat. He stripped off a surgical glove and slapped it in the white garbage pail.

"Thanks." Anne backed away. "I'll just stop and see Gary before I leave."

"You do that." He didn't look up.

Gary mentioned some concern with Geoffrey's appearance, his abruptness handling clinic patients, and the way the man's hands shook applying a dressing.

"I think he's worn out," she said. "He works all day and then comes here. And there's a great deal of pressure at Peralta."

Gary's green eyes were iridescent with scorn. "I know a stoner when I see one. He has all the signs."

Anne stiffened. "Geoffrey?" She couldn't believe Gary meant that. "You think Geoffrey is on something?"

He didn't answer.

"I think you're wrong," she said softly. "I think he's just working too hard."

But the idea bothered Anne. She dismissed it as an exaggeration, but the thought returned, uninvited and persistent.

Anne's father always said the easiest way through a door

was through it. And if Ammy wasn't the door to what had happened to her child, then it was certainly the hinge. The place to start was Peralta.

Tom Larkin was the night tech at Peralta. He fed the animals, refilled reagent bottles, and monitored any experiments begun during the day. And there was Chuck, the janitor. Anne hoped to avoid both of them long enough to get a look at Ammy's production and testing progress. And if she were seen, she was certainly no stranger to Tom or Chuck, even after seven months.

The back delivery entrance was unlocked at night. It wasn't *supposed* to be unlocked, but Tom usually ordered pizza around midnight, and the delivery man used the back entry. Anne remembered finding evidence of Tom's feasts. Wolton, a large Siberian-husky mix, smelled distinctly of Italian sausage, and even the guinea pigs had hoarded bits of pizza crust in their cages.

Anne tried the door, and it opened. She found herself in the bright utility hall that ran along the back of the main lab. She listened for Tom or Chuck, but only the long, white silence of PTI lingered in the hall.

Seven months previous, Ammy had been produced in a small lab off the animal room. Initially, amino acids such as alanine, leucine, glycine, and valine were mechanically linked to a base molecule in a glue-pot arrangement. Later they found that oxygen would bond the amino acids and an osmotic catalyst to the polymer, stabilizing the molecule until contact with an enzyme called relase, which broke the oxygen bond and freed the protein for introduction directly through skin and mucous membranes. Oxygen, at this point, was available for assimilation, equilibrating rather quickly. The discovery of the process was Geoffrey's brain child, ingenious and beyond their wildest hopes for a life-support medium.

When Anne opened the second door in the hall, she gasped. Lining the wall were huge glass vats of Ammy in which animals hung suspended: three rats, a gray tabby cat, six guinea pigs, a small terrier, and Xanadu.

Anne closed the door and examined the small white mouse,

upside down in the medium and gnawing viciously at a stump of a hind leg. Her head reeled. She tapped on the glass to distract him, if only for a moment, but the mouse continued his self-mutilation. Anne closed her eyes and turned away.

When she looked up, she noticed the familiar green notebook on the counter, the record of Xanadu's life in Ammy. Anne paged slowly through the notes until she came to a November entry: 3 cubic centimeters of blood removed. No reaction. Twenty four hours later, Xanadu was still eating normally.

She read a later entry: 2 cubic centimeters of blood removed. The mouse had circled the jar continuously for three days, but feeding was normal. Blood levels showed elevated serotonin on the specimen removed from Xanadu. Then the last entry. Monday morning, 1.5 cubic centimeters of blood had been removed and Raridine, an antihematopoictic drug, added to suppress the bone marrow, and Xanadu began chewing his tail and hind feet.

They'd bled the mouse to see if it would live in the medium. Xanadu's mangled hind leg didn't bleed. Disgust and pity swept over her. She quickly surveyed the other animals suspended in their glass cages. The tabby cat circled slowly. Had it been bled too? If the life of an animal could be sustained in Ammy without blood circulation, the medical advantages would be tremendous. Blood transfusion, heart-lung machines, and kidney dialysis would be a thing of the past. But the experiment wasn't working. Not at Peralta, at least.

Anne examined the contents of the small refrigerator that stood in the corner of the room. She couldn't stand to see Xanadu like that. Antibiotics and anesthetics lined one shelf, and brown boxes of capsules—red-and-blues, yellow-and-whites—sat in a rainbow array. Anne located the secobarbital, uncapped it, and poured the entire contents into Xanadu's jar. She started counting.

The mouse stopped gnawing, snapped his head from side to side several times, shuddered, and was still. Anne slid the lab notebook in her purse. No one would miss it until morning.

The hall was empty when she checked it, and the other doors were locked. If Ammy was being mass-produced somewhere inside Peralta, it had to be on the other wing, which meant walking through the main laboratory and certainly meeting Tom Larkin or the janitor.

She plunged ahead, barging through the door into the lab.

Tom Larkin looked up from the counter in surprise. "Anne. Anne Hart, isn't it?" He was pipetting a clear liquid into small plastic vials.

"Yes. Hello, Tom. I hope I didn't alarm you. I took a chance on finding Dr. Collier here." It was seven-thirty, and not an entirely unrealistic possibility. Geoffrey had often worked late, Anne remembered.

"It's Wednesday. He's at the clinic."

"Oh, of course. I must have forgotten." She glanced at the closed door to Geoffrey's office and then back to Tom. "What are you doing?"

"Hyaluronidase," he said, holding up one of the vials. "Makes the amino acids more available."

Anne nodded, but her mind raced ahead. More accessible to humans. To babies. "What's happening with Ammy now?" she questioned him with seemingly casual interest. "Are you on a production schedule now?"

"A hundred gallons a day," he drawled. "Two hundred by February. This'll be hot stuff when it hits the market. I guess they want to be ready."

Anne caught her breath. A hundred gallons a day? "What are they doing with a hundred gallons a day, Tom? The walls must be bulging."

"Stockpiling." He continued to fill the vials. "The truck comes Tuesday and Friday nights to pick up the drums. Things have changed around here since you left."

Anne chose not to pursue the subject. She was busy calculating the half-life of that oxygen bond in Ammy. It was one hundred and forty-four hours. Ammy *wasn't* being stockpiled. If hundreds of gallons left PTI, hundreds of gallons were being used. By hundreds of infants? Her knees melted under her.

"Well, listen, I've kept you from your work long enough. I guess I'll try to catch Geoffrey at Unity Clinic," she told Larkin. "Good to see you, Tom."

Leslie Corbin, Jolie's replacement in the neonatal ICU, was as verbal as she was abrasive, and her criticism of Mrs. Sands and General Hospital were constant in the cafeteria at the two-A.M. breaks.

"I don't believe this place. Who ever heard of a no-code newborn!"

Some of the nurses argued that nonviable infants were better off dead than as surviving vegetables, existing on respirators and blood transfusions. One suggested that General Hospital, and the entire St. Helena Valley, saw more than its share of premature births because of the insecticides used for the fruit orchards.

"Are you kidding?" Leslie hooted. "This hospital has a premature-fetal-death rate six times the national average. And it isn't because of insecticides." Leslie Corbin liked to be the center of attention, and she certainly was at the moment. "If you ask me, some of those babies aren't even dead yet. We jam them in a jar almost before they stop breathing."

"Why would anyone do that?" Anne asked her.

She shook her head. "I don't have any idea. But I'm not stupid. The last nurse in Neo ICU killed herself, and I think she may have found out something." She sat back in her molded plastic chair and grinned. "The moral is, if you get pregnant in this valley, don't come to General."

Anne wasn't surprised to see Leslie Corbin's name on the surgical schedule when she came in to work on Wednesday. Leslie would undergo a tubal ligation at eight-twenty the following morning. Dr. Ben Springer was the surgeon. Anne guessed the young nurse had decided not even to *risk* a pregnancy in the St. Helena Valley.

By six-thirty that next morning Leslie Corbin had checked into the hospital, slipped on a white, airy gown, and sat cross-legged on the bed reading *Moonfire,* one of the latest science-fiction best-sellers.

"Do you believe all that futuristic stuff?"

She looked up at Dr. Springer. "There's more truth in fiction than you might think."

Ben laughed. "I suppose you're right." He laid the IV tray on the bed stand and removed the towel. "You all ready, Leslie? We'll have you in OR in about an hour. And by tomorrow you'll be back home, raring to go again."

He hung a bottle of saline and sank the butterfly needle deep in a vein on the back of her hand. Leslie winced and lay back on the pillow.

"I'll give you your preop. Are you allergic to any medications, Leslie?"

"No, not that I know of."

Springer injected the medication directly into the IV, and the effects were immediate. Leslie blinked slowly and then closed her eyes.

"Getting sleepy?" he asked.

"Um," she agreed, smiling slightly.

At eight o'clock Leslie Corbin was wheeled to OR, lightly anesthetized and the incision made for a tubal, which was quick and relatively simple. Dr. Springer looked up once at the anesthesiologist, who scowled down at Leslie.

"She's too deep," he said to Ben.

"She told me she didn't sleep much last night."

A Band-Aid covered the incision in the recovery room. Her blood pressure was slightly low, so they decided to keep her in Recovery until she was fully awake. Twenty minutes later her blood pressure had fallen dramatically to 80/42.

The Recovery nurse, June Ramos, looked worried. "She's hemorrhaging," she said to the other nurse.

The resident ordered a stat crossmatch for six units. Leslie Corbin was indeed hemorrhaging. Blood soaked the sheets and pad under Leslie.

They tried an expander in the IV and pushed in three units of blood, but her pressure dropped again, was undetectable ten minutes later, and Leslie Corbin was dead at ten-forty-six that morning without ever regaining consciousness. The resident stood at the bedside and pondered the dead woman. He checked the chart for preops. Leslie Corbin had received a mild sedative that morning; her CBC, urinanalysis, and coagulation studies had been normal. The doctor had no idea what had happened.

Thursday afternoon an autopsy was performed by Dr. Theodore Bell and one of the Path residents. The county coroner had ordered the postmortem, over Ms. Corbin's family's objections.

After a long midline cut and block removal of the organs, Ted Bell sectioned the liver for any abnormalities. Part of the liver was fixed in formalin for later studies. No gross anomalies were present in the tissue. Leslie Corbin had been an unusually healthy twenty-six-year-old woman. The only finding was that her blood wouldn't clot, and they knew that before they ever did an autopsy.

The official cause of death was listed as idiopathic athromboplastinemia, a fancy name for the fact that Dr. Theodore K. Bell hadn't the slightest idea why her blood wouldn't clot, but it wouldn't. The prothrombin time was normal, but the whole blood-clotting time was off the chart. That left only thromboplastin as the culprit.

"Her blood just didn't clot," Dr. Bell explained to Mr. Corbin, Leslie's father, after the post. "We think it was a congenital deficiency. Is there a history of bleeding problems in the family?"

"Bleeding problems?" Mr. Corbin asked in a numb voice. "No, not that I know of."

"None? I mean, do you or your wife have any difficulty with blood clotting? Say, after you go to the dentist? Or any of Leslie's brothers or sister?"

Corbin shook his head. "She had one sister. Glenda's had two children. No, there haven't been any problems. Until now."

The hospital corridors buzzed with news of Leslie Corbin's death, not because she was an employee and the staff knew her, but because the mortality rate from tubal ligations was extraordinarily low, and Leslie Corbin's statistical exception was a matter for conjecture.

Very early Friday morning, Ted Bell returned to the morgue at General Hospital. He had been unable to sleep, which was a rare occurrence in his twenty-seven-year career.

The body of Leslie Corbin was on slab number 17. Bell removed the corpse and laid it out on the post table again. She was scheduled for pickup by the funeral director in the morning, but that still gave Bell enough time.

He snipped the large, heavy stitches down the skin, which fell away like old leather. Brain tissue, stomach, remains of liver and bowel nested in the peritoneal cavity, but those were of little interest now to Ted Bell. Blood and tissue fluid oozed through the cavity. The blood still had not clotted. He turned on the hose at the head of the table and flushed out the thin pink fluid.

With a cast saw, small and precise, he cut neatly into the iliac crest of the pelvis, dipped the cannula tip of a bone marrow syringe deep in the bone, and pulled out a marrow sample. He collected blood from the femoral vein and labeled tubes for analysis. The samples would go by taxi to the county toxicology lab in downtown San Marco.

There had to be a reason for the bleeding, and Ted Bell was determined to find out what it was. Leslie Corbin had had no history of bleeding problems, almost impossible in a congenital deficiency of one or more clotting factors.

Lack of sleep and his own suspicions made his hand less steady than usual, and he wouldn't get an answer from the tox lab for two hours. He spent those two hours reviewing Leslie's medical history, looking for any clue, and then painstakingly repeating the post. Had he missed something? The question plagued him.

At five A.M. Dr. Andrew Jones, General Hospital's resident neonatologist, returned a fetal specimen to Pathology. He used the lab entrance to the morgue and was surprised to see a shaft of light under the door.

Ted Bell sat staring at his clipboard. He had propped his feet on the counter.

"Ted," Andy said with a grin, "what are you doing here?"

Bell looked up slowly. His eyes were bloodshot.

"I don't know who should go on the slab," Jones joked, "you or her." He nodded to the gaping cadaver that once was Leslie Corbin.

"You know that nurse that bled to death in OR? She was murdered," Ted Bell said evenly. "The tox lab just called. A massive dose of heparin."

"Murdered?" Jones read the notes over the pathologist's shoulder.

"They confirmed it with the protamine sulfate test. Definitely heparin."

Jones whistled softly. "Have you called Homicide yet?"

"Not yet. I've been trying to figure out if this could happen accidentally. She was Ben Springer's patient."

Dr. Andrew Jones's left hand edged toward the post tray on the counter. "Look, Ted, you're exhausted. I'll call downtown. Or have one of the residents call. Is anyone else around?"

"Not until eight."

Jones's hand was around the scalpel. From the back he hit the carotid artery with no difficulty. Post scalpels were longer than those in the operating room. He thrust the blade deep enough to sever the trachea at the same time. It was merciful. Dr. Theodore K. Bell hissed, bloody foam bubbling from the slit in his neck, and toppled off the stool.

The genius of Andy Jones was apparent not only in his medical expertise but also in the man's accumulation of sheer luck. No one barged into the post room that morning. No one noticed the light under the door to the morgue. The janitor had already emptied the trash on that floor, and the red plastic garbage bags waited in the barrel for their trip to the "dogshed," where specimens scheduled for disposal were burned every Friday. It was all very simple, and the garbage disposal helped, an industrial unit with blades sharp enough to chew a man's hand into a mealy slush and spit it into the sewage system with no trouble. And no trace.

By seven-thirty A.M. Leslie Corbin was stitched up and back on the cold slab. The trash barrel was nearly full. Later that day Larry Jessup would comment on the heavy load but trundle it out to the incineration shed anyway, where it would burn for three hours.

Anne was off work at eight. At the elevator to the basement she waited beside Dr. Andrew Jones, who looked over and smiled. A long streak of blood ran down the side of his lab-coat sleeve.

"Busy night?" he asked.

"Pretty slow. People like to stay healthy for Christmas, I guess."

By Monday Ted Bell was listed as missing. That Friday, when he didn't show up at the hospital, the residents figured he'd taken the day off. No one thought to check on the yellow Mazda parked in the subterranean lot until Saturday. Dr. Bell was divorced, and his ex-wife hadn't seen him for three months.

Sergeant Robert Nielson, Homicide Division of the San Marco P.D., put the pathologist's disappearance under investigation, and General Hospital returned to normal activity.

Anne had time to shower and change clothes before she left for Marc Rivers' office. She preferred a bath, but hot water pummeling her back revived her. She pulled on faded denims and a dark green sweater. In the mirror she studied her side view. She was only six weeks pregnant, and it would be at least another month before that undeniable lump appeared.

On her way out of the house she set the burglar alarm. The man had come from Protec yesterday and installed a "foolproof" alarm. It was expensive, the very best, although Doug had argued for a good watchdog.

Marc Rivers was waiting for her at the office. He looked exhausted. "Come in, Anne."

Gray afternoon light sluiced the room. A table lamp managed

to brighten only one corner. Anne crept into the bentwood rocker for a change.

"Are you still afraid?" Marc asked.

"A little. I had a burglar alarm installed in the house."

"But you aren't afraid of burglars."

"No, not burglars."

"Why would someone hurt you?"

"Why would someone hurt Jolie?" she asked him. "Or Leslie Corbin? Or Dr. Ted Bell?"

Lunch at Donahue's was a once-in-a-while tradition with Fay and Anne, marking birthdays, unexpected income-tax refunds, or a soothing salve for artistic egos battered by rejection of one sort or another.

The decor bothered Anne that Wednesday afternoon when she and Fay worked their way through crab louis. The wallpaper at Donahue's was red, flocked with deep maroon, the booths were cushioned in red, and a red candle flickered on every table.

Anne picked at her salad. The baby cried in spurts, just enough to annoy at this lunch meant to celebrate Anne's pregnancy.

"The disappearance of that doctor at General is pretty weird," Fay said, glancing at Anne's plate.

"They found his car in the lot where I park at night. And one of our nurses died in surgery. Bled to death."

It was hardly a celebration. The room circled several times, and Anne excused herself to go to the rest room.

Fay finished her salad, and the waiter brought two plates of sticky, rich baklava.

"Is your friend finished?" he asked, one hand on Anne's plate.

Fay nodded and realized Anne had been gone unusually long. She slid out of the booth and checked the women's rest room.

"Anne? Anne Hart?" There was no answer. "Did you see a blond lady?" she quizzed the other women in the lounge. "She was wearing a white wool dress."

No one had seen her. Fay hurried back to the booth, hoping Anne had returned. But she hadn't.

And an hour later Anne still had not showed up. The waiter was pleasant but wary. Donahue's didn't like scenes. Fay felt his eyes watching her while she ate dessert very slowly and watched the doors and Anne's portion of baklava sitting there like enticement for a ghost.

Finally Fay paid the bill, tipped the waiter, whose smile was more relief than gratitude, and called Doug. He hadn't heard from Anne. Her Datsun remained in its spot in front of Donahue's.

At five-thirty Doug called Dr. Rivers. He hadn't seen Anne either. So Doug and Fay began the eerie task of phoning hospital emergency rooms. Before they called the police.

The only thing Anne remembered was that she was bleeding in Donahue's. It was slight, but enough to send her out of the restaurant in a panic. She remembered getting lost. She told the ER doctor at General that she was looking for a hospital, a cab, a doctor, or something, and she panicked. When she was unable to explain her difficulty to a young clerk in Powell's Bookstore, he had called the police.

"I'm so afraid I'm losing the baby again," she said to the ER doctor.

He called Dr. Springer, and ten minutes later Ben stood beside her bed in the curtained cubicle. "The bleeding's minimal. I don't think you're miscarrying. Have you been taking the pills?"

She hadn't. She'd run out of them weeks ago. And it was still three weeks before her appointment with Bryant at University Medical Center. She looked up at Ben Springer's bottom lip, pink and wet beneath the trimmed mustache.

A tidal wave of nausea hit her. She clapped her hand over her mouth, but she vomited anyway, long and hard. They gave her a shot to stop the vomiting. She saw Springer shrug to the ER doctor.

Anne lay weeping and quivering on the gurney. The baby

screamed. "Don't touch me," she cried at Ben. "I don't want you to touch me!"

Ben Springer leaned his large dark head close to her face. "Unless you calm down, Mrs. Hart, I will have no choice but to hospitalize you," he warned her. "A seventy-two-hour hold on Six West might do you some good."

Horrified, Anne tried to stop her shaking. He was correct. He *could* have her admitted to Six West for three days for as little reason as observation.

"We were giving you progesterone," Springer explained severely. "The spotting was caused by a sharp drop in the hormone level when you stopped taking the pills."

She hated his tone of voice. "Please, will someone call my husband?"

"I'll give you enough medication to last a few weeks. You come into the office next week. Monday or Tuesday at the latest."

Anne nodded tearfully. "Please call my husband."

She spent the weekend swallowing the pills: Sedatrol, for the nausea; Protiol, which was the hormone; and a small red tablet with the number twenty-five printed on it. She couldn't read the name Springer had scrawled in the corner of the envelope.

The infant alternately screeched and whimpered at her all weekend, and a series of red dreams left her cold and dazed.

Monday she phoned Dr. Springer's office.

"I'm sorry, the doctor is with a patient," his receptionist said in a nasal diplomacy. "If you'll leave your name and number, Doctor will return your call."

"Just tell him my name's Anne Hart, and I'll be seeing Dr. Robert Bryant at University Medical Center from now on."

"How do you spell that?"

"B-r—"

"No, *Hart*. How do you spell *Hart*?"

"H-a-r-t," Anne answered patiently.

"And your phone number?"

"He doesn't need that. Just give him the message."

*   *   *

When Anne told Marc Rivers about blacking out during lunch with Fay, she noticed the furrows deepen in his forehead.

"I've stopped spotting," she said quietly. "And I'm going to see another obstetrician."

"You don't trust Dr. Springer?"

"He won't get this baby."

Doug crept in the house at six-thirty. Usually he orchestrated his arrival with a shout, his briefcase clattering across the mosaic-tile entry, and a resounding slam of the front door. But tonight she saw him coming and flipped off the burglar alarm.

"Hi. How was your day?" she asked.

He stood looking at her with soft, tired eyes. "Exhausting. How was yours?"

Christmas carols played softly from the stereo. Their tree, shining in the corner of the living room, warmed the house with multicolored lights.

"I seem to be so tired all day," she explained. The last three-day stretch at the hospital had left her numb.

"Why don't you resign from General?" he suggested. His yearly bonus had been substantial.

"I can't quit now," she protested. "I just *started* there."

"But you didn't know you'd be pregnant so soon," Doug argued gently. "They'll understand. It happens all the time."

"Not yet," she said. "Not just yet."

After dinner they made love, slowly, almost cautiously, exploring the smallest of neglected sensations, the backs of Doug's knees, between each of Anne's fingers.

Later, propped up in bed, they watched *White Christmas*, then made love again, hungrily this time. Warm and tingling, Anne lay back on the cool sheets, enjoying the last stretch of orgasmic visions of a lush green meadow.

"When this is all over," she said, stretching luxuriously, "let's . . ." She looked over at him. Doug was asleep. His breath came like a great machine winding down for the day. She kissed her fingertips and touched them to his cheek without waking him.

10

Christmas carols filled a small but comfortable ground-floor apartment in Sioux City, Iowa, two thousand miles from San Marco.

Tim Sheldon adjusted one leg in his wheelchair and read the letter again. A baby. A baby girl. He read it over and over, afraid that if he looked away, the words might disappear from the paper.

Tim tried to phone Nancy at the school again. He'd already tried twice since the letter came that morning. The secretary at Greenfield School said Nancy was busy and would have to call him back.

Tim Sheldon had been in a wheelchair since the Vietnam war and that mine field. He would never walk again. And he would never father a child. And a child was the one thing he and Nancy wanted badly.

He folded the letter carefully. Maybe he would find a red ribbon and give the letter to Nancy on Christmas Eve. Quite a Christmas present, he thought. A baby girl.

11

Paul McConnell, surly and unapproachable, was night maintenance man in OR on the second floor of General Hospital. His was probably one of the most responsible jobs on Maintenance at night. Each operating theater was flooded nightly with a bacteriostatic solution, then dried and buffed to a mirror shine. Operating tables and trays had to be disinfected, counters wiped down, and trash emptied. There had not been one case of bacterial contamination in the operating rooms since Paul McConnell came to General eighteen months ago.

Usually the nights were quiet. Night surgery was on an emergency basis—appendectomies, cesarean sections and difficult deliveries, or dire repairs on accident victims. But most nights Paul McConnell was left alone to clean.

When they brought up the motorcycle accident, McConnell watched from the door of one of the operating rooms. It would take a long time to get that guy back in shape, Paul knew. He wouldn't get into Number 6 until morning to clean.

That Saturday night after Christmas was slow for Anne in the lab until she got the crossmatch on James Simpson, a twenty-two-year-old multiple-trauma motorcycle accident. He was AB positive. She swore softly. AB positives should *never* be allowed on motorcycles. The blood type was rare and sometimes difficult to get hold of in quantity.

A breathless nurse from OR called and asked Anne to bring up four units of Simpson's blood just after one o'clock. Anne knew this was her chance to look around the operating rooms. She remembered Max had told her about some kind of research unit located *behind* the OR. And she'd tried every other section of the second floor without success.

She gathered four units of AB positive blood from the refrigerator shelf and one O positive. It was a chance.

The pneumatic crackle-glass door to OR swooshed open and closed behind her. Luckily the desk nurse was nowhere to be seen. Anne quickly donned a surgical green gown, mask, booties, and cap. The second set of doors glided open. She spotted a door at the end of the first hall. She'd try that one.

But first she had to get the blood to the operating amphitheater where James Simpson was undergoing surgery. She turned down the second hall and saw a light shining from one of the doors. Anne set the four units of blood in one of the hall refrigerators and looked into the lighted operating room.

A nurse looked up sharply. The patient was already opened. They were working frantically.

"I brought up Simpson's blood," Anne said to the nurse. "They're in the hall refrigerator. He's an AB positive, so be neat about this."

"Bring us two units," the anesthesiologist barked without looking up.

Anne's stomach churned, but she brought two of the units of blood and gave them to the nurse. James Simpson's own blood lay in puddles on the floor of the operating room. She slipped before she got out the door. Her breath came in gulps, but she turned down the hall to that door. She held the extra O positive unit of blood in her hand and tried the door. It was locked.

"Hello," she called softly down the hall. "Hello? Is anybody here?"

Paul McConnell leaned out of the door of Number 3. "That door's locked."

"I realize *that*. They called me to bring up a unit of blood for some research unit. In back of the OR. Are you Paul?" Anne held up the plastic bag of blood.

"Wrong door," he growled. "Through here."

Anne followed him into Number 4, where he unlocked a door and let her into a dark hall. "Thanks," she said softly. Before the door clicked shut, she caught it with her toe. Don't lock, she thought, please don't lock.

The dark hall was about forty feet long, with an old recovery room on one side. The OR had been remodeled several years ago, and this area was apparently walled off, except for that one door.

A pale bluish light gleamed from a door farther down the hall. Anne's heart crashed against the inside of her chest. She stood still, trying to calm herself, and once her heart stopped thundering, she became aware of a peculiar whirring noise and a lightness to the air, as if it had just rained in the hall. Ozone, she thought.

Anne edged down the dim corridor with her back against the wall. She felt her way until she was four feet from the open door. Over the steady vibrating pulse from within the room she heard a woman's voice singing softly: "If that mockin' bird don't sing, Mama gonna buy you a diamond ring . . ."

A metallic click made Anne jump. Calm down, she thought fiercely. This is no time to panic. She crossed the hall noiselessly in the surgical booties, remaining in the shadow to get a look through the door.

A nurse in a white uniform stood in front of a row of silver metal tanks, like diving bells, fronted by wide glass windows, each with a movable metal cover. Two of the windows were open. The nurse bent to peer in one, and Anne caught a glimpse of a dark mass behind the glass.

She tiptoed closer. The nurse rose and wrote on the clipboard she held in one hand. Then she moved to the next window. A blaze of lighted dials on the front of each tank made them look like small rockets ready to launch.

Suddenly Anne's breath caught. She thought her lungs would explode. She was standing in the full light of the door. Through the window she saw a tiny iridescent arm. She saw the fingers grasp. Then a shoulder appeared, and finally Anne saw the face, the shriveled, wizened face of a human infant.

A cry escaped from her. The nurse whirled around, her face white and frightened. Anne recognized Muriel Bennett, the nurse in charge of employee physicals. But with the OR mask and cap, Bennett probably wouldn't recognize Anne.

Nurse Bennett rushed toward her, blocking her view of the tanks. "How'd you get in here?" she demanded angrily. "Who are you?"

"I . . ." Anne gasped.

"You're not allowed in here," Bennett continued, pushing Anne back into the dark hall. "This is a research unit."

"I had to bring blood up for OR," Anne explained, her head searching madly for an excuse. "I guess I took the wrong turn . . . or something. Where am I?"

"How'd you get in?" Bennett demanded again.

"Through the door. I thought I was going out, but I ended up in here."

"Well, you're not *allowed* in here. This is a sterile area. Are you from the lab?"

"Yes," Anne answered meekly. "I'm new here."

"Well, you'd best not go wandering around where you don't know your way."

"Yes, well, I'm really sorry."

Nurse Bennett's mouth was set in a straight, thin line across her narrow face. "You can't go back that way," she said to Anne. "I'll have to put you on the elevator to the first floor."

With a firm hold on Anne's upper arm, she ushered her down the hall to the elevator. Bennett slipped a key in a lock lit by a small bare light bulb. The elevator rumbled up toward them.

"What kind of research do they do here?" she asked the nurse, trying to keep her voice casual.

The answer was curt. "A variety of things."

The doors parted. They stepped into a small anteroom, not the elevator. Anne glanced around, puzzled. The doors closed, and a second set slid open to the elevator. A buzzing pink light overhead made her slightly dizzy.

On the elevator, she turned to see the doors close on Bennett's glare. Anne inhaled sharply and leaned against the smooth, cool wall of the dropping lift. She stripped off the surgical garb and dashed back to the lab when she arrived on the first floor.

The phone was ringing wildly on the desk. She picked it up. It was OR. They needed more blood, uncrossmatched, but type-specific, for James Simpson. She said she'd bring it up.

"He's gone bad in there," the OR nurse said, referring to Simpson. She grabbed the three units of blood before she disappeared through the sliding doors. Anne hurried back to the lab. It was nearly two A.M.

Her fingers tingled. Too much oxygen, she thought. Slow down the breathing.

It was human. A baby. No doubt about it. In a tank of Ammy. She beaded the realizations together quickly.

That was what she had thought she'd find. And more than she expected. They were supporting human infants in tanks of Ammy. But for what? Anne knew she didn't need to answer the question. She could report her discovery. Now someone would believe her. Someone who could do something about it.

When Anne woke Sunday afternoon, the memory of a child enwombed in a silvery mother was etched in her mind. She picked up the newspaper from the coffee table in the living room. She rarely read a paper. She thought there was enough trouble in life without knowing about everyone else's. And Doug told her anything important that was going on in the world. He understood riots in Ecuador, political elections, bus strikes, and grain embargoes, and, more importantly, that all of these were related somehow. It was a gift, she thought to understand how the world worked.

Anne read for diversion, to give her mind time to sort out the discovery of the last night, but that picture on page two of the General section looked vaguely familiar. She read quickly. Christine Springer, daughter of Dr. and Mrs. Benjamin C. Springer, was killed Saturday afternoon in a fall from her horse at the San Marino County Horse Show. Anne read it again, leaned back on the sofa, and closed her eyes. She remembered the picture of the child on Ben Springer's desk. The girl and the horse. Now the child was dead.

Anne was sorry for Christine Springer, but a surge of bittersweet justice pulsed through her. And would another child replace Dr. Springer's daughter? she wondered. Would he give her up, forget about her, and go on living as if she never existed, as he had advised Anne to do with her child?

And what if the answer was yes. She might not know how the world worked, but her own deep and biting fear about a child she lost and the one she carried illuminated a bit of reality called a respiratory distress syndrome research unit.

Larry Jessup hauled the barrel of burnable specimens from Pathology out to the dogshed behind General Hospital. He opened the door of the incinerator and began to toss in the red garbage bags that reeked of formalin and irritated his two-day-old hangover from the New Year's Eve Party.

In the light something glinted from the ashes. Something gold. Very carefully he reached into the gray ash and plucked out a tooth. He turned it over in his hand. It was a gold crown. By stirring through the ashes, he found two more crowns and three teeth. Larry Jessup had burned specimens at General Hospital for twelve years, and he knew that this time something was very wrong. That was when he called Sergeant Robert Nielson at Homicide.

"Teeth don't burn," he told Nielson. "I don't have no idea how they got there. But there they were."

"You and I know teeth don't burn," Nielson said, "but somebody obviously didn't."

"I saw a baby in a tank," Anne told Marc Rivers. "They're keeping babies alive in that RDS unit."

Marc listened without comment to her account of finding the research unit.

Anne prowled the office, stopped at Marc's desk, and absently picked up a smooth clay ashtray. She turned back to the maroon chair. "I made an appointment with the hospital administrator. Someone has to know what's happening at General Hospital."

"John Wanaker, you mean."

Anne stood at the window and gazed out. "I'm afraid if I go to the police I'll never find my baby."

After she left the office, Marc sagged back in his chair. The treatment of Anne Hart was proving long and difficult, particularly since she refused medication and clung steadfastly to the belief that her child was alive. No reason prevailed against the entrenched delusion.

So when Douglas Hart called and asked to talk to him, Marc agreed readily.

Doug Hart was not exactly what Marc expected. From Anne's description he would never have guessed that the boyish-looking man in a brown tweed jacket and sand-colored slacks who sat in his waiting room was Doug.

"*Is* she getting better?" he asked Marc anxiously. "I mean, she's so driven. And she doesn't sleep. And . . . I don't know, I'm just so worried about her."

"Does Anne know you planned to come and talk to me?" Marc asked him.

Doug shook his head. His brown hair moved like water around his head. "No, I didn't tell her."

"I hope you will. Anne feels there are so many secrets in her life. One more could only add to her mistrust."

Without compromising Anne's confidentiality, Dr. Rivers explained that Anne was unable to accept the death of the baby. And so she was on a hero journey, a crusade of sorts, to find the lost child.

"She is acting out the loss of the baby. Your wife feels compelled to search General Hospital and the people involved in the loss, her doctor, nurses. . . . I hope in the end she will exhaust the possibilities and deal with her grief."

Doug's hands knotted in each other. "I don't know what will happen to her if she loses *this* baby, too. You know she's painting again."

Marc tried to find some logic between losing a baby and painting. "Painting is a good affective outlet for Anne," he said mildly. He puffed on his pipe. "Do you object to it?"

"She's painted the face of a baby! It scares me. I mean, it's like she has a baby, but on a canvas. And I can't get her to eat enough or rest enough to take care of the real child she's carrying." His voice quavered. "How long will this go on, Dr. Rivers?"

"Until it's finished. That's all I can tell you. But maybe the painting is a transition from searching for the baby to *having* a baby. Do you see what I mean?"

"Then she is getting better?"

"Yes, I think so. But it will take time."

Time was the one thing Ben Springer knew about. He stood naked in front of the full-length mirror in his home in the Monte Verde foothills, and he ran his dark hand over the very nearly flat stomach. Not old, he thought, not yet.

Benjamin Craven Springer was forty-nine, to be exact. He'd grown up in Georgia with his grandfather. The old man raised Ben on stories about rum-running, opium routes, and privateers he's known.

There'd been years of schooling, St. Martin's Academy, college, and finally medical school at Johns Hopkins. Ben had learned his lessons well. He'd learned that his grandfather's money made the path straight—straight to a degree, a two-year residency in Obstetrics and Gynecology, and finally, his practice in San Marco.

He shivered in front of the mirror and grabbed a towel

from the chrome warmer. The bathroom was always too cold to suit him, not like those balmy Georgian nights. But his bath was a nightly ritual. It cleansed the day, washed off every particle of the world. His grandfather used to say you started over in life every day. Yesterday didn't matter. Or tomorrow. Ben thought he was right about yesterday, at least.

He let the towel drop to the floor and slipped into a double velour robe. Addy would have coffee ready by now.

In the living room a fire blazed in the stone fireplace, making a filigree of light on the bare wood floors around the edges of the room. An Indian rug, woven of soft golds, red, and brown, carpeted the sitting area, which consisted of a white sectional sofa and throw pillows. A grand piano stood in the far corner of the room.

Ellen, his first wife, had designed the house, and as the walls went up, their marriage crumbled into bitter accusations and a hollow shell of feeling between them. Before the roof was on, they were divorced, and a year later Ben married Addy, who preferred comfort to elegance. Ben sank to the plump sofa.

Adele Springer, dressed in a long kelly-green robe, brought two cups of coffee for them. Her hair hung in wisps at her ears, and when she bent to set the cups on the wood shipping trunk that served as a coffee table, he noticed her hair grayed at the roots.

"Dammit, Ad," he growled, "will you go to the hair dresser's."

She ran her long, pale fingers through her hair. "I just need some time."

Some time to what? Wander around the house like a recluse, living on memories? He poured brandy in the cup. "Why don't you pack up Chrissy's things and give them away?"

"Because . . ." She sat down stiffly on the sofa opposite him. Her arms moved like a wind-up toy. "Because I need to be here with all of them. You know, I found that lovely little velvet dress she wore for Christmas one year. Do you remember? She must have been three. It was green, with tiny white flowers embroidered . . . .'' Tears squeezed out of the corners of her eyes.

"For God's sake, stop living it all over again. What's past is past.''

Addy kept her head down and took several quick sips of the coffee.

He hardly thought about his daughter at all. He tried to remember her face, but it was difficult. Like the jump that day, higher than she and America, her sleek roan thoroughbred, had ever attempted. And then that strap on the saddle that gave way at the wrong moment. She should have checked her gear, he thought. Chrissy had always been too casual about details. She would have preferred to ride America bareback around the foothills all day in her old blue jeans and a flannel shirt.

Ben had pushed jumping—the shining black leather boots, her blond hair tucked carefully under her black derby, and that red jacket, not to mention all the blue ribbons that still hung in the den. Chrissy hadn't wanted them in her room.

"Listen, Ad,'' he said, softening his voice, "I know it's hard. I've been thinking about selling the house. The market's up. We could get a good price.''

"Where would we go, Ben?''

"I don't know.'' Actually, the thought of selling the house had just occurred to him. "Maybe a place in the mountains.''

Addy sat in a shroud of silence.

"Or another child. We could adopt, Ad. We're not old.''

Her face filled with horror. "You think we can just replace Chrissy? Is that what you think?'' Her voice cracked uncontrollably, and several choked sobs escaped from her throat. "It isn't that easy.''

Easier than she might think, he knew, but he didn't say anything.

Addy finished her coffee in a forced gulp. "I'm going to go out and feed America. I won't be long.''

The sweat started under his robe. That horse in the back corral irritated him. He hadn't wanted to bring it home after

Chrissy's accident. "I still think we should sell that damned animal. Get him off the place."

"Chrissy loved America. I can't . . ."

In one swift move Ben was out of the sofa and at his desk. He removed the loaded twenty-two revolver. "Well, I can."

"Ben, no, please . . ." she whimpered.

Still barefoot, he brushed past her on the sofa and slid open the back patio door. "Son of a bitch," he swore when his feet hit the painful gravel outside.

America tossed his dark head in greeting. That animal was just one more trapping of death, one more reminder for Addy that the child was gone. If he had to, he'd pack up all those filthy stuffed animals, every velvet dress, blue ribbon, and picture of Chrissy in the whole house. Yesterday didn't matter.

At the corral fence America nuzzled Ben's hand. He heard Addy's footsteps on the loose gravel behind him.

He rested the muzzle of the gun just below the horse's left ear and pulled the trigger.

He thought he heard Addy scream, or it may have been the horse, crumpled in a flail of hooves. In the moonlight, blood spouted from a black hole in its head. Ben leaned down and fired three more shots. America was still.

It meant another shower and a clean robe. He hoped Addy'd done the laundry. And when the phone rang at ten-thirty he was almost relieved. It was Muriel Bennett.

"I have to go to the hospital," he said at the closed door of Addy's bedroom. "Ad, did you hear me?" He knew she wasn't sleeping.

"I heard you."

"I'll be back soon. But don't wait up."

"I won't."

When he arrived at General Hospital, Ben took the basement elevator adjacent to Central Supply. These elevators were for staff use and were generally inaccessible to the public.

In the elevator he inserted his key in the lock above the

"Door Open" button. The key jammed. Ben felt his armpits drench in sweat. He twisted the key sharply, and it gave way. He pressed the button for the second floor.

With the key, the elevator would stop on the second floor as usual, but the doors would open to the west, to the anteroom of the research unit. Without the key, the east doors of the elevator opened to Second Main and the east wing of the hospital. It was a clever system, designed for use when the research unit had been part of the OR. Patients could be easily removed from Recovery back to their rooms. Or, without much fuss, to the morgue.

But Ben worried that someday the system would malfunction and the wrong person would step off the elevator to the anteroom. A person who might ask questions. And if Muriel Bennett was correct and the door between the research unit and OR could be accidentally left open, the elevator door could accidentally open the wrong way, too.

Stop worrying, he instructed himself. This is no time to worry. Things are going well. In six months or so, by the end of the summer, the project will be finished.

The elevator bumped to a stop, and the west doors opened. Ben stepped into the cool, ozone treated air of the small room, lit by long-wave fluorescence to control bacterial contamination. There was an infrared alarm, too. He knew the signal would alert the research unit that someone had entered the anteroom. It was a good system. Ben relaxed a little.

Muriel Bennett was waiting for him in the hall. He beckoned her into one of the rooms adjacent to the main unit.

"How much did she see?" he demanded.

"I'm not sure. Not much, Ben." Muriel Bennett looked at him with eyes like a wild squirrel.

Not so many years ago he'd found her eyes interesting, or at least unusual. But at the moment the woman's timidity annoyed him. And she'd grown thinner now, less to his taste. He didn't like bony women.

"Did you have any of the pods open?" he quizzed her.

"Two. Only two."

"Only two?" he sneered, bending toward her. She was

supposed to keep the metal covers down unless she was actually checking the infant inside.

"I'm sorry," she said quickly. "It won't happen again. The woman surprised me."

"I'm sure."

"She told Paul she was supposed to bring blood in here. That's why he opened the door for her."

"And why didn't you mention this before?" He leaned close to her face. "You know what could happen if she saw one of our . . . guests."

"She didn't see anything. I didn't think it was important enough to . . . to worry you, not so soon after your daughter's accident."

Ben dismissed her with a wave of his hand, and she fled. He would speak to Paul. But first he had to talk to someone else. He picked up the only phone in the research unit. When their grant gave out, eight months ago, the other phone had been removed. He checked a number in his address book and dialed.

"This is Ben," he boomed. "Our friend from the lab may be up to something. She walked in the unit from OR . . . yes, through the door. She tricked Paul. Listen, buddy, you take care of this. You hear me? Divert her or get rid of her. Or I will. Yes, Geoffrey, I'll have your stuff on Monday. As long as you do your part."

He snapped the receiver back on the hook. Even in the cool temperatures of the research unit, Ben felt his wet shirt cling to his armpits. Sweating was such a nuisance. It meant another bath later tonight. Or maybe just a quick shower in the doctor's lounge before he went home.

He stopped in the main room of the unit. Muriel was adjusting the flow rate on the calcium gluconate. He appraised the calf of her leg for a moment and then turned to Matt Treble, a male nurse moonlighting from Good Shepherd Hospital.

"Hi, Matt," he said. "Seen Dr. Jones around here yet?"

"Nope. He usually doesn't get here until after I leave."

"How are our guests tonight?" Ben asked, glancing at the silver tanks lining the wall. "Everybody comfortable?"

"Pod Three was a bit shocky earlier. I increased the calcium gluconate. He looks fine now." Matt picked up the chart from the central workbench. "And the O_2 on One was forty-three at nine tonight. I increased the oxygen to sixty-five percent."

"Have to be careful of that oxygen, Matt," Ben warned him. "Too much, and you knock out the optics. What's the O_2 now?"

"Fifty-six."

"Okay. Watch that tonight, will you, Muriel?"

She nodded. Her eyes flicked up at him and back to the maze of plastic tubing that trailed to the pods.

"Anything happening on the floors?" he asked Matt.

"We got a sixteen-week-old late this afternoon." He checked his clipboard. "It expired at six-thirty. I put it on the dummy to Pathology."

Ben nodded. "Too early. No sense wasting a pod on anything that premature. Anything else?"

"There's a threatened abortion in Labor and Delivery. Been here since morning. Twenty-six weeks."

"Who's on that case?"

"Wellman."

Ben smiled. "I think I'll see if I can give Wellman a hand—speed things up, perhaps." As head of Obstetrics at General, Ben had immediate access to any patient. "Have we got a pod ready?"

"We're filled at the moment," Matt replied. "But Two is term minus two weeks. She must be ready to graduate soon."

"I'm not sure about the arrangements for it yet," Ben said. He unsnapped the clips of Pod Two and slid the cover aside.

Through the portal a human infant was visible, suspended in the thick gel. Its face turned to the window. The mouth sucked at the medium, and then it floated away.

Ben closed the window and moved to Pod One. The infant inside was shriveled and yellow. Its limbs jerked convulsively. Ben checked the bilirubin readout of fourteen, still low enough to preclude brain damage. He guessed the infant had other central nervous system problems.

"Muriel," he said, snapping the portal of One closed, "if you get that abortion on the dummy tonight and it looks viable, pull Pod One. I don't think it'll make it, anyway."

"Not on your life, doctor," she snapped. "That's murder."

Dr. Robert Bryant was younger than Anne expected, tall, with a disconnected gait and ready smile. He seemed to fit in well at a university hospital, with his headful of unruly black hair jutting from the crown of his head, and dark, intelligent eyes. Anne noticed his hair had begun to thin in a small pink circle barely visible beneath the undisciplined thatch.

Bryant smiled absently at her and read through the medical history she'd filled out earlier. Anne could tell when he reached the part about three previous miscarriages. His eyes darted up at her.

"You've lost *three* babies?" he asked.

"Yes, three. And I don't want to lose this one," she told him. "Dr. Springer was giving me hormones—"

"Hormones?"

"Progesterone. To maintain the pregnancy."

His eyebrows shot up. It was an insulting gesture. "You don't need hormones, Mrs. Hart."

"He said if I quit taking them I could lose the baby."

Bryant shrugged. "Maybe. Maybe not. Our experience at University has been that oral additions of progesterone do not maintain a pregnancy. What was the prescription you were taking?"

Anne fished in her purse for the three envelopes. "Protiol," she said, and handed him the packets.

"It wasn't a prescription?"

"No, he gave me samples."

Bryant shook the few remaining pills out of the envelope marked "Protiol" into his hand. He peered into the other two envelopes, too. "Sedatrol. And what's this other one?" He held up the packet.

"I don't know. I couldn't read the name either. It's an antispasmodic."

"Well," he said, "we'll continue you on a low-dosage hormone for another month. A sharp drop in the hormone level could conceivably cause premature labor. I'll write you a prescription."

"I don't want to lose this baby," Anne said again, holding his gaze.

"And I don't want that either. I do want you to relax, take care of yourself, and get enough sleep. Are you working?"

"Part-time."

"Stop."

"Stop working? I can't. Not for a few more months."

He nodded and wrote something in her chart. "Some of the most recent research on multiple miscarriages seems to indicate an antibody formation—the mother may be 'allergic' to the fetus. By damping down the immunological system, we are having rather remarkable success with mothers in premature labor. Do you have any known allergies?"

"I'm allergic to the HISS test."

"The hepatitis-detection test?"

"Yes." Anne watched Bryant's face. "I had a terrible reaction to it. Could those antibodies cause a miscarriage?"

"I don't think so. A positive just means you've had hepatitis, possibly subclinical, at some time. And you shouldn't ever have another test. Did you know that?"

"Yes, they warned me."

Bryant closed the file. "Should you experience any discomfort, spotting, or cramps, I want you to come to University Hospital immediately. Don't try to call. Grab a cab and get to the hospital. And I don't want you to worry."

The reassurance sounded like a litany to Anne, but she agreed, adding, "I'll probably worry anyway."

He patted her arm on his way out, and the smile seemed more friendly. "I'll see you next month, Anne. Oh, and sign the release form for your medical records at the front desk. I'll send for them from General Hospital."

*   *   *

Two days later, January 10th, Anne had an appointment with John Wanaker, the hospital administrator, at ten o'clock. She didn't take time to go home after work and come back, but sat in the hospital cafeteria with a cup of coffee and an order of soggy toast and decided what to say to him. She'd thought about it for days, but after the long night in the lab, all her well-formulated ideas were jibberish. For an hour she made notes on the back of a napkin to organize her thoughts.

Anne wandered down the hall maze to the administrative wing of General Hospital. She had ten minutes to spare. But John Wanaker's door was ajar. She looked in. The secretary's desk was empty, but the door to his office stood open. John Wanaker was visible, bent over the desk. He looked up.

"Hello," he said.

"I'm Anne Hart. I have an appointment at ten."

He stretched his left arm out of the pale blue suit coat and checked his watch. "Yes," he said to her, "come in. I'm almost finished here."

Anne closed the door quietly behind her and took one of the institutional-gray metal armchairs by his desk. John Wanaker continued writing. He was a large man with overly delicate features for his bulk, a receding chin, and hair that he wore like a saddle blanket lopped squarely on the top of his head. He did not look up at her.

Anne reached down and took a paperback novel from her purse, located her place, and began to read. She was too tired to be affected by John Wanaker pulling rank, introducing slight annoyances to establish control, a common enough practice among executives.

Wanaker obviously noticed. "I'll be with you in a moment," he said. "I just have to finish this memo."

"Take your time," Anne said politely. She went back to her reading.

He finished with a flurry, tucked the memo in a file folder, straightened the stack of papers, and finally checked the calendar open on his desk.

"Well, now," he said, "what can I do for you this fine morning . . . ah, Mrs. Hart, isn't it?"

"Yes. Anne Hart." She closed the book and stuck it back in her purse.

"You're one of our night techs, aren't you? How are things in the lab these days? Not that I know much about the lab, I'm afraid. It really isn't my particular expertise. All those machines . . ." He shook his head. "I'm much better at talking the board into paying for that paraphernalia than trying to understand it." He chuckled softly. "How long have you been at General, Mrs. Hart?"

Anne opened her mouth, but Wanaker continued with barely a pause.

"This is my third year here," he said solemnly. "There have been so many changes lately. From day to day I hardly recognize the place. But then, I'm sure I don't have to tell you about change, not a lab tech."

She couldn't decide whether to nod yes or no. Her courage was rapidly failing. John Wanaker was nervous and unreflective. Maybe she'd made a mistake by coming.

"Well, now, enough about that. What can I do for you, Mrs. Hart?" He brought his thick hands together in a prayer posture.

"How much do you know about the RDS research unit back of the OR?" she asked quickly.

Wanaker froze. Anne guessed it was a pose of deep thought.

"We have some of the best research in the state here at General. I just read the bulletin on vitamin research from our dermatology department. Fascinating. Vitamin A. Have you seen it?"

"No, I—"

"Are you interested in research, Mrs. Hart?"

"I'm interested in the research unit back of the OR, Mr. Wanaker. And I think you should be, too."

"Let's see . . ." He brought his fingertips to his heavy lips. "The research unit back of OR?"

John Wanaker listened to Anne because he couldn't afford not to—not with the rumors that riddled General, rumors about the disappearance of Dr. Theodore Bell and whisperings about two dead nurses from the neonatal intensive care unit. He'd taken a week of ribbing at the NHA convention about an employee suicide rate triple the national average. So he listened to Anne's story, her suspicions, and at the mention of Muriel Bennett's name, Wanaker jotted a few notes.

When she finished, an irritable-looking flush had crept over his shirt collar. "Well, I don't know what to tell you. Maybe you'd had a difficult night. Believe me, I know how rigorous you lab people have to be to keep on top of things. Perhaps you thought you—".

Anne stood up. "Mr. Wanaker, I'm telling you I saw a human infant in one of those tanks. I want you to stop that research. Before it's too late."

His pink pads of eyelids blinked steadily. "Well, I certainly do appreciate your coming to me first with this bit of information. I assume you haven't mentioned this to anyone else. And you can be sure I *will* check on the matter."

Anne was still standing. "When?"

"Immediately, of course."

"You know, I checked in Pathology. My baby never went there. You can check for yourself. My name isn't on the log in August." She noticed a silky veil of sweat on his left temple. "I wonder how many other names are missing from that log, Mr. Wanaker."

She didn't close the office door when she left. John Wanaker's secretary, one of those middle-aged women with too much red lipstick, straight hair the color of an aging cocker spaniel, and clear plastic-framed glasses that are winged at the outer edge, sat at her desk and watched Anne leave. Out in the hall, Anne stopped and listened at the door.

"Grace? Grace!" she heard John Wanaker boom. "Get me a file. Anne Hart. Lab employee."

Panic seized Anne. She'd said what needed to be said. Now it was up to Wanaker. Her employee record was flawless. She knew that. And he had no reason to look at her medical chart. She drove home with a small headache, the kind that can become an enormous headache, wedged between her left eye and the bridge of her nose.

*   *   *

She swallowed two aspirin and collapsed in bed, but there was little possibility of sleep, not because of the terrifying red dreams now, but the questions. How many other women's names never appeared on the Pathology log? How many? And how could she find out?

Sleep eluded her, even that night, tucked up against Doug. In that first delicious delirium of falling asleep, the baby began a clamorous cry in the far corner of the bedroom. Not now, Anne thought, leave me alone. Please. She tried drifting, imagining herself at the beach lying in the warm sand. The infant squealed, and then shrieked. She wrapped her arms over her head, and the crying softened. Then it stopped. She waited, hoping she would fall asleep before it all began again. But she couldn't. One arm was numb. She uncovered her ears, and the cry was like a nail driven through her head. By four A.M. she was still awake. Exhausted, she thought about Dr. Rivers. She had an appointment for that morning. Maybe he could help.

She held herself under the thin veil of near sleep, rising and falling with each breath, an act of discipline practiced since college, when academic pressures or tuition deadlines prevented sound sleep. Now, stretched out on the daybed in the living room, she rode the waves of the infant's cry, cresting and then sliding down to silence, only to begin again. The drapes brightened slowly, as if they were on a dimmer switch. Luminous gold light seeped through the room, found the corners, and settled in for the day.

Anne wrapped herself in her terry robe and made coffee in the kitchen. She heard Doug thump to the bathroom. The child was silent at last.

And later that morning Marc Rivers listened silently while she described her inability to sleep because of the baby.

"Infants have a long history of disturbing their parents' sleep," he finally said without a smile.

She glared at him. "That doesn't help! Why don't you believe me?"

"Would you believe me if I told you that you *don't* hear a real baby cry?"

"I want you to make it stop. I want you to hypnotize me and tell me I'll never hear it cry again."

"Hypnosis isn't magic, Anne."

"I've never asked you for magic."

If Rivers wouldn't help, then maybe Geoffrey would, so Anne called and invited him for lunch.

"I'll buy," she offered.

"You're on."

He met her at the front entrance of Peralta, and they drove to Angelo's, a small Italian restaurant with outdoor tables in the summer and a glassed-in veranda for winter dining. Fountains of green ferns hung above the tables spread with red-and-white tablecloths. Anne ordered minestrone, and Geoffrey, after several furtive glances at the menu, said he'd have the same, with a side order of lasagne.

His pale, dry face hovered above his shoulders. He looked older than he had before. Several strands of hair hung in front of his ears. The rest was pulled back to a sailor's knot at the base of his neck.

"So, what's this all about?"

"Are you all right?" she asked impulsively. "You look terrible."

"Thanks a lot. Did you invite me for lunch to insult me?"

"Of course not." She felt her cheeks burn. "I'm just concerned about you. You look exhausted."

His smile seemed forced. "Hard work does that. And you don't look so hot yourself. Are those circles under your eyes?"

"Probably," she said. "I haven't slept much in the last few days. But then, I have an excuse. I'm pregnant."

"Yes, of course."

In that old camaraderie, reminding Anne of the time they had spent brainstorming together about Ammy, she asked him directly if the life-support medium was shipped to General Hospital for experimental use. And if he was aware that H. M. Schwartz was listed as funding a respiratory distress research lab.

The waitress interrupted her, balancing bowls of soup, a

plate of lasagne, two small loaves of herbed bread, and wine on a tray. The smell of warm butter and garlic rose in a moist cloud from the arms of the dark waitress. Geoffrey broke open one of the loaves and tore hunks of steaming bread away, dropping them one by one in the soup.

"They're keeping babies alive at General. Just like Xanadu. I saw it."

Geoffrey raised his bland blue gaze to her. "I won't give your idea credence by even discussing it with you. I think you're more tired than you know, if you imagine anything like that could possibly happen in a hospital. Ammy is still in the animal-testing stage at Peralta. It hasn't even been *scheduled* for human testing."

"*Some* of it goes to General," she insisted.

"You're mistaken. I can account for every fluid ounce."

"Every hundred gallons, you mean."

He gave her a twisted smile, announced he wasn't very hungry after all, and they drove back to Peralta in silence.

"It's too bad about Xanadu," she said just before he climbed out of her car, and although she didn't turn to see his reaction, she caught a glimpse of the painful surprise on his face as she sped away.

12

Anne woke up Thursday morning with a distinct queasiness eddying around her stomach. Nerves, she thought, tracing the roller that surged from her stomach to her throat. Dr. Rivers had finally agreed to try hypnosis.

She arrived at his office ten minutes before her appointment. Questions about the hypnosis clamored at her. Would she be unconscious? Would she be able to go under at all? Some people resisted hypnosis entirely. And even if she could be hypnotized, could she remember a time when she was under an anesthetic? Would she go back to that stuporous cloud, the black void, or worse, the red dreams? Too many questions, she thought.

Marc opened the door. "Hello, Anne," he said. He was dressed in a soft gray cardigan, gray slacks, and a white shirt. "Well, are you ready to try some hypnosis?"

"I'm a little nervous."

"Why are you nervous?"

"I've never been hypnotized before."

His smile implied that her nervousness was equivalent to convincing a barefoot child that walking in the grass wouldn't hurt its feet.

"It isn't as dramatic as you might think," he explained.

"A hypnotic state is a very relaxed condition that frees the mind to remember more clearly."

She nodded. Dr. Rivers talked just like Mrs. Stuart in the third grade. Anne relaxed.

"I'd like to know what you expect to remember. What you anticipate from this experience."

"I . . ." She stumbled on her own thoughts. "I want to remember what happened that night I lost the baby. I want to *know* what happened. Is that possible?"

"I'm not sure. We can try." His voice was serious and calm. "We'll put you in a very light trance state and move back to August."

"August 4," she said.

"You won't remember anything you don't want to, Anne. Will you keep that in mind? And you can stop anytime you become uncomfortable or do not wish to remember," he said, chantlike. "If you want to wake up, you will clasp your hands and pull them apart. When your hands come apart, you will be awake."

He paused. She concentrated on his face. Her hands felt very heavy.

"You will never go so deep that you lose contact with my voice. You will always hear what I say to you."

She blinked an acknowledgment.

"Now, I want you to take three deep breaths and let all the air out slowly. Then breathe normally."

A neck muscle spasmed. She took a lungful of air and let it out. "Have *you* ever been hypnotized?" she asked him.

"Yes. Some people can't be hypnotized at all. About a third go into a very light, pleasant state, and another third can enter the deeper levels of hypnosis."

She consciously relaxed her legs and arms and took another deep breath. "Which third are you?"

"The last."

Her hands felt warm and even heavier. She took the third deep breath. That neck muscle jerked again.

Marc paused. The air in the room was very still. "You are completely at ease," he finally said. "Your arms are getting very heavy and warm. Your face muscles are smooth and completely at ease . . . your legs feel heavy . . . your back is relaxed . . . the muscles are very loose. Close your eyes now, Anne . . . you feel very good . . . completely at ease.''

She drifted. The picture of still water appeared on her eyelids. On hot summer days in Iowa they swam in Little Dipper Lake. The water was as smooth as glass in the early evenings. She remembered easing herself down in the cool water, barely making a ripple.

"When I count to three, your right hand will begin to feel light . . . very light . . . one . . . two . . . three.''

Anne thought it sounded silly. Her right arm was as heavy as a telephone pole.

"Your right arm is getting lighter and lighter . . . there are balloons tied to your right wrist . . . blue, yellow, and red balloons . . . you feel completely at ease. And your arm is getting lighter and lighter. . . .''

His voice droned around her. She thought of it as a tent, a big blue tent.

"The balloons begin to raise your arm off the chair . . . your arm is growing lighter and lighter . . .''

A giggle rose in her throat. Her right arm was riveted to the armrest of the chair. She knew it was. She could feel it. Yet she saw balloons floating above her, blue, red, and yellow ones.

"Your arm rises slowly . . . higher and higher. You will touch your forehead . . . and when you touch your forehead, you will be very pleasantly asleep . . . your hand is almost touching your forehead now. . . .''

This is crazy, she thought. I can't do this. But she didn't want to stop. Not yet. She concentrated on her right arm resting solidly on the chair. Anne squeezed her eyes shut tighter.

Something warm touched her forehead lightly, like a feather, and she felt herself drop down, as if the chair sank. She suddenly realized her left arm was at her forehead.

That's funny, she thought. I'm sure he said my right arm.

But it didn't matter. She felt very good. There was nothing frightening about it, she told herself. She felt sure she could wake up at any moment, even without clasping and unclasping her hands.

The baby cried, but very distantly. The cries were sad.

"You're in a light sleep," he continued. "You feel calm . . . and completely at ease, Anne."

She inventoried her muscles. Nothing jerked or twitched. Nothing hurt.

"I'm going to count backward . . . and as I do, you will move back in time, month by month . . . ten. It's yesterday now . . . nine . . . this is January. You are moving back in time as I count, Anne . . . eight . . . December . . . Christmas . . . seven . . . now it's November . . . Thanksgiving."

A gray curtain draped over her mind. She felt empty except for glints of color as he counted, and certain smells, cold air, pine boughs, cinnamon, a hot iron on linen. . . . She wondered if that was moving backward.

"Six . . . you are moving back in time, Anne, and now it is October. Where are you, Anne?"

"In the supermarket. Buying apples."

"You feel completely at ease . . . five . . . September . . . where are you now?"

"Home. I'm reading." The answers came clear and strong. They surprised her.

"Four . . ."

Something jarred her.

"It's August . . . August the first . . . Anne, it's August *first*. Where are you today?"

"Marilyn's Maternity Shop."

"What are you doing there?"

"Buying a shirt. It's very hot."

"You are very calm . . . now the days are moving forward, Anne, one day at a time . . . in August. It's August 2, in the morning . . . what are you doing, Anne?"

"Having coffee with Fay."

"How do you feel today?"

"I'm fine. I'm getting big."

"Now the days move ahead again . . . it's August 3 . . . and now it's August 4 . . . very early in the morning . . . what time is it?"

"Five-thirty. Too early to get up. I don't feel well."

"Why don't you feel well?"

"Cramps."

"Now it's afternoon, Anne . . . August 4. Where are you?"

"In the hospital." She twisted uncomfortably in the chair.

"Why are you in the hospital?" he asked.

"I'm bleeding." She was increasingly agitated. She tried to calm down. "I'm losing the baby." Her voice cracked.

"You will remember losing the baby," he said louder, "but you will remain calm and completely at ease while you remember, Anne. Very calm now. . . ."

Green lights swam above her. She felt very tired. Too tired to care about the lights.

"You are deeply asleep now . . . you are very calm and deeply asleep. They are taking you to the operating room."

A row of soft white lights passed over her. Honey-brown doors slid by. A rush of cold, clean-smelling air hit her hot face. But she felt her stomach and arm muscles tighten. She didn't want to go into OR. Panic rose in her, and she wanted to wake up.

"You are deeply asleep . . ." Rivers' voice intervened. "You will remain calm, Anne, while you remember the operating room. You will not feel any of the pain or the fear . . . you can tell me what is happening to you without experiencing any of the pain or fear."

The panic ebbed. She wanted Rivers to go on talking. She clung to his voice and decided not to wake up just then.

"What is happening to you in the operating room, Anne?"

"I'm cold. They put a warm blanket on me. It's hard to think."

"You can remember, Anne . . . without any pain . . . you are not afraid now. You are cold, and they wrap a warm blanket around you. You're warm now. Are you warm, Anne?"

"Yes."

"You're in the operating room . . . you're very calm . . . and there's a light over your head. Concentrate on the light . . . you will not experience any pain. What is happening to you?"

"Pain. It hurts. I'm losing the baby. It's coming out." Her voice seemed flat and separate from her.

"Are you asleep?"

"No. Yes. Something over my face . . . sort of awake . . . very sleepy."

"What's happening now, Anne?"

"Bad smell. No . . ." she cried. Her neck snapped back. And every muscle in her body seemed to contract with it. There was no pain, only a black hole that opened. She fell down and down.

"Anne." She heard his voice from far away. "Anne, listen to my voice."

"I want to wake up," she cried to him.

"You can wake up whenever you want to. Listen to my voice. If you want to wake up, you can."

He was getting farther and farther away. She struggled to wake up.

"Put yours hands together if you want to wake up now," he called to her. "I'll help you pull them apart. When your hands pull apart, you will be awake, Anne. *Listen to my voice.*"

She heard the urgency of his voice. She braced herself for the end of the fall. But it didn't come. The pit opened to a green-and-yellow fuzz, like the paper shreds her mama put in the Easter baskets.

"Where are you?" Marc Rivers asked. His voice was closer now.

"I don't know. . . . Voices . . ."

"What are the voices saying?"

"I don't know. I can't hear them."

"You can hear what they are saying now, Anne. Tell me what they're saying."

She listened. "They say, 'Got it. It's breathing. Jar it. Quick,' " she repeated the voices.

And then the cry, a high wavering, mindless cry pierced her and drove deep down inside her. "My baby!" she cried, and slid back in the black pit.

"Listen to my voice," she heard as she tumbled through the void. "Listen to my voice, Anne."

She was dizzy.

"You are deeply asleep. You are completely at ease," he said.

The somersaults slowed.

"Your body is completely at ease. Your mind is calm and peaceful. You are having no difficulty hearing my voice."

She stopped falling.

"You are in the operating room, Anne . . . you are very calm. . . . I want you to tell me what you see. . . . What do you see in that operating room? . . . You will remain completely at ease as you tell me."

"Dr. Springer . . ." she whispered. The sea-green room swam around her. "Faces . . . with masks . . . I see . . . Jesus, God, help me!"

"You will not experience the fear, Anne. You can tell me what you see in that operating room. Are you awake, Anne?"

"Yes . . . I'm awake. There's a silver metal. A tray. I can see the baby. In a jar. On the tray. I try to reach for the baby. She moves. Her arms move in the jar. I try to get up. They push me down. I can't reach the baby . . . I can't . . ."

"Listen to my voice, Anne. You are not afraid. Listen to my voice. Now you are leaving the operating room . . . it's all over . . . and you are going to a very peaceful place . . . a garden. Listen to my voice."

Flowers, blue irises with yellow tongues, blossomed around her. Pink roses burst like firecrackers.

"There are yellow daisies and green grass. And water in the garden. It's very peaceful there. You rest for a few minutes in this garden."

She sank to the soft grass. The herbal fragrance of spring washed over her.

"You will begin to walk through the garden. There is a path. As you walk down the path, you will begin to wake up. Do you see the yellow flowers, Anne?"

"Yes."

"You are walking down the path that leads out of the garden. When you leave the path, you will be in a very light sleep . . . a very pleasant state."

"Vermont."

He laughed softly. "Yes, Vermont is a very pleasant state."

The path was moss-covered. Tiny yellow flowers sprung up at the edges of the green moss.

"You are leaving the garden now. You're almost at the end of the path."

She was sorry to leave. She could see the end of the path, where a gate stood.

"When you leave the garden, you will be back in the office, sitting in the chair. You will be completely at ease . . . very peaceful."

She opened the gate.

"Once you leave this garden, Anne, you will never hear the baby cry again . . . never again. You are leaving the garden now. When you are back in this room, the baby will never cry again."

She stood at the open gate and turned back to the garden. She tasted the tears that rolled down her cheeks. She waved. "Good-bye," she called, and closed the gate behind her.

"You said good-bye to the baby, Anne. There is no need for it to ever cry again." His voice was thick. "Now you are back in my office. You are in a very light sleep . . . almost awake now. I'm going to count to three. And when I finish counting, you will wake up feeling very peaceful, completely at ease. You will remember only what you wish to remember about this experience, Anne. I am beginning to count now. One. You are waking up. Two. You are almost awake. Three."

She opened her eyes. A tear slid from the corner of one eye. She brushed it away with her hand, then stretched and smiled at Marc Rivers.

"Hi," he said.

"Do you ever get tired of saying 'peaceful' and 'completely at ease'?"

"No." His eyes glistened in the sun. "How was it for you? How do you feel?"

"I'm not sure. I feel good. Completely at ease, as you would say. You sounded scared once." She sat up straight in the chair.

"I thought you weren't listening to me."

"It's funny. Your voice sounded like you were talking through a megaphone next to my ear. Except that once . . ." Her eyes filled with tears again.

"We still have a few minutes left."

She stared at him. Her mouth dropped open. "Oh . . ." she gasped. "My baby. It cried. A girl. Oh, God, I saw it move!" Something broke inside her, a cleft down the middle of her body. Her breastbone ached terribly, then seemed to split and gape wide. "I couldn't do anything . . ." she cried to Marc. Her hands reached out to him. "I couldn't help the baby."

She choked. She tried to get her breath. Anne lunged from the chair, but Rivers caught her and held her securely with his arms wrapped around her shoulders, but not tight. She pressed her face against his chest. His cheek rested on her hair. Sobs wrenched out of her like vomiting. She cried until she was empty and still. He rocked her slightly, as a child would be rocked and held. Finally she drew back slowly.

"I'm all right," she said, glancing at him through residual tears.

"Of course you are." His face was brimming with tenderness. "You are a very brave lady, Anne."

"I guess I needed to cry."

He nodded.

"I'm sorry. I got your shirt wet." She clung to the soft gray sweater at his back. His white shirt was soaked with wet splotches.

"It'll wash out," he said softly.

Anne let go of the sweater. "I'm so tired. I want to go home now."

"In a few minutes. I want you to sit here for a few more minutes."

She lowered herself into the maroon chair again. The leather back was still warm.

"Are you sure the baby was a girl, Anne?" he asked her. "How do you know, for sure?"

"I saw her," she said. Anne cocked her head as if she were listening to some distant music. "And someone said that. They said in the OR that it was a girl."

He nodded thoughtfully. "That's rather curious. I checked in Pathology in December, and apparently there was some confusion about whether the baby was a boy or a girl. The autopsy proved your child was female, however."

After the session, Anne sat in the car and counted trees planted in concrete squares around the parking lot while her mind did dizzy loops. A girl. A baby girl. She saw the pinched face again, eyes closed, and the doll-like hands wave, paddling in the thick gel of the jar. Ammy, she thought. The baby was alive in Ammy. What did they do to her? Is she still alive? Is she all right?

She remembered the cry, the thin, frail cry like a razor blade, the same cry that had perforated each of her days since August.

Anne considered the police. If John Wanaker didn't do something about that research unit, and soon, she would go to the police.

13

On January 16 the phone call came. Harriette and Jim Thoms had waited a long time for that call.

Early in December they had received the letter telling them there *was* a baby for them, and they'd rushed to town and bought the best crib available, a soft pink blanket, six tiny rib-knit shirts, diapers, and diaper pail. The letter said the baby was a girl. That was six weeks ago.

They sent part of the money required to an account in a New York bank, and wired the last payment three weeks ago. Twenty thousand dollars was a lot of money for a baby, Harriette thought, but their wheat ranch made more money than they could spend the last few years. And Jim was forty-six years old—too old to adopt a baby, they were told by the state and several private adoption agencies.

Two years ago the Thomses had taken in a foster child, Rodney, who had lived with them until last summer, when he returned to his mother in Fargo. The Thomses tried to get in touch with Rodney's mother, but the landlord told them the boy had gotten sick and they'd moved. He didn't know where. They hadn't heard anything since. A picture of Rodney sat on the television set. He was nine years old, with straight, shining black hair and large brown eyes.

That was when they answered a magazine ad for a private

adoption agency in New York State. The age limit was considerably higher, and the waiting period was estimated at only three to six months. They were turned down by that agency also, but two weeks later they'd received a letter from a second firm, indicating they *did* qualify. From then on, it was a matter of a three-page form, two checks, and finally, the letter about a baby girl for them.

The phone rang at eleven-thirty that night in January. They were to pick up the child at the Fargo International Airport the following evening.

Snow blanketed North Dakota, and more snow accumulated during the afternoon. They drove to Fargo through a blizzard, inching along, one mile after another. Jim stared into the blinding snow and hoped the van wouldn't get hung up on any of the drifts piling rapidly across the Interstate.

"The plows will be out soon," Harriette said, but Jim wasn't so sure.

By the time they could see the lights of Fargo, the worst of the storm had subsided. It was getting dark on the prairie, and flurries of snow careened out of the deepening sky.

"Do you think the plane will get in through this?" she asked, peering up through the windshield at the sky.

"It isn't due for two more hours," Jim said. "By that time, maybe the storm will have blown over completely."

The airport was closed down when they arrived. No plane had been able to land or take off for four hours. Passengers sat around in heavy parkas with their feet on suitcases and plastic garment bags. Children played tag around rows of blue and yellow plastic chairs.

At the Northwest desk they were told that Flight 67 had been diverted into Minneapolis, due to the storm. Passengers from that flight were expected on Flight 809 from Minneapolis to Calgary. Arrival time was estimated at eleven-sixteen P.M.

So Harriette and Jim waited again. The cafeteria was crowded, but Jim found a table, and they ordered turkey sandwiches and coffee.

"It seems ridiculous to be so impatient now," Harriette said softly, "after we've waited this long."

Jim's handsome, rough face cracked open in a slow smile. "I never got used to the waiting," he admitted.

By ten-thirty the storm was over, leaving the airfield under a black umbrella of stars. They stood at the wide windows and watched Flight 809 land. Jim carried the diaper bag for Harriette.

"Are you sure you like the name Sarah?" she asked him for the hundredth time.

"Sarah Thoms is the most beautiful name I can think of for a little girl."

The baby was beautiful, tiny and pink, wrapped in layers of blankets against the cold night air. A young couple brought her to Fargo. The woman laid a sleeping Sarah in Harriette's waiting arms.

"Everything's in order," the man said, shaking hands with Jim. "Good luck to you."

The couple disappeared into the rush of travelers. It was so easy, Harriette thought. No one seemed to notice that ten minutes ago she carried only her purse, and now she held a baby in her arms, her own baby. No one in the Fargo airport, aside from Harriette and Jim, had witnessed the almost miraculous change.

Jim brought the van to the front entrance while Harriette waited inside the terminal with the baby. Too excited to think about sleep, they started home across the expanse of clean white land. The van was warm and cozy.

Sarah drank six ounces of prewarmed formula at two A.M., burped loudly on Harriette's shoulder, and fell asleep again.

That same night at Park State Hospital, Claire Anderson sat on her bed with a faded blue chenille spread. In her arms she cradled a small orange pillow, elaborately diapered in a white pillowcase.

"If that mockingbird don't cry," she crooned softly in a slow, childlike voice, "Mama's gonna buy you an M 16 . . ."

None of the other five women in the ward looked up at Claire. They'd heard that same song for months.

A nurse glided through the door. "Time for bed, ladies.

Lie down, Mrs. Oltman. Come on, Claire. That's a dear.''

Claire Anderson held out the pillow. ''Isn't he beautiful, Miss Sutherland? Isn't he the most beautiful baby you ever saw?''

Nurse Sutherland took the pillow and plopped it on the end of Claire's bed.

Her anxious dark eyes blazed. ''Don't lay him on the bed! He could roll off and kill himself. Don't you know anything about babies?'' She snatched the pillow-baby from the bed. ''Now he's crying! See what you made him do.''

''Claire,'' Nurse Sutherland soothed her patient, ''it's time to sleep now. Lie down, dear.''

Claire Anderson clutched the pillow to her breasts. ''If that diamond ring don't shine,'' she screeched, ''Mama gonna buy you a twenty-two semiautomatic.''

''Good night, ladies,'' Sutherland chirped.

''Promise you'll never lay him on the bed like that again!'' she called when the overhead light was off and only a night light glimmered in the ceiling fixture. ''Promise me, you bitch,'' she whispered to the closed door.

Sighing, she stretched out under the thin spread and snuggled the orange pillow to her cheek.

Sunday night Anne studied the hospital's new annual report, but it was tedious, scanning column after column. And lab requests interrupted her every few minutes. There had to be an easier way to get information.

She entered the results of a urinanalysis in the computer, okayed it, and pressed the transmission bar. The information was gobbled from the screen and would print out in the emergency room.

The computer. Of course.

On her way to the nursery to draw a blood sugar on a newborn, Anne stopped in the computer room.

Sidney Velasco sat dozing, his arms folded comfortably over his chest and his feet propped on a second chair. He bolted upright when he saw Anne.

''Hello, Sid. Slow night?''

The computer filled the room with a soft hum, and every few minutes the terminal printer clattered and clacked out more data.

"Pretty slow. I'm feeding in night reports," he said in a weary voice.

"Listen, Sid, I need a favor." Anne held out the blue-covered annual report. "I can't make heads or tails out of this thing, and I need some information."

Sidney's smile spread across his face like butter on warm toast. "It took me two months to get that into a form very few people would understand. 'Noncomprehension' is the word. You're not supposed to get information from that report."

Anne told him she was in an M.A. program at the university and was writing a paper on the correlation between laboratory services and neonatal survival.

"So, what do you need?" he asked.

"I need the names of every Pathology specimen from Labor and Delivery last year."

"Simple."

"And the ones from Neonatal ICU," she ventured, since he was so cheerful about the whole thing. "Of course, I won't use any real names in my paper. I just need to follow a few cases to correlate the lab work, so all I need is fetal specimens received in Pathology."

"I shouldn't give anyone that information," he said gravely. "But since it's you, I guess it'll be okay."

"How long will it take?"

"Give me a couple of hours."

"Good, I'll stop back." Her breathing had relaxed considerably.

Sidney's eyes narrowed slightly. "You'll never mention where you got your information."

"You can trust me, Sid." She waved the annual report at him. "If anyone ever asks, I'll tell them it's all in here. I dare them to prove me wrong."

Anne left the computer room and took the elevator to the nursery. She leaned against the cool green wall. The rest of the information would have to be dredged from the annual report, like the total number of admissions to Labor and Delivery, and the number of fetal deaths at General, plus expired infants in Neo ICU. It would take hours, long weary hours, but if her suspicions were correct, the numbers wouldn't coincide. And then John Wanaker would have to listen to her. John Wanaker believed in numbers; she was sure of it. Police liked them too. As well as newspaper people.

The elevator jerked to a halt and startled Anne's attention back to the job at hand, a capillary blood glucose drawn from a heel stick on Baby Rymer.

Susan Hinshaw was night nurse in the nursery. Most of the infants were normal, full-term, squalling babies in clear plastic bassinets.

"Hi," Anne said to her, "I'm here for that glucose."

Susan Hinshaw looked up from the rocking chair where she was feeding one of the babies. "Rymer baby. Is it four already?"

"On the dot." Anne grinned.

Nurse Hinshaw squinted at the remaining formula in the bottle and laid the infant back in its bassinet. The baby shrieked.

"Oh, shush," she said. "I'll get back to you and your dinner in a minute." She picked up another infant and carried him out to the long stainless-steel counter in a small room adjacent to the nursery, where Anne waited. "Baby Rymer," she said, plopping the bundled child on the counter.

"Bad night?" Anne asked.

Susan shook her head. "We've got a full house, and the lot of them are bawling every ten minutes."

Anne laughed and pricked the baby's heel. She filled two small glass capillaries easily. "You always think babies are fussy."

"But that's not all. Did you hear about our in-house butterfly-net case?"

Anne taped a Band-Aid on the baby's foot. "What?"

"We got a real kook tonight. Walked in off the street yelling about how we'd stolen her baby. She actually got as far as the door there before they shot her full of tranquilizers. Enough to keep her horizontal for a few hours.''

A sharp sliver of ice ran down Anne's back.

Susan Hinshaw shook her head. ''A real crazy.''

''She came all the way to the nursery?'' Ann asked.

''Yipping and yammering about her baby, bottles or jars or something, and cursing Dr. Springer.''

''What's the girl's name?'' The room was spinning around Anne at a dizzying speed.

''Phillips. Nina Phillips.''

Anne returned to the lab. Her heart sputtered and throbbed while she spun the capillaries and injected serum into the Beckmann. The glucose was 42 mg%, much too low. She called Susan Hinshaw immediately.

Susan was breathless on the phone. ''You know that psycho I was telling you about? She's dead. They just found her in her room. A penicillin reaction. I guess she had a urinary tract infection. Besides being crazy.''

''Didn't they know she was allergic? Most people wear a bracelet or something.''

''I guess not, but they know now.''

At eight o'clock that morning Anne slipped the computer printout Sid Velasco had given her into her purse and left the lab. When the elevator doors opened to let her off in the basement, she looked straight into Ben Springer's face. He smiled fiercely at her. Anne's lungs shrank inside her.

''Hi,'' he said, backing up no more than three inches to let her off the elevator.

''Good morning, doctor,'' Anne snapped. She tried to get past him, but he blocked the way.

''Tough night?''

''Yes, as a matter of fact, it was. And I'd like to go home now, if you don't mind.''

He threw out his hands, indicating he wasn't restraining her. She started to walk around him, but he caught her face in his hand, holding her chin just enough to hurt.

''You look pale. Are you all right?''

''No,'' she said between her teeth. ''I'm not all right. Nina

Phillips *died* last night.'' She watched his eyes, but there was not a flicker of recognition at the name.

"Actually, I'm more concerned about you." His thumb stroked her cheek. "You missed your appointment last month. We aren't going to have any trouble over this, are we, Anne?''

She had to get away. "I wanted to tell you how sorry I was about your daughter.'' She forced the words up from her quivering throat. "Chrissy, wasn't it?''

His hand dropped to his side. "Yes, Chrissy.''

Anne fled down the hall to the parking ramp door. When she glanced back, Dr. Springer was still watching her.

Ben Springer had never seen Andy Jones sweat, but that night in the RDS unit's small office, Ben detected the pearls of perspiration on the doctor's anguished face.

"Calm down, Andy. A few questions don't mean a thing.''

Jones tugged at his ecru shirt, open at the neck. He was one of those bright boys, the ones grammar-school teachers single out right from the beginning as exceptional. Jones's college professors and certain of the faculty at Harvard Medical School agreed that Andy Jones was a genius. His two ex-wives didn't share that opinion, unfortunately, and his present wife was kept in blissful ignorance by her husband's casual gracefulness and choirboy smile. But the murder of Dr. Theodore Bell was not so easily charmed away. Andy Jones was unraveling like a ball of yarn before Ben's eyes.

"I have no idea *why* they're asking me about Ted,'' Andy whined. "We rarely worked together. That police officer even asked if I was right- or left-handed!''

"Routine. Stop worrying,'' Ben said.

"The Hart woman saw me that morning. At the elevator. If she remembered . . .''

"Anne Hart?'' Ben sat down across from Andy.

"How much longer will she carry that baby?''

"Shouldn't be much longer, buddy, but you know she's seeing another doctor now.''

"What happened?'' Andy asked, sounding irritated.

"It's no problem," Ben assured him. "She's just a little skittish at the moment. Don't worry. She'll be back."

"When the progesterone level drops, you mean, and she aborts."

"Just like last time," Ben said.

"And then we won't have to worry about *her* anymore." Andy Jones leaned back in his chair and took a deep breath.

The administration of progesterone to selected patients, early in their pregnancy, and then a sudden withdrawal, had precipitated enough spontaneous abortions to provide the RDS lab with adequate subjects for more than two years.

"I'm not even sure we need Mrs. Hart's baby," Ben continued. "All we really have to do now is keep cool and wait for the publication of the paper. When *is* that deadline, by the way?"

"June. June 15."

That still gave them five months, plenty of time. The work with those fetal cats last fall had provided the data for the paper, announcing Ammy at the AMA convention in San Diego in August, and assuring their own personal fortunes as well as fame. Given a choice, Ben would have chosen notoriety. He'd never lived without money and could hardly envision its absence in his life.

"Except for the oxygen-level problem," Andy reminded him cautiously. "We have to repeat the work with the cats under reduced oxygen levels. Just too much scarring of the optic nerve."

Ben shrugged. "A few more months should do it."

Actually that reduced-oxygen-level work should have been done at Peralta, but they were off on another tangent at PTI, supporting an organism without blood supply. They hoped to revolutionize open heart surgery, eliminating the use of the heart-lung machine. They thought they could also introduce Ammy as a substitute method for kidney dialysis. Ben remembered the bitter debates in the board meetings at Peralta. And old H. M. Schwartz had won, agreeing only to supply medium for the research at General Hospital at an ever-increasing price. And a cut.

Then there was the use of Ammy on the burn unit at General. An emergency situation, the severe burn of a twelve-year-old boy, had forced a provisional permission to use the medium on a human being. It was also a convenient cover for the RDS research. No one asked any questions about the drums of Ammy arriving weekly.

Things had gone well up to now. Ben wanted it to stay that way.

"You took care of that Path specimen, didn't you?" he asked Andy.

Jones nodded. "I checked the Hart PSD and replaced a male specimen on the shelf. It's all taken care of."

"I hope so." Ben stared at Andy, frowned deeply, and gazed out the window. "You're sure that Hart baby was a boy? Seems to me—"

"I *checked* the PSD!" Jones snarled. "The infant was male."

When Ted Bell had come sniffing around for a misplaced specimen last month, they realized a flaw in their system. So Andy Jones regularly collected specimens scheduled for scientific disposal, or burning in the dogshed, froze them at -70 degrees, and whenever a baby arrived in the RDS unit, Jones thawed a specimen and sent it to Pathology a few days later.

But something about the Hart case still bothered Ben. He wasn't sure what it was. That night had been confusing. Anne Hart woke up almost fully once, and they weren't sure how much she saw until later, in the recovery room, where she carried on about the baby. Ben had spent his time taking care of Anne, and Andy did the paperwork for the baby, getting the father to sign the PSD and later concocting an autopsy report to place in her file. And finally replacing the infant in Pathology.

"You're just damn lucky you have such easy access to the incineration barrel in Pathology," he told Jones.

Andy smiled. He was obviously more relaxed. " 'Talent' is the word." His expensive shirt expanded and settled back over his chest. Even sweating, the man was elegant. "Listen, Ben, I hate to bring this up again, but . . . ."

"You need money? What is it this time? Horses, or tables, or tail?" Springer's tone was not amused.

"We only got seven grand from that last baby. I counted on twelve."

"How much do you need, Andy?" Years ago Ben had learned that it was easier to keep Jones rich and happy. It seemed to lubricate his brilliance. And damp down his nerves.

"Eighty-five hundred."

Ben nodded. "I'll have it for you late Friday."

"We can't afford to give up those babies yet," Andy said. "I figure seven or eight more will see us through to August. Including that Hart baby."

"We'll have to use some of the pods for the cats," Ben reminded him.

"But you can't sell cats."

As he left the unit, Ben glanced into the main room. All six pods were filled, but three of the infants wouldn't make it. Two others were questionable. Only one was a sure thing. One baby they could sell to keep the research going and finance Andy Jones's hobbies. The latter was by far the worst liability.

And then there was the Hart baby. He hadn't mentioned anything more to Andy, but what she needed was another child. Not a replacement, of course, but something to get her mind off Chrissy. And there *was* the Hart baby. A good genetic package. And it would be so easy. This time Anne Hart wouldn't realize the infant was missing. He would make sure of that.

He jammed his key in the lock, pressed the button, and listened to the elevator rumble up toward him.

For hours Anne and Doug worked at the kitchen table with the computer printout spread in front of them, the annual report from General Hospital, an expensive calculator, and Xanadu's green lab notebook, the detailed record of the maiming and torture of a small white mouse to test the furthest scientific boundaries of Ammy, the miracle substance.

Doug, drained of all color, worked grimly on the statistics

gleaned from the annual report, comparing them with the figures from the printout, which provided not only statistics but also names.

"Your name *is* here," Doug said, keeping his finger on the place. "Hart, Boy, 12-12, #3673."

Anne stared at her name. "December! Hart, *Boy*? How can that be?"

When Anne had told Doug about the hypnosis and the birth of their daughter, he'd said a doctor asked him to sign something—permission for scientific disposal, he thought it was called.

"The doctor asked if we wanted to bury the baby. We hadn't talked about it," Doug had said softly. "So I signed the form, but I'm sure it said the baby was a boy."

"It was a girl," Anne had said. "*I'm* sure we have a daughter. Somewhere."

"He told me the baby died. A nonviable fetus."

"I think he was mistaken," Anne had said, ending the disagreement.

But there it was in black and white, "Hart, Boy," on the computer printout. She couldn't explain it. And, as Anne expected, there was no easy explanation for the fact that the statistics from the printout and the annual report didn't coincide, but they didn't. Of the total number of admissions to General's Labor and Delivery, 336 fetal deaths occurred, about one a day. These were spontaneous abortions or miscarriages. Therapeutic abortions or abortions not admitted to Labor and Delivery for one reason or another were not included. The number of Pathology specimens received from Labor and Delivery totaled 288.

Forty-eight infants were not accounted for in Pathology. Four babies a month. Even if parents requested the fetus for burial, Pathology performed an examination to determine cause of death. What had happened to forty-eight infants?

Anne and Doug worked feverishly. These were hard, cold statistics. John Wanaker would understand these numbers.

Infant deaths in Neonatal ICU totaled eighty-four. Only

sixty-nine Path specimens were received from Neo ICU during the last year. Another fifteen babies.

A total of sixty-four infants was missing. The enormity of the number almost paralyzed Anne. She and Doug gazed numbly at each other across the kitchen table. It was nearly four A.M.

"You could be right," he said softly. "Jesus, Annie, you could be absolutely right."

And Marc Rivers agreed when she told him about the discrepancy.

"Hospital statistics don't always agree," he said, flipping through the annual report of General Hospital. "It's often a source of embarrassment to the administration. But sixty-four infants is an incredible number. I think John Wanaker should hear about this immediately.

Fay leaned on the doorbell, jabbing Anne awake with the syncopated ring. She stumbled to the door.

"I never see you," Fay complained, "unless I come over here and drag you out of bed. Pregnant women tire easily, but this is ridiculous."

Luckily Doug had made coffee and left it on the warmer. Anne poured two cups, and Fay grimaced and swallowed hers whole, like raw oysters.

"Here's to waking up!" Fay said, toasting Anne with the cup. "Though with Doug's coffee, there's hardly a choice. It's strong enough to make your eyelashes fall out. So what's happening? How'd it go with the administrator? Have you talked with him yet?"

"Not yet." Anne sipped her coffee. "He's off on another convention. He'll be back next week."

"How are you feeling?" Fay ventured, peering at Anne as if she were studying the glaze on one of her pots. "Have you been eating your wheat grass?"

"Religiously. I feel fine. The nausea is better, and I keep busy and don't have much time to think about it." Anne set down her coffee cup. "Listen, you haven't seen the paintings. I finished the palette knife a few days ago."

Just inside the door of the studio, Fay pulled up short. She stood staring at the painting. "I could almost fall into that one," she finally said, indicating one of the five foot canvases painted in deep shades of magenta and black with metallic explosions on one of them. "I don't think I've ever seen anyone paint holes before."

"Here, take a look at this one." Anne turned the palette knife painting toward Fay. Sharp colors were well defined into a beautiful, but haunting face. Each feature, by some clever knife strokes, combined texture and color in a way that made the face change, as if the individual features had been painted double. Subtle shades of ocher and raw sienna filled in the dark green background.

"Annie, it's really very good," Fay said in an almost reverent tone. "Really good."

Anne stepped back to study the face again. "I've been working on it for months."

"This is so different from anything else you've done," Fay continued without taking her eyes from the painting. "And that red shadow on the forehead is stunning. Or is it a cap?"

Anne frowned at the painting. "What shadow?"

Fay outlined a deep crimson cowl over the left forehead of the face.

"Oh, that. I'm not sure what that is. It just seemed to belong there. I didn't finish the painting until after the hypnosis with Dr. Rivers. I was in some kind of far off place for a few days, I guess."

"At first I thought it looked like a baby's face," Fay said, squinting her eyes.

"It was," Anne admitted. "But I just kept putting on paint, and the face changed, grew up maybe . . ."

"Yes, it's like a face you can see from infancy to adulthood. Fascinating, Annie."

Anne sank to the beanbag chair against one wall. "I'm really glad you like it."

"I love it!" Fay's eyes softened in the constancy of the studio's northern light. "Can I call David and ask him to look at the paintings? He isn't filled for the February show, and I think he'd be interested.''

David Farah ran a small but very successful gallery downtown. Fay exhibited her pottery there, and she valued David's opinion. But the few times Anne had met him, he went out of his way to ignore her, even when Fay pointedly told him Anne was a painter.

"Oh, sure,'' Anne finally agreed. "Why not?''

And two days later David Farah called to see if he could look at her portfolio.

"My what?''

"Your portfolio. You do have one, don't you?''

"I might, if I was sure what it was,'' she said.

"Photographs of your work, a bio, and descriptions of technique and media.''

She was insulted by him again. He spoke as if he were telling a three-year-old how to use a table fork at dinner.

"No.'' She yawned pointedly into the receiver. "I don't have one of those.''

"Oh, dear,'' he sighed, "that certainly complicates things. But I guess Fay did say you were an amateur.''

He stopped by the house to see the paintings and talk to her. Luckily Fay was there with coffee in hand. Anne knew David Farah's rough edges would rub up against her own jagged places, and Fay was the only hope for a buffer.

He stood in her studio in front of the paintings for a long time, looking uncomfortable and out-of-place in a loose white cotton shirt, gray suede jacket, and exquisitely cut French blue jeans.

"I have a few spots left in the February show,'' he finally said, "and they're yours if you want them. That portrait is really quite extraordinary for a beginner. What kind of price do you have in mind for it?''

Anne gasped. "I don't want to sell it. I mean, I couldn't possibly sell that one.''

Farah ran his hand through his mound of curly graying hair. "Fame and glory.'' He groaned. "That's all you painters want. What's wrong with money?''

Fay intervened quickly. "It's okay," she said, smoothing the tension that was as thick as petroleum jelly and about as pleasant. "We can set the price high. Don't worry." She looked from Anne to David. "You can make your money on the other two paintings."

He picked up an avant-garde metal sculpture and whooped in amusement. "*What* is this?"

"A sculpture," Anne explained in an overly patient voice. "I call it *Birth*."

"Jesus," he whistled softly.

"I want that shown with the paintings," Anne said, her patience wearing thin. "Frankly, I think it's the best thing I've done."

"You're not serious!" he jeered.

"Perfectly serious."

"I'll take the three paintings. Leave the pop art at home," he told her, but she insisted, and he finally gave in, raising his hands in helpless surrender.

After Farah left, Anne stamped around the studio railing at him. The sculpture was constructed from bits of plastic tubing trailing in and out of household gadgets, a furnace thermostat, around a series of large bright screws, and finally out the end of a garden-hose nozzle.

"Maybe I'll call it *Hard Relief Form* or something like that," Anne stormed.

Fay picked up a dusty plastic rose and stuck it in the nozzle. "Or *Who Knows How the Flower Grows*."

The last week in January, Harriette Thoms wrapped the baby in three blankets and covered Sarah's face when they trekked out of the house. A bitter wind swept the Dakota plains, taking Harriette's breath away as she picked a path to the van. The wind blew snow over the sidewalk as fast as they could shovel it away.

Jim had warmed up the van for nearly thirty minutes before it was time to drive to town for Sarah's checkup with Dr. Mathison. Jim helped Harriette, cradling the baby in her arms, up to the front seat.

"Whew!" she gasped when he climbed to the driver's seat beside her. "That wind is stiff."

"Sarah didn't mind," Jim said. "She didn't even cry."

Harriette peeled back the blanket, revealing Sarah's pink face, oblivious of the below-zero temperature outdoors.

"She doesn't mind being bundled up or even having the blankets over her head," Harriette said, smiling down at the baby. "You're such a good baby, aren't you, little Sarah?"

Dr. Mathison examined the baby gently, running his finger down the soles of her feet, checking her hand grasp, and flashing a light in her ears and eyes. Harriette watched admiringly. Dr. Mathison wasn't a baby doctor especially, but out here there were only two doctors in a hundred miles. They had to take care of everyone. Dr. Mathison clucked and cooed at the baby.

Harriette had explained to Dr. Mathison on the phone that the baby was her sister's daughter's child, and she and Jim had agreed to rear the baby because the girl was only sixteen and unmarried. The arrangement was not uncommon, and he hadn't questioned her further.

"She's beautiful," he said to Harriette when he finished the examination. "You're doing a fine job."

"She's such a good baby. She hardly ever cries."

"You can get her dressed now," Dr. Mathison said. "I'll write you a prescription for vitamins, and you can start her on milk. Mix it with the formula, half and half for now."

"You mean four ounces of formula in four ounces of milk?" Harriette felt stupid asking, but she wanted to be very sure she understood Dr. Mathison's instructions.

"Yes, that's right," he reassured her.

Harriette dressed Sarah in clean diapers and the pink knit dress and matching pants. Her sister, Kate, in South Carolina, had sent it to the baby when they heard about the adoption. Kate *did* have a sixteen-year-old daughter, if anyone cared to check, and besides, South Carolina was a very long way from North Dakota, Harriette reasoned.

When Dr. Mathison came back with the prescription, Jim followed behind him.

"All ready to go?" Dr. Mathison asked the baby.

Harriette glanced at Jim's anxious face.

"I asked Jim to come in because I wanted to talk to both of you," Mathison said, looking from Harriette to Jim. "I don't think it's anything to worry about, but I'd like Sarah seen in Fargo by a pediatrician, Dr. Luke Morrow. I went to school with him. He's a fine doctor."

"Why?" Harriette and Jim chorused.

"It's only a suspicion, you understand." The doctor cleared his throat. "Some of her visual responses are not quite normal, and I seem to detect some scar tissue at the base of the optic nerve. Have you noticed if she watches things that move in front of her eyes?"

"No . . . I . . ." Harriette stammered.

Dr. Mathison shot his hand very close to Sarah's face. She didn't blink or follow his hand. "Do you see what I mean? But she's only three months old, so we can't be sure."

"Sure of what?" Jim asked quietly.

"That she's blind."

The words made Harriette's ears ache. "No . . ." she said, holding Sarah close.

"It's only a suspicion," Mathison said.

Jim picked up the baby's bundle of blankets. "Will you set up the appointment in Fargo? As soon as possible."

"Yes, as soon as possible," Mathison assured them.

They huddled in the van. Jim idled the engine to warm it. He fussed with a panel of knobs to extract every bit of heat possible from the engine.

"Must be twenty-five below now," he said.

Harriette sat in silence, clutching the baby. Tears dripped down on the blankets.

"It'll be all right," Jim said softly.

She was rigid. She shivered once. "How can they tell? They can't tell for sure . . ." She looked up at Jim's face. All the lines around his eyes and mouth curved down when he was sad. The lines were like planting furrows for the wheat, not straight, to protect the grain from the merciless wind. "They can't tell for sure," she said again.

But they could. A week later they were told by the pediatric ophthalmologist in Fargo that Sarah was blind, except for one area of peripheral vision in the right eye. Dr. Luke Morrow said she was lucky. She could learn to use that small patch of vision.

They were instructed to hang a mobile of bright colors on the right side of her crib and bring her back at six months.

"We see this sort of thing when too much oxygen is given at birth," Dr. Morrow said. "Do you know how much oxygen she had when she was born?"

Panic paralyzed Harriette's thought. "I don't know," she murmured.

"How premature was she?" Morrow questioned her gently.

"Premature?"

The doctor's eyebrows knitted quizzically, as if he were speaking in a foreign language. He turned to Jim.

"The baby is my wife's niece's . . . a teenager . . . you know. We agreed to raise the baby. They didn't tell us she was premature. Or anything like that."

Morrow nodded, but his expression was one of disbelief. "Well," he said, "she seems like a very bright baby. She can learn to compensate for her blindness."

Harriette hated that word. Her chest tightened every time she heard it.

She didn't relax until she saw the farm from the end of the lane. Fargo, this Dr. Luke Morrow, and South Carolina were a long ways away. But blind, that was closer, as close as the two weeping willows near the house, or the storm door that kept out the prairie cold all winter.

She didn't care. Sarah was their baby now. Harriette bit her bottom lip, but gently. Sarah would grow up beautiful and strong. And blind.

14

An Ace Transport truck pulled up to the loading dock at
Good Shepherd Hospital. It was two-thirty A.M. Skipper
Mullins, a wiry, nondescript man in loose denims and cow-
boy boots, opened the back of the truck, leaped in like he'd
done that all his life, and loaded three ten-gallon drums on
the old red dolly. He bumped his way down the platform and
jolted across the concrete dock. The door to Supply opened
when he knocked, and he disappeared inside.

Twenty minutes later he returned to the truck, lit a cigarette, and leaned against the cab. He had two more deliveries
to make. This was the usual Tuesday and Friday hospital run.
The only difference tonight was that white Volvo that had
followed him since the pickup at Peralta.

Old H. M. Schwartz paid well, and Skipper Mullins knew
that Volvo meant trouble. Whoever was driving it hadn't
managed to conceal themselves from him, either, but then, he
could spot a tail like the smell of rotten codfish.

Skipper finished the cigarette, ground it into the concrete,
and climbed back in the truck.

He could lose them. Down on Snelling, a back street in an
industrial section of town, and next to the railroad tracks. The
area was a maze of alleys through huge, dark buildings, large
lots for overnight truck parking, and stoplights on every

corner. If he could lose them at all, it would be on Snelling.

Twenty minutes later he pulled the truck sharply into a parking lane. The white Volvo was just turning at the light onto Snelling. He killed the lights and engine and waited. The Volvo drifted by.

Skipper Mullins watched the car do a Y turnaround and cruise back down Snelling. From the street he knew they couldn't possibly recognize the Ace truck.

When the Volvo turned at Yolo Street, away from Snelling, Skipper started his engine and crept down the lane without lights. It was easy. A hard left at Seites Manufacturing would put him back on his route.

The Volvo was nowhere in sight. And Skip Mullins still had two deliveries to make that night, one to San Marco General, and the other to University Hospital. He also had the license number of that white Volvo.

Sergeant Robert Nielson sat at his desk at police headquarters that morning. He turned a gold-crowned tooth over and over in his hand.

Gary Caldwell, San Marco P.D., Special Forces, sat in front of the desk. Gary wore a thin red-and-black flannel shirt, blue jeans, and sneakers. His green eyes followed the flash of gold in his boss's hand.

Nielson replaced the tooth in a small envelope in the top drawer of his desk. "I think they're related, this Unity Clinic and the murder of Dr. Bell. I just don't know how yet. Bell tried to tell us. Whoever murdered him missed that one sheet of notes. Something about an anticoagulant."

"That's not much to go on," Gary said softly.

"The body of the Corbin woman will be exhumed next week. We'll know more then." Nielson leaned back comfortably in his chair. "What have you been able to pick up at the clinic?"

"Not much, so far. Except Dr. Collier has a drug habit as big as a battleship and almost as unmanageable. And he refers his patients to a Dr. Ben Springer at General."

Nielson drummed on the desk lightly with his pencil. "At

General?'' He thought a minute and then thumbed through a small file in one of the side drawers of his desk. Finally he pulled out a small white index card. ''Here it is. A young woman came in here about a month ago with a very bizarre story about losing a baby at General Hospital. I dismissed her as a crock, but I think I'll try to get in touch with Miss Nina Phillips again.''

When it rained in the St. Helena Valley, which it did often during the winter months, Marc Rivers' hands stiffened painfully. Between medication for the arthritis and exercises, however, the affliction didn't stop him from his daily routine.

On one of those drizzling February mornings, he met Ben Springer in the hall at General.

''Marc,'' Ben boomed. ''How are you?'' Springer extended his large hand.

Marc shook it with as much grace as he could muster, considering both hands felt like bear claws. ''Ben. I'm fine. I've been meaning to speak to you. I'm very sorry about your daughter.''

Ben seemed almost confused for a moment. ''Yes, well, thanks, Marc,'' he said in a jittery string of acknowledgments. ''It's difficult, of course. But you know Addy's pregnant again. Four months.''

''No, I didn't know.''

''Quite a surprise, as you can imagine.'' The fabulous Springer smile played across Ben's face. ''Addy nearly lost it after Chrissy, but things are fine now. Just fine.''

''When's she due?''

''Late June. Early July. You know babies. About as predictable as interest rates.''

''Indeed.'' Something about Springer nettled Marc. Maybe it was the fact that at nearly fifty Ben was starting a new family. Of course, Addy *was* younger. And Ben was certainly practicing what he preached. If you lose a child, have another one. ''Well, then, congratulations are in order,'' Marc said politely. ''Your child is due about the same time as Anne Hart's.''

"Yes." Ben's response was stiff. He directed his gaze at Marc's hands. "You still having trouble with the arthritis, Marc? You might speak to Dr. Tam. They're doing surgery for that now. Releasing the tendons . . ."

Anne stared at the olive-green phone on the nightstand beside her bed. She picked up the receiver and then glanced at the clock on the dresser. Seven-thirty in California would be nine-thirty in Iowa. Her father went to bed at ten. She would have to phone now or wait until tomorrow.

She dialed and listened to the series of musical beeps.

"Hello?" her father's voice finally answered.

"Dad," she said, her voice cracking. "It's Anne. How are you?"

"Annie! I'm fine. How nice to hear your voice."

"Dad, I wanted to ask you . . . I thought maybe you could come out this month for a visit. With the snow and all, you might enjoy some sun out here." Tears dripped from the rims of her eyes and ran down her face. She didn't want to sniff.

"Annie? Are you all right?"

"I'm fine, Daddy," she said, but her voice rose to a squeak. "I miss you. I want to see you."

"What's wrong, Annie? You're crying. Tell me what's wrong."

"Daddy, I'm pregnant again. Nearly four months. I waited to tell you this time. And I'm so scared." Her words were barely controlled sobs. "I need you here."

Her father's silence was long and painful for Anne.

"Are you and Doug having trouble?" he asked in a tight voice.

"No," she whispered. "It's just that—"

"Why don't you come home for a visit? Fly back for a week or so?"

A week or so? She was afraid she might scream.

"I promised I'd help out with Linda's girls. Shelley has her tonsils out next week. Did Linda write you? Maybe after that—"

Anne hung up very gently. She pushed the two white buttons on the top of the phone down so slowly it was like a fade-out, until the only sound was a white hum. She held the receiver in her hand and kept the buttons down. He might call back. She didn't know if she could talk to him again. At least not tonight. Anne watched the phone for a long, long time. It didn't ring.

At ten-thirty the burglar alarm shrieked a long A-sharp-minor "Eeeeee" when Doug returned from an evening of racketball and Scotch and sodas in the club lounge. He stripped off the toast-colored sweatsuit and stood in the bathroom, looking out at her, huddled under the quilt.

"You okay?"

"Fine." She shivered. Everything was fine. She'd just phoned her father, cried like an idiot, and hung up on him. Dad wasn't young anymore. She shouldn't do that to him. And Doug, fuzzy-edged from exercise and Scotch, believed they were back to their old lives again. He pitted himself against enough worldly obstacles, at work, in a mirror, or on the racketball court, to have that easy confidence that comes with experience. He thought things would work out. She knew they hadn't.

"Did you get a chance to talk to John Wanaker again?" Doug asked her from the doorway.

"Have you ever talked to a grapefruit rind?" she snapped. "He says the discrepancy in numbers is caused by multiple admissions. Women admitted several times for premature labor."

Doug's long hands rested on his hips. "But the problem is with the number of babies who *died* and the number listed in Pathology."

"John Wanaker won't listen to me," she said. "I'm going to the police, Doug. I have this terrible feeling that someone's watching me. Waiting . . ."

"Why don't you quit your job now?" Doug suggested gently.

Her hands tingled from clutching the quilt. "I can't quit yet. Not yet."

But in six weeks she would *have* to resign from General. There was a rule about pregnant women not working after the fifth month of their pregnancy. And six weeks was not very long.

Later that week, she told Marc Rivers, "They're going to get this baby, too. I can't stop them." Her hands were very still in her lap. Usually they tore at threads in her jacket, twisted the upholstery tacks, or tangled locks of her hair. But today they lay like two dead fish on her navy blue slacks. "I think they're watching me. Sometimes I can feel it."

"Why would you be singled out?" Marc asked, knocking out his pipe in the ashtray. "There must be any number of pregnant women in the valley. Did you know that Dr. Springer's wife is pregnant? Their baby is due about the same time as yours. Why would he be watching you, Anne?"

"Because I'm easy. I don't run."

Monday morning John Wanaker cornered Ben Springer at General Hospital and invited him into the office for a few minutes.

"First," the administrator said, folding his hands, "I want to tell you how sorry I am about your daughter, Ben. A terrible accident. Now, I know you've had a little time to adjust, but if there is anything I, or Mrs. Wanaker, can do, you know we'd be glad to."

"Of course. Thank you." Ben acknowledged the sympathy, but he shuddered thinking about Carol Wanaker's gravel voice and squat, peasant fingers. She wore three rings on each hand. And she'd even consulted him once about the unproductive union between herself and John. Ben doubted he would ever want Carol Wanaker to do anything for him.

"But that's not what I wanted to talk to you about," Wanaker continued, "particularly. A month or so ago I had a young woman in my office asking questions about this research unit upstairs. She says she saw something."

Ben kept his eyes level.

Wanaker lowered his voice dramatically. "She thinks you may be using live infants for your research."

"As a matter of fact, we do."

John's mouth dropped open. Ben figured his systolic pressure rose at least fifty millimeters, the way the man's face flushed.

"You're using babies?"

"Of course. Baby cats. Kittens. Why?"

"Oh," Wanaker sighed. "Cats! She thinks you have *human* infants!"

Ben snorted. "That would be convenient, but impossible, as you know. Was the woman Anne Hart, from the lab?"

Wanaker looked up quickly. "As a matter of fact, it was."

Ben shook his head. "She wandered into the research unit in the middle of the night. She may have seen one of the kittens in a pod."

Wanaker relaxed his shoulders. "I couldn't ignore it completely," he said, "not after the bit of trouble last fall with that nurse in Maternity. The one who thought someone was stealing babies in the OR. These things have to be checked out. Nipped in the bud. Rumors are as damaging as facts."

"Of course, John," Ben soothed him. "I understand your concern." His heart thudded several times. "Anne Hart lost a baby seven or eight months ago, and she's been distraught ever since. A very unfortunate situation. She's been under psychiatric care since August."

Wanaker looked thoughtful. "I see," he said.

"Mrs. Hart is a reactive depressive with schizophrenic tendencies, I'm afraid. Paranoia, hallucination . . ."

John Wanaker's head jerked up. That's what Ben counted on, John's sensitivity to any trouble at General. There'd been enough of that lately, and having a schizophrenic lab tech was nothing any administrator needed.

"You might ask for an evaluation of her, John," Ben offered. "She *is* an employee. You can easily require a physical exam as a condition of continued employment. Anne Hart is pregnant again, you know." Springer leaned back in the chair and stretched his legs out in a wide V. "Protect the hospital from any liability. Just in case she aborts again and decides it was caused by her employment here. You know the sort of thing . . .'' He let his voice trail off, drawing John Wanaker along by the leash of implication.

"Would you do the physical?"

"Of course, if you'd like."

"Good," Wanaker agreed happily. "I'll talk to Muriel Bennett. Schedule it soon."

"Well, John, if that's all . . ."

Wanaker sat back in his chair. He asked Springer if he might take a look at the research unit. Wednesday morning, perhaps. He admitted he was a bit surprised to learn the unit was still functioning after losing its funding. Ben chided him for not reading his own annual report. Funding for the unit was all in black and white in the report. Ben felt the sweat start under his arms.

He sauntered out of the office, winking at Grace, and went down the hall to First Center. He buttoned his sport coat. The rings of perspiration extended down his armpits past his ribs. A dead giveaway, he thought, but he'd played it right with Wanaker. Damned woman. She was too determined for her own good.

He took the elevator, but two nurses stepped in at the last moment, and he didn't risk using his key. On the third floor the two stepped out.

"The grrrreat doctor," one quipped before they were out of earshot.

Ben crammed his key in the lock and pressed the button for the second floor. John's chat, the sweating, and that nurse's comment irritated him.

Peter, the day assistant, smiled at Ben as he stepped from the anteroom to the research unit.

" 'Morning, Peter. Is Jones here?"

"In the office."

"How's our registration this morning?" Ben referred to the babies as motel guests. It made it easier to talk about them. Andy Jones preferred a garden-patch analogy, speaking about the infants as turnips and tomatoes.

"Only two."

"Don't fill any more pods," Ben instructed him, and burst into the office.

Andy Jones was dozing, but both feet hit the floor when he heard the door.

"You been here all night?" Ben stormed. "That's a bad habit, buddy."

Jones's mild blue eyes blinked steadily. He scanned the desk, stacked high with books, manila folders, and blue lab notebooks. "I was busy."

"Andy," Ben grunted, "we've got problems. John Wanaker is coming up to take a look at the unit Wednesday morning. If he sees anything but fetal cats in those tanks, there's going to be hell to pay. You get rid of those babies."

"Be reasonable, Ben," Andy said. "We need the money—"

"Apparently you didn't hear me. John Wanaker will be here Wednesday morning. I want those infants out of here by the time I come back tomorrow. Or you can forget about the eighty-five hundred we talked about."

Jones paled. "You haven't transferred those funds? For God's sake, Ben."

"You take care of this, and I'll have the cash for you tomorrow night. I'll pick up a pregnant cat or two at the SPCA. We'll fill the pods tomorrow."

Ben left the unit via the door into OR. Using the elevator this time of day was too risky. On Obstetrics he felt better. Obstetrics was his unchallenged turf. He approached the nurses' station, where Mrs. Wright pored over the charts.

"Oh, hello, Dr. Springer," she said, smiling. "Mrs. Lester is about ready for you."

But Ben wasn't feeling up to Mrs. Lester at the moment. He wanted to go home, sink deep in a hot tub, have a couple of reds, and sleep. He didn't want to think about John Wanaker, Andy, or those two infants still in their pods, or fetal cats, or even Chrissy. Ben's breath caught in his chest. His heart thundered. It had been doing that more lately. Periodic aventricular tachycardia. He needed a few days off, less drugs, less booze, more sleep, but that would have to wait.

Mrs. Lester was delivered of a whopping nine-pound-two-ounce girl who had inherited her mother's unfortunate pink rolls of fat.

Afterward Ben ate a quick salad in the doctors' cafeteria at the hospital. The food was supposed to be better than in the regular cafeteria. He doubted that. Pale, limp lettuce and three coral wedges of tomato did nothing to entice his appetite, and he counted six shrimp scattered in the bed of greens. There may have been seven. He couldn't decide whether one pink fleck was shrimp or something else he preferred not to think about.

By two o'clock he was in his office. And he was exhausted. The first patient was late. Ben dozed in the chair, folding his arms over his chest. He let his mind wander, never dwelling on any one thing particularly. Sometimes that helped him fall asleep, though not often anymore. Not even the sleeping pills worked anymore. Tonight he'd take three, instead of the usual two, but just this once, he promised himself. Just one night of sound sleep was all he needed.

He heard footsteps and voices in the hall and knew his first patient had arrived.

A few minutes after five, Ben dialed Peralta. "Hello," he said dryly. "This is Ben." He stretched out in the leather chair and crossed his feet. "Anne Hart went to John Wanaker, who now wants to see the unit, Geoffrey. . . . That's right, buddy." He rubbed his forehead with his fingertips. "And I have to tell you, your allotment will be delayed this month. A little trouble with the shipper. I'm sure it'll all be cleared up soon. As soon as we take care of Anne Hart. . . . I never threaten. You know that."

Tuesday evening Ben showered and slept for two hours. Addy hadn't dressed all day. She wandered around the house in a mouse-colored bathrobe and old blue slippers.

"Get dressed, won't you?" he growled. "We'll go down to Casio's for a bite of dinner."

"I made lamb stew," she said. "It's in the Crock Pot in the kitchen. I think I'll just have some of that."

"I have to go to the hospital tonight for a while. I should be home by midnight."

She nodded absently and shuffled past him to the kitchen. A few days before, he'd asked her why she didn't set the table for their meals anymore, and she'd said, "I still put on three plates."

So Ben drove the ten miles to General Hospital with Beethoven's Concerto in D Major for Violins playing on the tape deck. The music took his mind off things.

At the hospital, Muriel Bennett scuttled in and out of the main room of the research unit, scowling and muttering softly to herself.

" 'Evening, Muriel," he said. "Has Andy been here tonight?"

"Earlier," she mumbled.

"John Wanaker's coming up for a little tour in the morning. Everything's going to be shipshape for his visit, Muriel, a kitten in every tank." He held up a cardboard box.

Muriel's face distorted. "Not cats again!"

"Fill all six tanks—we do have *six* tanks empty tonight, don't we?" We'd better, Ben thought.

"Five. Dr. Jones—"

Ben's fury exploded. Muriel shrank back, and Ben threw open the metal cover of each pod until he found the small occupant of Pod Four. In one swift movement he picked up a white enamel pan from the counter, yanked open the top hatch, and scooped out the fetus, dripping clear gel and wriggling like a fish in his hand. He slapped it in the basin and looked straight into Muriel's face, frozen in horror. "Don't say it," he snarled.

Feeble choking came from the pan. Muriel turned away. Her lips were dead white. Ben filled a syringe from the vial of sodium Amytal in the refrigerator. He plunged the needle deep in the infant's abdomen. The gasps stopped. The fetus shuddered and lay still.

"Where's a plastic bag?"

"In the drawer. Second drawer from the wall."

He bagged the dead infant in a red plastic sack and knotted

the end. Ben deposited the sack in the silver bin for burnables.

"You finish filling the pods and reset the parameters for felines," he instructed her. "I'll section the cat."

"I wasn't hired to take care of cats."

"Muriel, sweetheart, you were hired to take care of anything I damn well please." He wasn't up to a tantrum tonight. "Don't give my any trouble. Okay?"

Ben retrieved the box from the hall. He carried it to the back room, spread newspapers on the metal tray by the sink, and removed the first tranquilized female cat from the box. Just before the cesarean section, Ben rubbed the head of the unresponsive gold tabby. He injected it with a lethal dose of barbiturates.

An hour later all six pods held fetal cats. A small electrode was inserted into the umbilical artery and then plugged into the pod to produce a constant readout of vitals. All six kittens floated peacefully in the transparency of the gel medium.

"Will you clean up back there?" he asked Muriel, motioning to the back room.

"No, you do your own dirty work, doctor."

Ben angrily dumped the dead cats, two of their offspring, who probably got some of the barbiturates, and a wad of newspapers in another garbage sack. He hosed down the tray, put the scalpel and hemostats in a cup in the sink, and threw the garbage bag in the trash, along with the dead baby.

"Will Paul pick this up tonight?" he asked Muriel.

"He comes in at two, when he finishes in OR. Don't worry. It won't be here in the morning," she hissed.

It was nearly one o'clock. He remembered he'd told Andy he'd be home by midnight. Not that it made much difference. She never waited up.

"Tell Peter that John Wanaker and I will be here in the morning, so be ready."

"Yes, sir."

He didn't like the saucy tone of voice. "Do you know what Andy did with the other baby? Did he get in touch with Pearson in New York?"

"I'm sure I don't know, doctor."

"Good night, Muriel," he said pleasantly. When he looked back, just as the first set of doors opened to the anteroom, Muriel Bennett was still glaring at him.

John Wanaker pulled on the stiff green surgical gown, mask, booties, and cap to go through OR to the research unit with Ben.

"Our assistants shower in a germicide before they come on duty," Ben explained as he also donned the isolation garb. "But unless you want a shower, this is quicker."

The administrator looked uncomfortable. He shoved the mask back over his nose several times. "It's been a long time since I've been in this getup," he murmured, but good-naturedly.

"It isn't too bad, once you get used to it."

"No, I suppose not."

They entered the unit through the door in OR. Ben decided that would create less fuss than showing John how the key still worked in the elevator. The dark hum greeted them, and they walked the hall like Halloween ghosts.

"We use these other rooms for office and storerooms," Ben explained. "And this is the main unit."

Wanaker's eyes were wide at the sight of the pods, which whirred and gurgled softly. Peter was cleaning out one of the tanks.

" 'Morning, Peter," Ben said cheerily.

" 'Morning, doctor."

"What happened?" Ben asked, indicating the empty pod.

"Six died early this morning, I'm afraid."

"Six?" Wanaker asked, puzzled.

"Pod Six," Ben explained patiently. "These last few fetal cats were very young."

A stainless-steel basin sat on the black countertop. Springer peered down into it. The pale, fingerlet kitten lay dead in a pool of thick gel. Wanaker looked in too, jerked his head back, and stared at Ben with watering blue eyes.

"You okay?" Ben asked him.

"Uh . . . yes, I'm okay."

Ben noticed the man's pallor. "Each tank is an artificial uterus. Andy Jones designed them, and they were built by Wells and Wells in San Francisco."

Wanaker ran his hand over one of the pods. "Very interesting."

"The pods are filled with a life-support medium that supplies oxygen, nutrients, even antibiotics if necessary—orally and also through the skin—an enzymatic ion transfer. The gel also acts as a kidney, filtering wastes, and a lung, throwing off carbon dioxide."

"Don't they breathe in the stuff?" Wanaker asked.

"A fetus *doesn't* breathe," Ben reminded him with a smile. He snapped open two of the windows. Deep in the pods, the kittens hung suspended. Wanaker glanced inside. One of the kittens drifted to the window.

"Is that what Mrs. Hart saw?" he asked, drawing back.

"Probably," Ben said. He indicated the array of dials on the front panel of the pod. "With an electrode, we get a readout of vitals on each fetus. Here, I think the implant is intact in this kitten." He grabbed the steel pan and held up the animal bulging with a metal pin and a long red wire.

John Wanaker turned away and leaned heavily against the counter.

"John? Are you all right?"

"I'm not used to this," the administrator admitted in a weak voice. "I feel sick."

Peter was grinning wickedly. Ben winked at him, and the smile faded. Ben clapped John on the shoulder and said, "Let's get some air."

They walked back down the hall and retreated through OR to the small doctors' lounge in Recovery. Wanaker sank in a leather armchair and pulled off his mask. He was still pale and sweating. "Whew," he panted. "I'm sorry. I didn't expect . . ."

"Think nothing of it," Ben said. "I'm afraid I forgot that you aren't accustomed to these things. Please don't apologize. It happens to many of us at first."

"Well, I certainly didn't see any human babies." Wanaker giggled nervously. "No, sir, not a single one."

"But you can imagine the shock of seeing even a fetal kitten, especially after a miscarriage."

"Ah, yes, I certainly can."

"This entire affair was simply an unfortunate coincidence," Ben continued. He bent and removed the green cloth boots from his shoes. "Complicated by Mrs. Hart's delusional tendencies."

The color was returning to Wanaker's face.

"She overreacted with a very active and disturbed imagination."

"Quite so," Wanaker agreed. "I sent a memo to Personnel, requesting a physical exam for Mrs. Hart—make it look routine and all." He was still taking slow, deep breaths. "They tell me in the lab that Mrs. Hart is an excellent tech. They haven't noticed any particular difficulties with her work at night."

"Job problems are often the last symptom in a case like this," Springer said.

"I suppose you're right." John Wanaker untied his gown in the back. "She pointed out a remarkable discrepancy in the annual report. Last year, sixty-four fetal deaths were not recorded in Pathology." Wanaker shook his head. "I told them two years ago that the computer was no substitute for the human brain."

"And you're absolutely correct," Ben assured him.

"But it is a remarkable discrepancy, don't you think, Ben?"

"I'll believe anything is possible with computers," he said grinning. "Shall we go get a cup of coffee?"

Saturday Anne woke up at two thirty P.M. to a cold, steady rain pelting the bedroom window. Doug was at his Saturday class in physics at U.C. and had evidently turned down the heat when he left that morning. The bedroom was freezing.

She made a wild dash for the thermostat in the hall, flipped it to sixty-five degrees, checked to make sure the burglar alarm was on, and dived back under the quilt, curling into a ball and shivering violently. The warmth of the bed seeped into her slowly, and she dozed and woke again. This was the best part of working all night, she decided, this luxurious waking in the afternoon.

The opening at David Farah's Ocher Earth Gallery was only three and a half hours away, and she hadn't decided whether she wanted to go or not.

But by nine-fifteen, dressed in a powder-blue dress, a rose lace shawl, navy shoes, and huddled in a lined raincoat, Anne was propelled through the door of the gallery. The room thronged with clots of women in pale turquoise chiffon and salmon Qianas, men in black suits or elegant jackets with leather lapels, mingled with a few Indian-headbanded guests and several wearing cotton tunics. The sweet bouquet of champagne misted the air.

Doug disappeared momentarily with their coats. Anne gazed around the gallery. The Ocher Earth was a converted delicatessen, with an added loft for additional display space. The walls were paneled in grayed barn wood strewn with flourishing green ferns. Anne stood on tiptoe to see where her paintings hung, but what she saw was David Farah's anxious face bulldozing through the crowd. Fay wove along behind him.

"Christ," he murmured frantically, "I thought you'd *never* get here. The painting sold. I can't believe it. One of the collectors walked in here and paid eight hundred without blinking an eye."

Anne glanced at Fay's face, stiffened with misery.

"What?" she cried to Fay. "It sold?" Doug was beside her again. She reached for his arm.

Fay thrust a plastic glass of champagne in Anne's hand. "Drink one, quick," she said softly, "or ten. You might feel better hearing the news if you're drunk."

David Farah began to pull Anne through a break in the crowd before she could ask who bought the painting. "Come on," he coaxed them along. "Dr. Springer's been waiting to meet you."

She dug her heels in the carpet, and David jolted to a halt. "Who?" she demanded.

"Ben Springer bought the painting," Fay said quickly, as if a swift stab was less painful, or less deadly.

The room swayed with garbled conversation. "Why would *he* buy the painting?" she demanded angrily.

A woman with a well-behaved auburn pageboy and crinkled blue eyes turned to her. "Exactly what I was thinking. So crude. Primitive, don't you think?"

Anne curdled the woman's expression with a fierce glance. "I want to go home," she said to Doug.

"You're almost famous," he whispered. "Enjoy it."

"Doug, please . . ." she pleaded, but David Farah had maneuvered them into the circle around Ben Springer. Anne's stomach stirred with alternating hot and cold rushes, and Farah kept a tight hold on her elbow.

A woman with piles of blond hair was hinged to Ben Springer's elbow, and she diverted Anne's attention for a moment. Was this Ben's wife? Heavy Pan-Cake makeup covered the woman's age, detracting from an elegant scarlet silk dress, gathered softly at the shoulder and flowing to ample hips. One hand, gleaming with red nail polish, rested delicately on Ben's arm, and the other hand was apparently an integral part of the woman's speech patterns, conducting the conversation around her.

"Oh, I rarely come to these shows," she was saying. "What do *I* know about art!"

Laughter bubbled through the knot of men, punctuated by a slippery wiggle of the lady's hips. At that moment Ben looked up at Anne and smiled.

David Farah had been waiting politely for a break in the conversation. "Here she is," he announced. "Dr. Springer, this is Anne Hart."

"Hello again," Ben said, raising his glass in a toast.

"Have you met?" David Farah looked distinctly disappointed.

"We've met." Ben's thin lower lip widened in a dark smile.

"Ohhh," the woman, still attached to Springer's arm, squealed. "The painter of faces! We were just talking about your woooonderful paintings."

"I understand you now own one of them," Anne croaked.

The woman's face congealed in a mixture of surprise and confusion. Ben glared at Anne. The woman blinked several times, and then her face resumed its hard serenity.

"I'd like you to meet a friend of mine," Ben said. "This is Sinclair Williams."

Anne felt her face flush. "I'm sorry," she apologized to the woman.

"Oh, *don't* be sorry. *I'm* not a bit sorry about being Sinclair Williams." Another chord of laughter accompanied the statement.

Anne's knees were liquid. She backed away from Ben, but he swayed toward her.

"Your painting is quite remarkable," he said, his eyes black and malignant. "Quite remarkable."

She shivered, and she suddenly caught sight of her paintings on the wall. The aging infant's face was formalized by the frame and a soft lighting. Unframed, it had the feeling of something raw and unprotected. Now the face was cool and sheltered, warmed only by the distinct red shadow over the forehead and left eye. A dead face, in a coffin. No, not a coffin. She caught her own thoughts with a shudder. Not a coffin.

"I want to go home," Anne said to Doug again, but with a finality that cut off any objections.

"Anne?" She heard Fay call her name. When she turned, her friend looked numb. "I'm sorry, Anne. I didn't think it would sell."

Anne half-smiled at Fay. "It's all right. We're going home now. I'm exhausted."

Laughter and trailing discussions followed them as they worked their way to the door. Faces loomed, faces that seemed familiar, but she couldn't say why, faces that called to her, faces that smiled, and then Marc Rivers, whom she recognized with relief.

"I'm so glad to see you," she said, suddenly chilled and shaking visibly.

"Hello, Anne," Rivers said. The same quiet concern was evident around his eyes. "I would like to introduce my wife, Moko."

Anne's gaze left the comfort of his face and rested on the Oriental woman beside Marc. She was plump, the roundness of contentment, with silver-veined black hair and dark, merry eyes.

"Mrs. Rivers," Anne said, struck by the woman's eyes.

"Please call me Moko," she said pleasantly.

"Moko." Anne nodded. The shaking stopped.

"I have seen your paintings tonight," Moko said, smiling with self-assurance. "They are very good, especially the portrait."

"The portrait," Anne repeated, as if she wasn't sure what the word meant. She looked back to Marc. "The face . . . Dr. Springer bought the painting. I didn't want to sell it." Tears collected in her eyes.

"It is sad to be a painter sometimes," Moko said in her gentle voice. "Much like being a parent, I think. We lose our creations to the world eventually, where we can't control or protect them anymore."

Anne's rage dwindled. "Yes," she agreed. "Like children."

"Don't worry about Ben buying the painting," Marc told her. "He is an avid collector. With very good taste, I might add."

Moko Rivers laid her exquisite hand on Anne's arm. "I am particularly interested in the crimson caul on your painting. I think the effect is quite unusual."

Anne reeled backward slightly.

"The caul is a sign of nobility or special gifts in some countries. And protection against drowning. Years ago the captains of ships bought them at enormous price. If a caul was not secured for a voyage, the crew often refused to sail."

For one instant Anne thought she heard the high singsong cry of a baby, weeping a comfortless mourning, over the jumbled voices of the gallery. "No," she said, "I didn't know that."

At home that night, Anne slept fitfully, waking every hour, it seemed, to some strange noise outside, and drifting back to an alert slumber after mentally reviewing the locks on the doors and windows. The burglar alarm was silent. But then, she wasn't willing to trust her life, or her child's, to electronics. So Anne half-watched the world because it had changed dramatically. She couldn't even name the change that night, but she knew that if the tiger had no name, he had a territory, a well-defined turf that was undisputed. And she knew she had stepped over the line into that arena. And all alone.

15

Albert Daniel Resnick sat on the paisley velvet sofa holding Rachel, his three-month-old infant, in the cup of his huge hands. He was a big man, with thinning brown hair and a full beard, whose salt-water-blue eyes gave away the gentleness inside.

The baby's fingers grasped at the air. Those tiny fingers fascinated him. He could almost count the capillaries under her tracing-paper skin.

Sally, Al's wife, banged around in the kitchen. Sally never did anything quietly. Her body wouldn't let her. It insisted on disrupting every atom possible, regardless of the activity. Al smiled, thinking about Sally. Even when she read, she whipped each page of a book or newspaper across with a snap, announcing her accomplishment. He loved her for her energy, but he was softer, being content to disturb as little as possible in the world.

The baby yawned. "You sleepy?" he asked the child, half-expecting an answer. "Hungry? What? You can tell your old man, kid. I'm not as tough as I look."

He settled Rachel on his lap so he could look at her, and clasped his hands at the back of his neck.

"You two okay?" Sally called from the kitchen.

"I think she's bored with me already," he said. "I haven't gotten a smile for ten minutes."

"You have to try harder with us girls," she called back. "Sing to her. She loves that."

"You like singing?" He studied the small, serious face before him. "Got any favorites? I don't do hard rock, you know." He hummed a few bars of "Swanee River."

Rachel turned her head away.

"Don't like the golden oldies, I see. Burns? You like Bobby Burns?"

And in a full, rich baritone he sang "Flow Gently, Sweet Afton," the words rolling through the apartment, hanging on the smell of cooking beef from the kitchen, mixing with that strange winter darkening late in the afternoon. The baby turned her head to him.

He smiled and rubbed her cheek with his hand. His fist was as big as her head.

"You sure are a little mite," he said. "I had no idea you'd be so small. What are you looking at? You think that bookcase is talking to you?"

The baby's eyes were transfixed on the rows of books against the side wall.

"Don't get any book fixations," he said, almost in a whisper. "After what you cost us, kid, I doubt I'll be able to send you to college. You'll just have to work in the deli. Anyway, for eighteen grand, you should come with a sheepskin for diapers. What *are* you looking at?"

He twisted slightly to see what she continued to stare at, but there was nothing to see except the bookshelf. He looked back to Rachel and frowned slightly. "Maybe they gave you a short course on TM at that California agency. I understand that's the big thing out there."

Al gently turned the baby's face to his own, but her eyes wandered past him. "Hey!" he said with a laugh. "You missed me!" He waved both hands at her, but she did not seem to notice.

"Sal?" he called. "Can she see yet?"

"Of course, silly."

"Could have fooled me," he murmured.

Rachel's gaze meandered around the living room of the apartment in the Towers, furnished with soft low furniture in warm patterns of red, blue, and gold. Sally's energy trans-fused a lush window of ferns, dracaenas, prowling vines, and a rubber plant. Now, with the baby, they were talking about finding a house in the suburbs, but neither of them had much heart for that. This was home.

"You like the place?" he asked Rachel, trying to trace her wandering gaze. "You approve?"

She smiled, even though her eyes never lit on him.

"That wasn't gas, was it? And you haven't had one bite of your mother's cooking! Just wait. Then you'll find out what gas is." He wrinkled his nose. "I hope you're Jewish, kid. Otherwise, you won't last two days at Sally's table."

He traced Rachel's small nose with his finger. Her fists jerked, startled. "Are you Jewish? You don't look Jewish, you know." He rubbed the thin shock of blond hair on the baby's head. "At least your hair curls—a little. Maybe we can pass you off as a Belgian Jew. How does that sound?"

Rachel blinked slowly several times.

"Ah, Rachel, you're pooping out," he said, laying her on his chest. She snuggled down with a sigh. Al liked the baby smell of her head, a clean, warm smell. It reminded him of his brother Jud's hair when they had slept in a tangle in that big bed in the house on Sixty-fourth Street. His brother's crown of red-brown hair always smelled like caramel candies, the soft kind.

But Jud was dead, murdered by a gang of street hoodlums, and it had almost killed Al, too. He'd spent ten months at Riversedge State Hospital, and years learning how to live again without being afraid. He shivered.

The baby's breathing was shallow and even. He stroked her back gently.

There were all those interviews when he and Sally decided to adopt children, after trying unsuccessfully to have a baby of their own. As soon as the agencies discovered his stay at Riversedge, the Resnicks had been politely but decidedly turned down for a child.

But that was all over now. They had Rachel. He rested his hand on her back. It had been easy. They answered a small ad in *Davida*, a magazine of Jewish home life, for childless couples interested in adopting. They were turned down initially. Then there were the phone calls, a letter from a California agency, a second mortgage on the deli, two checks, two months, and finally Rachel. His eyes misted again when he remembered the first sight of Sally holding the baby at the airport.

"Is she asleep?" Sally asked beside him.

He was startled. He hadn't heard her come in the living room.

"I think so," he said, trying to see the baby's face. "If she isn't, it's a pretty good imitation."

Sally gathered the infant from his chest. "Come on, little one, time for bed."

"Sally?" He sat up slowly. "Have you noticed if she looks at you? I mean, she never seemed to see me. You think her eyes are okay?"

"Of course her eyes are okay . . . aren't they, Rachel?" She nuzzled the baby. "I'll put her to bed. Dinner's almost ready. Be right back."

He ran his fingers through his own hair. She was probably right. Sally usually was. Besides, what did he know about babies?

16

Late February warmed the valley to a soft hue, hinting at spring with a few premature bursts of blossoms on the plum and acacia trees.

Anne stood in front of the Medical Building and watched a jogger in a gray sweatsuit work his way down the sidewalk toward her. His arms swung loosely and then tightened when he pushed himself into a run. He passed her, and Anne smelled the clean, sweet sweat and saw his straining neck muscles.

She wouldn't run. She knew that, sensed it as something basic in her nature to stay and fight. She'd given up thinking about *when* she would feel safe, but *if* she ever would again.

"Why would Dr. Springer buy the painting?" she asked Marc Rivers in his office in the Medical Building.

"Maybe he liked it."

"That wasn't his wife."

"No, it wasn't," Marc answered. "I understand Mrs. Springer has not been feeling well. I think I told you she is pregnant."

Anne traced the familiar row of upholstery tacks on the chair. "Yes, you told me."

"Anne," he said quietly, "I found your paintings very

interesting, and I have a hunch about the face. Will you let
me hypnotize you once more?"

She nodded, and Marc took a gold pen from the table
beside him.

"Just watch the end of the pen. You are feeling completely
at ease . . ."

His voice swept her into the undercurrent of a warm, heavy
relaxation. Her feet felt like two stones at the ends of her
legs. The gray curtain drew over her mind while he moved
her back in time, back to August again and the operating
room.

"You're in the operating room now, Anne . . . you're
deeply asleep. You will not remember the pain or the fear,
but only what you see and hear around you. What do you see,
Anne?"

"I . . ."

"Listen to my voice. You're not afraid, Anne. What do
you see?"

"Eyes . . . they wear green masks."

"Do you see the baby, Anne?"

"No . . . Yes . . ."

"You can see the baby. What does it look like?"

"Can't see it. They rip something—something around the
baby. It's bleeding . . . It's head . . . I . . ."

"Anne? Tell me what you see."

"Like a skin. They rip off a skin."

"A caul? Was the baby born in a caul?"

"Yes, a caul."

"And they tear it off the baby. Is the baby alive?"

"It's crying. I can't reach it. Why is it crying?"

"And is the baby a girl or a boy?"

"A girl. Someone says it's a girl."

When she was awake, Marc sat watching her somberly.
And Anne remembered the strange red shadow over the
forehead of the haunting face she'd painted. The remnants of
the birth sack. A caul.

"That's why Dr. Springer bought the painting," she said.

*   *   *

Dr. Ian Gillespie's office in Pathology had a sanitary finality. Colors didn't match—turquoise chairs against yellow walls, a brown Formica-topped desk above which hung a modern print of hazy blue fog, institutional-gray tile flecked with black—and a fluorescent light fixture flickered overhead. It could be a holding tank for hell itself, Marc Rivers thought grimly.

He was waiting for Dr. Gillespie to bring the specimen to the office. The smell of formalin pinched Marc's nose. Finally Dr. Gillespie eased through the door, cradling a jar in his arms.

Through the glass Marc saw a shriveled yellowish-gray fetus, so small he could have held it in one hand. The infant was still curled, its small arms folded across its chest, the knees in full flexion. It had been slit open from the groin to the left side of its head. And the face, dehydrated and creased, had been preserved in its fleeting history, one moment of horror. A large section of the head, removed during the post, lay peacefully in the bottom of the jar.

"Was this baby born in a caul?" Marc asked the pathologist.

Gillespie turned the jar. "No. Otherwise the tissue would have been kept with the specimen."

Marc looked down at the label, which was now visible. "Hart, Boy," he read silently. "Dr. Gillespie, Anne Hart gave birth to a girl in this hospital, August 4, and the child was born in a caul."

Dr. Ian Gillespie checked the specimen and swallowed hard. "This is definitely a boy. I don't know what to say. I guess—"

"The autopsy report on Mrs. Hart's chart states the infant was female." Marc's voice was calm but insistent. "I don't know what's going on around here, but I think we'd better find out."

They checked the permission for scientific disposal, signed by Douglas Hart. The PSD listed the child as male. But the autopsy report said Anne's baby was a girl.

Marc called her at home. "I think it's time you went down

to police headquarters and talked to Sergeant Robert Nielson,'' he told her. ''As soon as possible.''

Anne was scheduled to work that evening. She and Doug would go downtown to police headquarters to talk to Sergeant Nielson the following afternoon.

At one-thirty A.M. she got a call to bring two units of blood to the OR, stat. Breathless, Anne looked around for the desk nurse, but no one was in sight, so she gowned and carried the blood back through the pneumatic glass door herself.

A light was visible from one amphitheater down the hall, but when she stepped into the operating room, no one was there either.

Confused, Anne turned and looked into the face of Dr. Ben Springer. He pushed the door closed and barred her way. Anne's heart stammered.

''I want to talk to you,'' he said quietly. ''This was the best way.'' He spoke deliberately, menacing each word with a dark stare.

Her breath came in great gulps, and she was feeling slightly dizzy. She backed up and hit the operating table. ''I don't want to talk to you.''

''Sure you do,'' he said in a silky voice. He stepped closer to her.

Anne's voice was a hoarse whisper. ''What do you want?''

''I want you to stop making a fool of yourself by asking these ridiculous questions about the research here.'' He reached the end of the table and picked up a black anesthesia mask. ''I will *not* allow you to injure my work at General. Do you understand what I am saying?''

She bumped against a row of colored tanks.

''You are jeopardizing your pregnancy. All this stress and worry. In fact, I'm somewhat surprised you've carried it this long. But you must not let your emotions influence your judgment.''

''Don't hurt me . . .'' She could feel the warmth of his breath with every word. His eyes were bloodshot and angry.

''Hurt you? Why would I hurt you?'' He towered over her

like a stone giant. "I'm going to show you the research. I think you'll be very interested, Anne."

"I've seen it," she hissed.

Springer grasped her arm. "I don't think so."

Instead of dragging her through the door from OR into the research unit, Ben prodded her on the elevator, and they got off on the fourth floor.

Ben half-led her, half-dragged her to the burn unit of General Hospital. Inside the doors, the smell of charred flesh almost knocked her over.

"Breathe through your mouth," he told her.

One of the rooms in the unit was glassed, totally isolated from the rest of the patients. Ben Springer stopped at the wide window.

Inside that room lay a child immersed in a flat Plexiglas pan of thick gel. The gel was Ammy.

"This is Jeremy. He's twelve."

The boy, who had been hideously burned, slept peacefully, at least the part of him that looked like a boy—his head and right arm. The rest of Jeremy appeared to be finely ground hamburger molded into a loaf torso and only the vaguest hint of two legs.

Anne closed her eyes. "Why didn't you just let him go?"

"Because he's in no pain, and he plays a helluva game of chess. And you know what else? His skin has begun to grow. Look at his chest. You see that pale stripe? And we're hoping he's healing on the inside, too."

Anne's eyes were wide open now. It was possible. Nutrients, antibiotics, and even painkillers would be accessible to the child's body through Ammy.

"You realize what could happen if we get any more hassle about our research. Jeremy, here, would start screaming. Have you ever heard a burned child scream, Anne?"

She turned away and started out of the unit. Ben followed her. The air on the fourth-floor pass-through smelled like spring lilacs compared to the burn unit.

She waited for the elevator, and when the doors slid open, Anne stepped in and smashed her hand into the button for the first floor. But Ben put his hand over the electric eye, and the door did not close. He glanced both ways down the hall.

"Have you changed your mind now?" he asked.

She didn't answer.

"In case you haven't," he said, his smile cadaverous in the overhead light, "what if I were to tell you your baby is still alive?"

The air was brittle. "Is she?" Anne whispered.

"And suppose I were the only person who knew where." His smile faded. "If anything adverse happens, any cops nosing around, or hospital administrators, you'd never find out, would you?"

He withdrew his hand, and the doors closed. Anne stood in numb horror. He did say it. He did say the baby was alive!

"You son of a bitch," she screamed at the enameled orange elevator doors. "I'll see you in hell for that."

The doors of the elevator closed, and Ben stepped back. Too bad she's only eighteen weeks. Twenty weeks is so much better, he thought.

The survival rate of sixteen-to-eighteen-week fetuses in the RDS unit was not good. But at twenty weeks, they brought seventy percent of them to term. To life.

And Ben Springer wanted that baby. It wouldn't be difficult. He'd covered himself with Addy's pregnancy. No one would ask any questions about the new baby at the Springer household. Especially not since Addy had left for three months for Switzerland with her sister. Ben had sent her gladly.

"It'll do you a world of good," he'd told her.

In the meantime, all he had to do was relax for two more weeks. Then there was succinylcholine chloride. Given intramuscularly, he'd have two minutes, three at the outside, to do a section on Anne Hart. The myocardium would not be affected, only the diaphragm and chest muscles. She would stop breathing. And best of all, after ten minutes, all traces of succinylcholine chloride would vanish from her system.

Anne hardly remembered driving home. At seven she'd

called Doug and said they had to see Sergeant Nielson that morning.

She screeched into the drive, and Doug was there waiting.

"He said the baby is alive?" he asked her.

"He said, what *if* the baby was alive and he was the only one who knew where she was." Adrenaline coursed through her, making her hands shake and her voice tight.

"We want to see Sergeant Nielson," Anne told the police officer at the information desk on the main floor at headquarters.

"Is he expecting you?"

"At two. But this won't wait that long!"

Sergeant Nielson met them at the door of his office on the third floor. "Come in," he said. "Have a seat."

The office was monochromatic blue-green, with matching gray metal chairs winging the desk like sentries.

"My baby was stolen at General Hospital," she said to Nielson. "Dr. Ben Springer told me last night that if I don't stop asking questions about the research at General, I'll never find out where she is."

Throughout the interview, Nielson jotted notes, asked questions to clarify any points, and after an hour he sat back in his chair. "Is there anything else, Mrs. Hart?"

"Geoffrey . . ." She hesitated. She hadn't intended to mention his name, but it was too late. "Geoffrey Collier is head of Research and Development at Peralta. He told me no Ammy was shipped to General for research. But we followed the truck one night. Three drums of Ammy were delivered to Good Shepherd Hospital. We lost the truck, but I'm sure the next stop was General."

"Is that the same Dr. Geoffrey Collier who's at Unity Clinic?" Nielson asked. His steel-blue eyes scrutinized her closely.

"Yes."

Nielson added one more line to his page of meticulous, perfectly spaced notes. "We'll have you sign a statement," he said. "And we'll be in touch."

"But . . ." Anne stammered. "They *took* my baby! And all you want me to do is sign a statement?"

"Can you prove they took your child?"

"There's a specimen in Pathology that *isn't* my baby, even if it has my name on it. Dr. Rivers can tell you about that. And Springer practically confessed," she cried. "How much more do you want?"

"We need more than your word, Mrs. Hart."

Doug and Anne sat out in the parking lot of police headquarters in numb silence.

"He didn't believe me." Tears of frustration and exhaustion trickled down her face.

Doug cradled her head on his shoulder. "We can leave, Anne. Maybe it's time to get out of San Marco. Away from Ben Springer, General Hospital, and Peralta, and all the bad memories."

She sat up and blinked her tears away.

"I think Dr. Springer was using our baby as a kind of blackmail to keep you quiet. But now you've told the police. It's up to them. Let's put the house on the market and get out of this valley."

Anne nodded slowly. She closed her eyes and leaned her head back. "I never told you that Geoffrey Collier offered us a baby through Unity Clinic. He told me that's how he got his son. But I didn't tell you. I didn't think you'd agree, knowing we could never adopt the baby legally."

She opened her eyes and saw a row of ornamental plum trees laden with snowy pink and white blossoms. When she looked at Doug, his piercing eyes stung her.

"I think I would have taken it," he said.

In his office, Sergeant Robert Nielson pulled the index card on Nina Phillips and shook his head. She was dead, due to anaphylactic shock caused by a reaction to penicillin. That was an unfortunate circumstance, now that this whole reasearch affair at General Hospital could cook up into a mess of stinking carp. Sergeant Nielson hoped Anne Hart didn't have any serious allergies. He sincerely hoped so.

*   *   *

Claire Anderson folded the old blue cotton robe and placed it alongside her slippers, worn through in several places. Leaving a state mental hospital was a meager affair. She slid the bottle of cologne she'd received at the hospital Christmas party into one of the small pockets of the suitcase. This was her last day at Park.

Dr. Fisher came down to say good-bye. "You've come a long way, Claire, from not speaking to us at all and then that orange pillow and that song. What was it?"

"Mama's Gonna Buy You a Mockingbird," she said softly.

"Do you remember where you picked that up? Once you told me you heard a woman singing that to babies in tin cans." He chuckled softly.

Claire Anderson smiled weakly.

"Well, you have a place to stay in San Marco, and I am sure you'll find some kind of work to occupy your time. You'll be back here every two weeks to see me, of course, but I think you're going to be fine, Claire."

"Thank you, doctor," she said. Claire Anderson had learned all the right answers.

When Dr. Fisher left, she snapped the suitcase closed and walked out of Park State Hospital.

Andy Jones sat at the desk in his office at General Hospital and stared out the black window. There was nothing to see out there this time of night.

He slowly rolled up the left sleeve of his very white shirt and around his bared upper arm wrapped a tourniquet, catching one end in his teeth and pulling it tight with his free hand. He watched his arm redden and the brachial vein distend.

He'd never been calmer. His hand was perfectly steady when he picked up the loaded syringe on the desk. He popped the cap and inserted the needle into the vein. Then he released the tourniquet.

Slow, now, he told himself. Go slow. He began to push five cc's of concentrated potassium-chloride solution, obtained from the calomel electrode of the blood-gas instrument. When the syringe was empty, he had twenty seconds before it hit.

There were reasons. The San Marco *Times* had carried the story about the murder of Dr. Theodore K. Bell, based on a police finding of three gold crowns in the hospital incinerator. Jones knew he'd made a mistake.

And that wasn't all. The body of Leslie Corbin had been exhumed, and the stitches that closed the body after autopsy had been executed by a right-handed person. Dr. Bell, the attending pathologist, had been left-handed.

Jones clutched his chest. His delicate features contorted.

He'd even mixed up a fetal specimen in Pathology. He was certain he'd checked the PSD, but Dr. Gillespie'd come into the office in a rage a few days ago. Jones explained it as a simple mix-up. But Gillespie said the infant had been born in a caul, and there were no Path specimens that fit that criterion.

And more than anything else, Jones discovered that all the fetal cats in the last experiment were blind, due to oxygen, even at the reduced level. Ammy would take more testing, more animal studies, before it could be announced. And Andy Jones didn't have any more time. He'd lost that magic touch that turned ideas into gold.

One hand clawed for the phone, but too late.

Three hours later, Sergeant Robert Nielson covered the body of Dr. Andrew Jones with a white sheet. It was six A.M. "Too bad," he said, sorting through the contents of Jones's pockets, laid out on the desk. "I'd hoped to talk to this fellow. Now, why do you suppose a nice young doctor would kill himself?"

John Wanaker, pale and looking like he might faint, wrung his thick pink hands. "I'm sure I don't know. But at least he didn't use cyanide."

Suspicion at San Marco General smelled like an old garlic charm. Two nurses and two physicians had died in the last five months. If suicide was a disease, the employees were afraid of catching it. And if someone was shoving bodies in the incinerator or slipping heparin into IV's, there was even greater cause for alarm. Rumors about a killer loose at General circulated through the halls.

When Anne arrived at work Friday night, she found a memo on the communications board for her. An exit employee physical was scheduled on March 21. Her final paycheck would be issued upon completion of the exam. She'd submitted her resignation only three days earlier.

"What's an exit exam?" she asked a few of the nurses at the two-A.M. break.

Susan Hinshaw looked up from her cup of hot chocolate. "They want to see if you're healthy enough to quit work! The only criterion for *starting* work at General is a temperature approximating 98.6 degrees and a more or less vertical position."

Everyone laughed, not because it was particularly funny, but because bureaucracies like General Hospital had a way of making trivia an inescapable truth, reinforced by the power of the paychecks they issued. In her fifth month of pregnancy, Anne felt she had to choose her battles wisely, and the exit exam would not be one of them.

Up on Fourth Central she drew a blood glucose at two-thirty A.M. and jumped at a shadow in the hall. One minute she was sure she saw something move, and the next, only open doors of the hall gaped back at her. She stopped at the nursing station.

"You okay?" Nurse Haus asked. "You look like you just saw a ghost."

"Did anyone go down that hall a minute ago?" Anne asked her.

"No, no one. It's just the jitters. Everybody's got them. Don't let it get to you."

Back in the lab, she ran the glucose, phoned the result, and busied herself restocking reagents for the next day. The Sequential Multiple Analyzer-12, a Plexiglas instrument full of color-coded tubing and dialyzing membranes, blinked at her from the corner of the lab. The "twelve," as it was called, didn't run at night, but reagent bottles on its lower shelf were in constant need of attention. The lab was very quiet.

She heard the door open with a characteristic "whuff," but tonight her heartbeat almost strangled her as she stood up to see who was there. Geoffrey, hunched up in his lab coat, stood glancing around the lab.

"Hi," he said without a smile when he spotted her. "Thought I'd stop by and see you."

Anne replaced a reagent bottle and walked back to the accession area. Geoffrey shifted nervously from one foot to the other. His eyes were networks of live red wires.

"At three A.M.?" she asked.

"Listen, Anne, I have to talk to you. There isn't much time. You have to *stop* this investigation of the research here. I'm serious."

Anne kept the desk between herself and Geoffrey. "I went to the police. I told them everything."

"About me, too?" He asked the way a small boy inquires from his mother the extent of her knowledge about a broken window.

"I told them you were head of Research and Development at PTI. That's all."

"Nothing about the clinic?"

"They already know you're at Unity Clinic. I didn't tell them about your offer, if that's what you mean."

Geoffrey's eyes were brilliant staring gems set in their dark sockets.

"You aren't . . . ? She stopped. "Geoffrey, you aren't *part* of this research project, are you?"

His hands shook. He jammed them deep in his lab coat pockets.

"They took *my* baby!" she cried at him. "One of those babies in the tanks of Ammy was *mine*!"

He mouthed the word "yours," but no sound came. Then he turned to the wall and pushed his doubled fist against it, as if testing whether walls would move under his force. It was a strange gesture, Anne thought, not angry, but helpless.

"And they won't get this one," she added. "I've resigned from General. We're selling the house." Anne sank to the desk chair.

Geoffrey paced the reception area, stopped, and absently

sorted through the tray of blood drawing needles, syringes, and stoppered tubes. His hand twitched.

"Geoffrey?"

He smiled faintly at her. At that moment the phone rang. Anne picked it up without taking her eyes off Geoffrey. She was needed in the emergency room for a CBC and throat culture. She jotted down the information, and when she glanced up at Geoffrey, she saw him slip something in his mouth. He stumbled into the bathroom, ran the water, and returned holding a paper cup unsteadily.

"Are you on something?"

He stared at her. "Don't be silly. You think I'm hooked?"

"Are you?"

The cup jerked, and water splashed to the floor. "Of course not." He crushed the cup viciously. "I've got a lot on my mind."

"You certainly do," she snapped. "Uppers all day and barbs all night." Anne brushed by him and picked up the tray of needles and syringes. She snatched the paper from the desk and glared at Geoffrey.

"I came here to talk to you!" he shouted. "You'd better listen to me." He collided with the swivel chair that crashed into a row of files.

Anne stopped beside the counter. Her heart hammered her throat.

"Anne . . . please. We have to get out of this mess."

"It's too late."

"No. No, it isn't." He edged toward her. "What do want to withdraw the charges? To forget all this. Say you made a mistake. Money? We can get you money."

"I don't want money. Geoffrey—"

"Your baby? Is that what you want? We can too."

He came toward her, fumbling his way along the counter. Anne reached for the scissors in her pocket. She backed away. At the end of the counter reach the back door of the lab, she thought. But

"Geoffrey, go to the police," she urged him. "Tell them what you know."

He shook his head. "I can't, Anne." He staggered forward.

"Did he buy you, Geoffrey? Is that a very expensive habit you have?" Her fingers were wet around the scissors. "All those pills? Or that terrific job at PTI? Maybe even your son?"

His mouth worked spasmodically. "My son is blind. But at least he's alive," he shouted. "You and I may not be so lucky. I only came to warn you."

With a last pleading look, he turned and jolted to the front door of the lab. Anne stood riveted in the aisle. The door opened and closed. She took a deep breath. She would have killed him if he'd continued to come at her.

After several long minutes she checked the accession area. Her hands were weak, and her heart continued to leap. Anne opened the door of the lab and cautiously checked the long, wide hall. She glanced at the elevators at one end, and then ⌐ard the main lobby, dimly lit this time of night. Geoffrey ⌐d in one of the lighted phone booths with his back to her. ⌐atched him, pressing herself against the door.

⌐hone booth burst open, and he staggered to the glass ⌐he hospital, the white lab coat flapping madly at his

⌐," she called softly, but he was already through

⌐ stroked his cheek, but Geoffrey shivered ⌐ General Hospital. He hurried to his car. ⌐back a few things, stop at PTI for more ⌐blues, and drive to Yuma to join Janet ⌐d sent them to his parents because he ⌐ht find out about his son. Someone

⌐s fuss about the research would ⌐wn and Anne Hart might come ⌐d it after their conversation. ⌐r own good.

Geoffrey stopped. Carl Sweeney was sitting in the driver's seat of Geoffrey's car in the lot. He wasn't used to seeing Sweeney at three in the morning, and the man's heavy-jowled face and narrow eyes at that hour alarmed him.

But Carl always brought what Geoffrey needed. The drugs. The cocaine, especially. Geoffrey had been surviving on whatever he could pick up at PTI and Unity Clinic for a week now, mostly barbiturates and amphetamines, but cocaine was the salvation. His body ached for it.

This time, however, Sweeney had something else for him. A surprise, he said.

A second man rose from the backseat. Geoffrey half-turned to see the long, bearded face. The man snapped Geoffrey's head back. He struggled, smashing his fists at the fingers that pushed deep into his throat. He bit on a metal guard inserted in his mouth, gagged, and fought, but he was no match for the burly Sweeney and those educated fingers in the backseat.

His vision blurred. It was all he could do to raise his arm. Sirens shrieked in his numbing brain.

"Feel better, Geoffrey, old boy?" he heard Sweeney whisper. "Pretty soon you won't feel nuthin.' Not one thing."

They'd forced drugs down his throat, into his stomach, and his only hope was to vomit, but he knew it was too late. His heart fluttered. The muscles of his chest were as heavy as concrete slabs.

And the whole time, he knew what they were doing. He didn't know why. He hadn't made any mistakes. Not like Jones.

His brain frayed, came apart like threads of an old coat. He heard the car engine start, and he let go, let his mind stray off into the dark.

By the time Anne pulled into the drive on Sawyer Street, shortly after eight that morning, she ached down to her toenails, and her eyelids felt like they were coated with ground glass.

The burglar alarm was silent when she unlocked the door. Doug must have switched it off last night, she thought.

The need to lie down with her head on a cool pillow was almost overwhelming. But *first* she needed to talk to Sergeant Nielson. She found the San Marco P.D. number and dialed. She wasn't sure what she'd say to Nielson. "They're going to kill me" was the only thing she could think of.

A fast-talking officer answered the phone and immediately put her on hold. Anne leaned against the kitchen counter and waited. The white noise of the phone lulled her. She closed her eyes.

Doug stumbled sleepily into the kitchen. "What's happened?"

"I'm calling Sergeant Nielson. Geoffrey came to the lab last night. He said they're going to get me."

Doug looked at her as if she'd told him she was trying to get reservations on the next moon shot. "They? Who's 'they'?" He ran both hands through his tousled hair.

"I have a pretty good idea. I want to talk to Sergeant Nielson."

Doug took the receiver from her hand. "They're going to get you?" he repeated in disbelief. He insisted she lie down while he tried to reach Nielson.

"Turn on the burglar alarm," she said before she fell asleep. "Don't forget to turn it on."

She thought she'd slept for only several minutes when she heard her name called through the vapors of her uneasy slumber. "Annie? Annie? Wake up. There's a policeman here."

Doug hovered over her. She blinked and sat up, still wearing her lab coat.

A policeman in a dark blue uniform waited in the hall. He was young, with sandy hair and dark hazel eyes fringed with thick lashes. "Mrs. Hart? I'm Officer Partridge, Homicide." He flipped open the plastic-coated I.D. badge. Anne glanced at it.

"Come in," she said, indicating the living room. She bundled the blue velux blanket from the sofa where she'd been sleeping. Homicide? Isn't that murder? Jolie? Her head blurred.

Partridge sat down in one of the wing chairs and took out a notepad and pen. "Do you know Dr. Geoffrey Collier?"

Anne hardly dared to breathe. "Yes."

"I have some bad news for you, Mrs. Hart. We found his body in his car this morning."

"His body?"

"Looks like a drug overdose. Possibly murder."

"My God." It was more of a moan.

Anne answered the questions, or as many of them as she could. Officer Partridge's expression never changed. He assured her his questions were routine and necessary, particularly since the police had been unable to contact Geoffrey's wife.

Doug, looking quite alarmed, sat on the edge of the other wing chair.

"I told Sergeant Nielson most of this," Anne said when Partridge asked her about Dr. Ben Springer.

"Do you have any proof that Dr. Springer and Dr. Collier were involved in any way with each other?" he asked.

"No," she said softly. "I'm afraid not. Nothing *you* would call proof."

"We suspect Collier was mixed up in a drug ring through Unity Clinic," the officer said, flipping through his notes. "It's odd, however, that he said they'd get you, too. You worked at the clinic, didn't you?"

"Yes, but not for very long."

"Where were you at three-fifteen A.M., Mrs. Hart?"

"In the lab."

"Are you accusing my wife?" Doug demanded.

"These are routine questions," Partridge continued in a professional drone. He glanced around at the cardboard boxes Anne had packed. "Are you moving, Mrs. Hart? I see you're packing."

"We were. We took the house off the market. My obstetrician says it's too risky for me to make a move right now."

He nodded. "Well, I think that's all the questions I have."

The phone rang. "That may be Nielson now," Doug

explained on his way to the kitchen. "I left a message to have him call."

Anne followed Partridge to the front door. She turned off the burglar alarm to let him out.

Partridge replaced his hat. "Thank you, Mrs. Hart."

In the kitchen, Anne, feeling vaguely indicted herself, took the phone receiver from Doug.

"Sergeant Nielson?" she said. "Dr. Collier came to the lab last night to warn me that they'll get me too. Officer Partridge just left. He told me Geoffrey's dead. . . . Murdered? Are you sure?"

She hung up the phone.

"What did he say?"

Anne felt the blood drain from her head. "He said somebody forced drugs down Geoffrey. They found gouge marks at the back of his throat."

She reached the bathroom in time to vomit miserably, kneeling on the cold tile floor. Finally she rested her head in her hands and flushed the toilet.

When Fay rang the doorbell, Anne leaped three inches. She watched the windows, bolted awake at the sound of a branch against the window, and studied every face up and down the aisles in the grocery market. But nothing happened.

She read about Geoffrey's death in the *Times*. The article said his death was accidental.

He was buried Tuesday morning in Yuma, a small town two hundred miles north of San Marco. Anne wondered if he grew up in Yuma. She vaguely remembered the town, a collection of gray concrete commercial buildings and tan houses with brave, thirsty geraniums. It was hot there, suffocatingly hot, all summer. And bitterly cold all winter. A place of extremes.

And considering extremes, she stepped on the scale in the bathroom and realized she'd gained ten pounds in a month. That was certainly a change. If she wasn't careful, she'd have to endure those lectures again about her weight.

But Dr. Bryant didn't seem concerned. "The weight gain

is perfectly normal during the second trimester," he told her.

Bryant looked relieved when she told him they'd taken their house off the market. "We'll wait and move after the baby's born," she said. "But then I'm leaving this valley!"

Anne had told him about her suspicions concerning her other child, the RDS research at General, Springer's threats, and the red dreams. She'd also told him about Marc Rivers, her hypnosis, and going to the police.

"I can understand your apprehension," he said nicely. "If the strain gets too bad, we can arrange to check you into University Hospital for a while. You let me know."

"Thank you, doctor," Anne said with a smile.

"And make another appointment for two weeks. I'll want to watch you closely from now on. You know all the drugs you took early in your pregnancy put this baby at considerable risk. I'll want to monitor for fetal distress, toxicity . . . regularly."

"Of course."

At the door he turned back to her. "Are you still seeing Dr. Rivers?"

"Yes. He's been a lifesaver."

Ben Springer sat at the oversized drafting table in the study of his home. The room had floor-to-ceiling bookshelves of dark mahogany on two walls, French doors hung with heavy burgundy drapes, and a thick Persian rug on the floor. It was nearly midnight.

Spread on the desk in front of Ben were the data of two years' work, proving the tremendous value of the life-sustaining gel Ammy. All that time, all that money, and the gambles would pay off soon. Except for one problem. Oxygen.

Ben read the post reports of the five fetal cats Andy Jones had autopsied just before he died. All five showed marked scarring of the optical nerve. It meant only one thing. Blindness. The oxygen parameters were still grossly elevated.

A year ago their success rate with three-hundred-gram fetuses was zero, until they increased the oxygen and calcium gluconate. Then the infants began to survive. Remarkably so.

One of their first successes was Geoffrey Collier's child, and he was definitely blind. But what about the five-hundred-gram babies? And the seven-hundred-grams? Were they all blind, too?

Ben went over the data once more, the lab notebooks, charts, and graphs. Other than oxygen, the experiment was an astonishing success.

Could he decrease the oxygen? He could try. There was one more baby that would be residing in the RDS unit soon, and still three months before the paper was due. If he succeeded and produced a perfectly sighted child from Ammy under reduced oxygen levels, that would be his greatest victory. And if he failed? He wouldn't fail.

He placed the papers and notebooks back in his open briefcase on the floor. And from the case he pulled a manila folder marked "ANNE HART" on the blue index tab. It was Anne's medical history from General Hospital. Ben had requested it in Medical Records that morning and never returned it.

Most of her record he'd read before, but he read it again, slowly and carefully.

By two A.M. and his third Seconal, he was tired and grumbling. Succinylcholine chloride would give him enough time to deliver her infant, and in ten minutes its effect would vanish completely. But if she died before the drug wore off, would autopsy show the presence of a fatal dose? He didn't know. He'd almost blown it once with Leslie Corbin. This time he needed something else, something less suspicious than heparin or succinylcholine chloride.

And there is was, right before his eyes. The answer.

17

Sunday night, March 20, was Anne's last midnight shift at General Hospital. She packed a book, instant coffee, and her lab coat at ten-thirty.

Doug sat in the recliner in the family room, watching the end of the news. "I think I'm getting a cold," he said to Anne.

"Take an antihistamine tonight so you can sleep."

"I may not go to work tomorrow," he called.

"I'll see you in the morning, then. We can have breakfast together. Except I'll be a little late. I'm scheduled for an exit exam at eight o'clock."

"An exit exam?" He padded into the kitchen in stocking feet.

"Stupid bureaucratic nonsense. But I can't collect my check until Personnel verifies that my heart is still beating and I breathe in and out with some regularity."

But at eight o'clock that next morning the physical wasn't much of a joke. Anne just wanted to go home, fall in bed, and not move a muscle for six hours at least.

She walked to the Employee Health Office, which took her through the administration wing. John Wanaker's door was closed. Anne was grateful. She didn't want to talk to him. She heard he'd been frantic when Geoffrey's body was found in his car in one of the back parking lots. And then he'd learned that Anne *had* gone to the police with her suspicions about the RDS unit. She wondered how he answered their questions about what was happening at General. At least he'd taken a police investigation seriously. She heard he'd talked to a number of employees about their observations of operating-room and neonatal ICU procedures for nonviable infants.

It was only a matter of time now, Anne thought. Soon, very soon, that RDS unit would be closed down and Ben Springer would have to answer for his research. All those infants. Sixty-four of them.

The olive-green door at the end of the hall read "EMPLOYEE HEALTH." Anne pushed the door open. She just wanted to get the exam finished.

Muriel Bennett sat at the desk reading. Slowly but deliberately she laid a chart over the magazine. "Hello." Nurse Bennett smiled. "You're right on time, Mrs. Hart."

The door closed softly behind her. She sucked in her breath. She'd forgotten that Muriel Bennett was the Employee Health nurse. How could she have forgotten!

"I don't need a check this bad," she murmured, turned, and threw open the door.

She stood staring straight at the wet bottom lip of Ben Springer. He didn't move. Anne backed away.

"Well, Mrs. Hart," he said in a low, almost melodic snarl, "what a coincidence. I'm scheduled to do employee physicals this morning." He reached out for her.

She felt his hand clamp down on her arm like the jaws of an animal, and he steered her toward an examining room. "Mrs. Hart's a bit nervous this morning," he said to Muriel. "We'll fill out her paperwork. You get the HISS test ready for me and then take a nice, long coffee break, Muriel."

"But, doctor . . ." the woman sputtered. "She . . ."

Anne tore her arm out of his grip, heard a snap like a branch breaking on a tree, and a pain so exotic and intense shot up her arm that she cried out. Her head spun.

"Just do as you're told," Ben said to Muriel Bennett. "I'll take good care of Mrs. Hart."

Dizzy and slightly nauseated, Anne felt him roughly guide her into one of the small rooms.

"The vial's in the refrigerator," Bennett said just before the door closed. "I'll have to fill it from there."

Anne stumbled against the exam table. She cradled her arm next to her body. The pain throbbed maddeningly. "Don't hurt me," she begged him. "Please don't hurt me." Her voice was barely a whisper.

"I won't hurt you," he said as if he were coaxing a frightened child out from underneath a bed. "We're just going to do a little exam this morning. Nothing to it."

She moved around the end of the examining table. "I have a positive HISS test," she said. "Another one will kill—"

"I didn't know that. Isn't that a shame, Mrs. Hart? I had no idea you had a positive reaction before. Now, I want you to get undressed. Or do I have to do that for you, too."

"I'll scream!"

"Go ahead. There's no one out there to hear you. Now, let's get you out of those clothes."

He grabbed for her, caught her lab coat, and she twisted away, screaming when her arm wrenched out of the sleeve. Anne's plaid shirt came away in his hands. He spun her around, and she caught a glimpse of the large jar of Ammy waiting on a tray in the corner of the room along with a row of scalpels and sponges.

"No, my God, no!" she screamed.

And Anne vomited, a thin projectile of foul coffee and remnants of a doughnut from her break.

"Oh, shit!" he swore, stepping away and brushing the pink spatters from his suit jacket.

Anne made a desperate lunge for the door. If she didn't get out of that room this time, she knew she wouldn't ever come out alive. But he tossed her back easily against the exam table. She crumpled, holding her arm.

"Now, where the hell is Muriel?" he shouted, opening the door and looking out. "Muriel?"

"Here."

All Anne remembered was a bright flash of something

metallic. Ben Springer dropped to the floor like a felled oak and lay there, dazed.

"Son of a bitch!" he bellowed.

Muriel Bennett hit him again. Harder this time, with the sharp edge of a metal chart clipboard. The first time, she caught him in the neck, and the second she brought down the saber-edged board against his skull, meeting metal and bone. Blood gushed from the side of his head.

Anne looked up and saw John Wanaker's crimson face behind Muriel. Then Anne fainted.

When she came to, cool hands held her head. She looked into the face of Muriel Bennett, kneeling on the floor beside her. "Don't get up, honey," Bennett cooed. "You're all right." She rearranged the tatters of shirt over Anne's shoulders.

Springer, on his feet now and holding a towel to the side of his head, was securely flanked by two police officers.

"What the hell is this!" he raged.

"You're under arrest. I must advise you of your rights. Anything you say—"

"Don't play cops and robbers with *me*!" he snarled. "What's the charge?"

"Attempted murder, for starters." Gary Caldwell of the San Marco P.D. held up the syringe of sera for the Hepatitis Skin Sensitivity test. "Are you all right, Anne?"

"I think my arm's broken," she said. The arm hung at an peculiar angle, but it was numb now.

Springer was hauled into the office, and Anne, with Muriel Bennett's help, managed to get to her feet and wrap herself in her lab coat.

"How far along are you?" Muriel asked, trying to button the coat over Anne's hips.

"Five months."

"You certainly are big for five months," she clucked.

"Mrs. Bennett, please, will you tell me what happened in that research unit? What happened to my baby up there?"

"Your baby? *Your* baby came to the RDS unit? One of those was *yours*?"

"Please, try to remember. Last August. The fourth, early

in the morning. Please try, Mrs. Bennett.'' Anne was feeling nauseated again, but she had to find out. "A baby with a caul."

Muriel Bennett gazed up at the ceiling. "Last August. It's hard to remember that far back. We had so many babies for a while. I wouldn't have any idea . . . There was one baby last summer. Yes, in August. I remember her. A baby with a caul. They're special, you know. Sacred babies in some countries."

"A caul? Are you sure?"

"Yes, like a cap over the forehead. Usually they remove it in Labor and Delivery, but I guess there wasn't time. But there were so many babies, Mrs. Hart. I would have no way of knowing which of them was yours."

"What happened to them in the unit? Please, I have to know."

Nurse Bennett looked so sad Anne wanted to cry. "Some of them died. Especially at first. And those that lived, well, after they were removed from the pods, Dr. Jones knew someone, who knew someone. Pearson . . . I can't remember exactly."

"And the baby with the caul? Did she survive?" Anne held her breath.

"Oh, yes." Bennett smiled. "She was a lovely little thing."

A policewoman opened the door and spoke softly to Anne. "Are you all right?"

Anne nodded, and the three of them walked slowly to the outer office, where Gary had Ben against the files. When John Wanaker saw Anne, he rushed to her, but the policewoman blocked his way.

Flustered, he asked Anne over the policewoman's shoulder, "Are you all right? We're going to get you checked over in Emergency. This is terrible. Why didn't you tell—"

"Excuse me," the policewoman insisted, and led Anne to one of the chairs. "Sit here for a minute."

Anne looked at Ben. His long, dark hands were humiliated in the handcuffs. The bleeding had stopped, and he stared down at the floor.

Muriel Bennett, in the company of a police officer, left the office and returned shortly with a red garbage bag, stiff and crackling from the freezer.

"I knew it was murder," Muriel said. "He told me to get the sack out of the unit before Mr. Wanaker came. I knew he was killing that baby to get rid of the evidence." She unwrapped the brittle plastic."After he left that night, I took the sack out of the trash and put it in the deep-freeze."

Anne crept to the desk and stood unsteadily beside John Wanaker, who was the same color as his white shirt.

"They sold the babies that lived," Bennett explained. "But there wasn't time for this one."

The small frozen body of the fetus lay curled in the red folds of the garbage bag. Wanaker turned aside.

"She's crazy," Springer said. "Absolutely crazy."

"The charge is Murder One," Gary said to him.

"I just couldn't let it go on anymore," Muriel continued. "They'd gone too far." She looked up at Anne. "And then, when Dr. Springer told me to get the HISS test for Mrs. Hart, I knew he was going to kill her too."

In the emergency room Dr. Keith Kyle set Anne's arm. While the cast dried, he examined her carefully. "Did you ever lose consciousness?"

"Not until I saw Muriel Bennett hit him on the head."

"She gave him a pretty good smack with that clipboard." Kyle laughed softly, and then his smile faded as he listened to the fetal heartbeat. "Everything sounds fine in there, but I think we'll keep you overnight just to be sure. The heartbeat is somewhat muffled, but don't worry. The baby's had a few jolts this morning. A good night's sleep should calm both of you down."

She fell asleep almost immediately, and when she woke, Doug was beside her. She was in a room in General Hospital. "What time is it?"

"A little after seven," Doug said. "How do you feel?"

"Like someone just broke my arm."

"They tell me you're okay. The arm was a clean break."

He stroked her hand. "And he didn't have time to give you that drug."

"He was going to take the baby," Anne said. "Then he would have murdered me with the HISS test."

"My God, Annie . . ." His voice cracked. "Dr. Bryant was here this afternoon. And Dr. Rivers. Do you remember?"

"No." The events of the morning were still hazy in her mind. What she remembered most were the terrible, sickening pain in her arm and Muriel Bennett's cool hands. "Mrs. Bennett said our baby lived, Doug. She said they sold her . . ." Hot tears spilled from her eyes.

"Sergeant Nielson promised they will do everything possible to find our baby, Anne."

The next morning's headlines in the San Marco *Times* read "BABY BLACK MARKET UNCOVERED IN VALLEY." The newspaper carried the story of a research unit at General Hospital and a dead infant frozen in a red garbage bag. There were indications that the baby ring was nationwide, the article said, robbing hundreds of women like Anne Hart of their premature newborn infants.

That afternoon, Anne went home. Dr. Bryant felt satisfied that the pregnancy was not threatened.

"Dr. Kyle said the baby's heartbeat was muffled. What does that mean?" she questioned Bryant.

"Muffled?" He raised his dark eyebrows. "The baby's heartbeat is fine. I want you to put your fears to rest now, Anne. Everything is perfectly normal."

And John Wanaker met her at the door as she left General. His smile was a very good approximation of genuine warmth, and he waved her final paycheck in his hand. "Let me know about the baby," he said.

The following Monday Anne sat in Marc Rivers' office. She clutched the obituary page from the San Marco *Times*.

"Jeremy died."

"Jeremy?" he asked.

"A young boy at General. In the burn unit."

Marc read the newspaper: "Jeremy Richards was twelve years old when he died Thursday evening from burns received in a Christmas Day fire at his home in San Marco."

"It's always sad when a child dies," Marc said softly.

"I hope he didn't scream."

April burst the St. Helena Valley into full bloom, underlaid by a plush carpet of green. By May, apricot trees were laden with promising green fruit and the mock orange simmered, filling the air with a heady sweetness mingled with rosemary, mint, and the season's first roses.

Beside Anne's house, volunteer nasturtiums leaned their sunny colors toward the morning light, and the last of the red tulips stood like weary guards at the edge of her garden.

The burglar alarm was turned off. Anne relaxed and watched her own burgeoning growth.

She hired Arthur T. Silverman to represent her as legal counsel, and he worked with the police to try to trace the infants who had disappeared from the RDS unit into the baby black market.

A total of eleven persons were involved in the ring in the valley: Dr. Ben Springer, Muriel Bennett, H. M. Schwartz, Paul McConnell, Mrs. Gloria Sands in the neonatal intensive care unit, four nurses at General, and two male nurses moonlighting from other area hospitals. Gloria Sands confessed to the murder of Jolie McKinley.

The infant, labeled as "Hart, Boy" at General Hospital, was incinerated, unfortunately, by the time Silverman checked with Pathology. Dr. Ian Gillespie was unable to explain the premature disposal. Most specimens were kept for one year.

On May 23 Anne testified before the grand jury about her drugged experience in recovery, discovering the respiratory distress syndrome lab, the hypnosis with Marc Rivers, and finally the attempted murder by Dr. Springer. Her voice was clear and even as she answered their questions.

"Do you remember someone saying 'IMI' to you?"

"Yes."

"Do you know what IMI is?"

"Yes. Imidazole methyl iozide. A synthetic lysergic-acid compound used as a post-op anticonvulsant in epileptics, particularly. And sometimes producing hallucination, paranoia" —she hesitated—"and psychosis."

"Are you epileptic, Mrs. Hart?"

"No."

"And you know for a fact you have a positive HISS test?"

"Yes, it's on my medical records."

The indictment by the grand jury was first-degree murder, attempted murder, child stealing, and conspiracy against Dr. Benjamin Springer, Muriel Bennett, and Gloria Sands. Conspiracy charges were brought against the other seven members of the black-market ring. Muriel Bennett agreed to talk, and there were rumors of plea bargaining.

On June 4 Ben Springer, in the company of two men, descended the steps of the courthouse on Third Street. Ben smiled casually. He was out on bail.

Parked on the street and idling was a dark green Plymouth, rusting and minus its rear chrome bumper. The car door opened slowly, and a small dark woman emerged. She rested one hand on the door, steadied the gun she held, and pulled the trigger.

Ben Springer dropped to the sidewalk, one side of his head a mass of cerebral tissue, shattered bone, and blood.

Claire Anderson walked around the car, across the grass, firing into the body of Ben Springer until the gun was empty. The two men who had accompanied Springer had leaped for cover and were unhurt.

Claire Anderson was arrested moments later as she stood staring down at the body. She made no resistance to the arresting officers.

Anne sprawled in the patio lounge chair in the backyard. Mid-June had turned hot and windless. She wore blue-and-white-seersucker shorts, and a sleeveless maternity top stretched snug across her abdomen. Several days earlier, Dr. Bryant had removed the cast, and her arm, although white and puckered, had healed perfectly.

The day's heat was just beginning to give way to cooler night air. Doug and Fay sipped iced tea beside her.

Anne leaned forward heavily and pulled a stack of photos and scraps of well-read letters from a long metal file case on the picnic bench. She compared several of the photos.

"I've almost memorized these faces," she said. "I never get tired of looking at them."

Through the spring, photographs of infants, sometimes accompanied by short, carefully camouflaged letters, arrived in the mailbox on Sawyer Street. The arrest of the black-market-baby ring had received national coverage, along with the story of the disappearance of Anne and Doug's child into that miasma. The letters expressed sympathy with Anne and Doug and assurances that if their child was indeed the Harts', they loved and cared for it as their own.

Some of the infants in the photos were boys, some girls, some were two years old or more, several of them were black, others Oriental. These were all children gained through the black market. But Silverman and the police were totally unsuccessful tracing even one of the infants from the RDS unit. Muriel Bennett remembered the name of Pearson, but that led them nowhere. They had even tried tracing the postmarks on some of the letters Anne and Doug received. But that was a dead end too.

"Listen to this letter." Anne read softly: " 'Please don't worry. If our baby is yours, we love her. She is so beautiful. I thought you might like to know. . . .' " Anne folded the letter and opened another. " 'It took us a long time to get Rachel. We'll raise her right. If she is yours, she'll be okay. I hope that's some comfort to you. . . .' "

"Is that any comfort?" Fay asked.

"Every time I see a baby, I search for something familiar in her eyes, the way she smiles . . . something. But the strangest thing is that she wouldn't have survived at all without Dr. Springer or Muriel Bennett. It's odd how things work out sometimes."

18

Tim Sheldon held his sleeping daughter in his arms. June was so green in Sioux City, Iowa, it hurt his eyes to look at the grass. And spring green was just one more thing his daughter wouldn't see.

He worked his wheelchair closer to the window without disturbing seven-month-old Kendra Lynn Sheldon. They knew now that she was blind, despite all the hopes and all the doctors. Tim wondered if it was only the color outdoors that made his eyes hurt.

"Don't worry," he whispered into the child's wispy, softly curling blond hair. "You'll be okay. I know a lot about the world, even if I can't get there very easy. If you do the running, Kendra, I'll tell you where to go. We'll make it okay."

19

Labor started late on the morning of June 17. Anne took a cab to University Hospital, where she was checked in and put to bed in a labor room.

She tried to hold back the tears and her urgent need to push too soon.

"This isn't catastrophic," Dr. Bryant told her. "Lots of babies arrive a few weeks early."

Doug stayed beside her, holding her hand and telling her it would be all right.

It was dark outside. Anne had no idea what time it was when Bryant brought a syringe and said, "It's almost time. We're going to put you out for this last part."

"No," Anne cried, looking around desperately for Doug, but even as she struggled, the drug pulled her down into sleep.

But there were no red dreams this time; no stuporous terror when she awoke.

"You have a fine son, Mrs. Hart," the nurse said. "Everything's fine."

"A son," Anne whispered.

They stood at the nursery window and watched Victor Marc Hart try to work his tiny fists into his mouth. At four pounds, six ounces, he looked like a doll lying in the incubator.

"Maybe we should have named him Victor Douglas," Anne said softly to Doug.

"There'll be other sons for that," he said, his smile handsome and proud.

Victor Marc Hart, his eyes squeezed shut, lay in one incubator at University Hospital, and down the hall, back through the delivery rooms and inside a much smaller nursery, reached through a narrow hall just off one of the delivery rooms, his identical brother rested in an identical incubator.

One wall of the room was lined with glass, aquariumlike tanks. Nurse Baker had just finished filling one with the warm, translucent gel. Twins were always the easiest, Nurse Baker thought, leaning over the incubator.

"One for them," she said, "and one for us."

About the Author

Mary Lundholm Hanner was born and raised in Round Lake, Minnesota. She attended Gustavus Adolphus College and the College of St. Scholastica and now lives in the San Francisco Bay Area with her husband and two children. Besides novels, she writes poetry and short stories, and has worked as a medical technologist for fifteen years.

Bestsellers from SIGNET

Buy them at your local
bookstore or use coupon
on next page for ordering.

Recommended Reading from SIGNET

Great Novels from SIGNET

☐ **MUSIC FOR CHAMELEONS by Truman Capote.**
(#E9934—$3.50)*
☐ **BREAKFAST AT TIFFANY'S by Truman Capote.**
(#W9368—$1.50)
☐ **THE GRASS HARP AND TREE OF NIGHT by Truman Capote.**
(#J9573—$1.95)
☐ **IN COLD BLOOD by Truman Capote.** (#E9691—$2.95)
☐ **OTHER VOICES, OTHER ROOMS by Truman Capote.**
(#E9961—$2.25)
☐ **FORGOTTEN IMPULSES by Todd Walton.** (#E9802—$2.75)*
☐ **FEELING GOOD by David D. Burns, M.D.** (#E9804—$3.95)
☐ **SUMMER GIRL by Caroline Crane.** (#E9806—$2.50)*
☐ **CHILDMARE by A. G. Scott.** (#E9807—$2.25)†
☐ **RETURN TO SENDER by Sandy Hutson.** (#E9803—$2.50)*
☐ **TWO FOR THE PRICE OF ONE by Tony Kenrick.**
(#E9807—$2.50)*
☐ **GLITTER AND ASH by Dennis Smith.** (#E9761—$2.95)*
☐ **THE EDUCATION OF DON JUAN by Robin Hardy.**
(#E9764—$3.50)*
☐ **LADYCAT by Nancy Greenwald.** (#E9762—$2.75)*
☐ **THE INHERITORS (Haggard #2) by Christopher Nicole.**
(#E9765—$2.95)†
☐ **"DEAR ONCE" by Zelda Popkin.** (#E9769—$2.50)
☐ **BITTERSWEET by Susan Strasberg.** (#E9760—$3.50)

*Price slightly higher in Canada
†Not available in Canada

Buy them at your local

bookstore or use coupon

on next page for ordering.

SIGNET Bestsellers You'll Want to Read